Jane Tara is the author of *The Happy Endings Book Club*, as well as three novels in the Shakespeare Sisters series: *Forecast, Trouble Brewing* and *Hamlet's Ghost*. She has over twenty children's books published in Korea, and runs a children's travel publishing company called Itchee Feet. She lives with her partner Dom and their four sons in Sydney. Jane can be contacted via her website: www.janetara.com.

Also by Jane Tara

Forecast: Shakespeare Sisters
Trouble Brewing: Shakespeare Sisters
The Happy Endings Book Club

Hamlet's Ghost

Jane Tara

First published by Momentum in 2014
This edition published in 2015 by Momentum
Pan Macmillan Australia Pty Ltd
1 Market Street, Sydney 2000

A CIP record for this book is available at the National Library of Australia

Hamlet's Ghost: Shakespeare Sisters

EPUB format: 9781760081027
Mobi format: 9781760081034
Print on Demand: 9781760300517

Cover design by Carrie Kabak
Edited by Kylie Mason
Proofread by Laurie Ormond

Macmillan Digital Australia: www.macmillandigital.com.au

To report a typographical error, please visit momentumbooks.com.au/contact/

Visit www.momentumbooks.com.au to read more about all our books and to buy
books online. You will also find features, author interviews and news of any author
events.

For Zika Nester, my teacher and friend.

And in memory of the Independent Theatre… as it was back then.

Prologue

"To be or not to be. To *be be be* or not to *be be be.*"

Kip Daniels took a deep breath. Everything was going to plan. The sacrifices, the shattered dreams—all worth it now. Persistence was about to pay off. His moment had arrived. He just needed to calm down.

"That is the question. The big, big, *big* question." His voice bounced off the dressing room walls.

Kip stretched and tried to calm his nerves. He was petrified—understandably. He was, after all, performing *Hamlet* in his very own theater. Opening night at the Hamlet Majestic with a performance of the Bard's greatest play. It was fate. He could feel it…along with the nerves.

There was a knock on the door and Martina the stage manager stuck her head into the room. "What are you doing?"

Kip hated stupid questions. "Hunting elephants. What do you think?"

"You're back on." She took in the number of talismans scattered around—a string of garlic, an upside-down broom—and rested on the pile of books about witches on Kip's makeup table. "You'd swear we were doing the Scottish play, Kip."

1

Kip glanced at the books, then at Martina. His dark eyes flashed. "I don't believe in any of that stuff."

"Sure you don't." She held the door open for him.

Kip followed her backstage and stood in the wings. He fingered the velvet drapes for luck. Yes, there were whispers about him being a control freak, but in this business, you didn't get anywhere while others held the reins. Control was key. And since he'd discovered he had quite a gift for directing as well as acting, he was finally in control.

He allowed himself a quick fantasy about settling old scores. The thought flamed the fire in his belly. This would show all those bastards in New York! Everyone who had uttered those soul-crushing words—"Thanks...we'll be in touch"—would wish they had. They'd sit up and take notice when they heard that Kip Daniels had opened his own theater and given the greatest interpretation of *Hamlet* since Olivier. And he'd done it in a town *called* Hamlet. That in itself was a stroke of theatrical genius.

Hamlet, Massachusetts, would be on the map. This speck of a town would soon be recognized as the home of the greatest regional theater in America. The Hamlet Majestic would become the starting point for Broadway shows, a springboard for future theater stars. And as the owner/ artistic director, he would have the power that had been stripped from him, piece by painful piece, in that soulless jungle. He would, finally, be the man he knew he was capable of becoming.

Kip felt a small hand slip into his. He looked down into the excited face of his son, Tad, the driving force behind his desire to succeed. Tad was a five-year-old version of himself. With his dark hair and eyes and never-ending energy, Tad could be—and most probably would be—him in twenty-five years. Didn't we all become our parents, no matter how hard we fought against it?

Kip loved being a dad, although it had come as a huge shock initially. He'd hoped a two-week gig on a daytime soap would lead to bigger and better things. It had, but not work wise. Instead, a one-night stand with the show's star had led to fatherhood.

Kip did the right thing and proposed to Collette. She did the right thing and told him to fuck off. They ended up being great friends. They were very much alike, although Collette thought Kip's passion for theater was a bit pretentious. She didn't care for Strasberg or Meisner. The method to her was what her dermatologist did once a month to keep her looking young. She wasn't an actress; she was a soap star. And nothing would get in the way of that. So while she loved Tad, she simply didn't have time for him. She paid Kip to look after him.

A couple of years of night-time feeds and nappy changes and single parenting, mixed with daytime rejections from casting agents and directors finally took their toll and Kip began to wonder if it was all worth it.

That's when his sister told him about an old theater for sale near where she lived. It was like a light going off for Kip. He'd still perform, he'd just take control of what he performed. And give Tad an upbringing near family, away from the insanity of New York. He was determined that Tad would have an incredible father to model himself on. So Kip bought the theater—with Collette's money, admittedly—and took his son to live in Hamlet.

He renovated the theater himself. He taught acting classes and met some other locals who had theater backgrounds. Bit by bit, the community came out to support him. Being a single parent wasn't always easy, but it had cemented his relationship with his son. It was the two of them against the world. Nothing could damage it now.

"You're gonna be great, Dad."

"Are you going to go and sit with your mom?"

"I wanna watch from here. Can I, Dad?"

"Sure you can."

Kip realized the Queen had just exited. He kissed Tad on the head and ruffled his hair. "It's my time." He moved into the wings and jiggled his legs a bit. He needed to go to the toilet again. Nerves! He waited until the King and Polonius left the stage and then turned and winked at Tad. "I'll be seeing you, buddy."

The stage lights beat down on him, making him perspire. He sensed the audience although the house was deathly silent. A good sign, he thought. He glanced downstage and could see the bobby socks and sneakers of his niece in the front row.

He began. "To be or not to be…"

Everything faded out of focus and he found that core inside himself that belonged to Hamlet. The Prince took over his body.

"That is the question. Whether 'tis nobler in the mind to suffer; The slings and arrows of outrageous fortune; Or to take arms against a sea of troubles; And by opposing end them?" He was so in the moment he forgot where he was, who he was.

Kip felt the zone close around him and swallow him whole until he was aware of nothing but the emotions of a man who until this moment had been fictional. Kip breathed life into him and became him. He knew nothing but Hamlet. "But that the dread of something after death…" He didn't notice the heat, or the bored swinging of his niece's legs. He certainly didn't notice that loud crack that roared through the theater, or the moan as the roof gave way.

"Be thou all my sins remembered…"

"Oh my god, *no!*"

Kip finished his monologue to mayhem, rather than the awed silence he had hoped for. The audience was screaming.

People rushed around yelling and crying. Kip looked at Tad, frozen to the spot, his face pale, his eyes full of horror. What had he missed?

Kip turned and the room began to swing. He felt strange. He followed Tad's gaze to the center of the stage, the spot where he thought he was standing, and instead saw a pile of rubble where the roof had fallen. Under it lay his own crushed, lifeless body. His empty eyes stared straight back at him, mocking him.

As he watched from a strange, altered distance, Kip realized he was floating above everything. He saw Collette rush to their son and cover his eyes. He watched his sister scoop his niece up. He could see his own body, broken and alone. All the actors stood around staring, bar one, who screamed for a doctor. When no one responded, Chandler ran from the theater himself to call one.

And then his girlfriend, the woman he'd been in love with for a while but only just realized, went to him and took his pulse. She whispered his name.

"I hear you," he whispered back.

She looked up to the skies, toward him...straight at him, as though she could see him. Her face crumpled and she let out a wail of pure grief.

She really loves me, thought Kip. Don't cry darling, I'm here. I love you too.

Suddenly he sensed the light. It was warm and welcoming, beckoning him to go home. But then he remembered *her*. He knew without a doubt why this had happened. It was because of her. He was helpless. He didn't even try to go towards the light. He knew he was stuck. Darkness rose and the light vanished.

And then a tsunami of sorrow washed over him and he turned and drifted back to his dressing room.

Chapter 1

Rhiannon Dee felt like she was having an out-of-body experience. It was almost too much to comprehend. She shook her head, but they were still there, naked, unaware she was watching. Her best friend, Victoria De Whittaker, had her legs splayed across the coffee table, while Chandra, Rhi's boyfriend of two years, crouched between them like a very eager dog.

"Oh, Chandra, what are you doing to me?" screeched Victoria.

Rhi had seen enough. "Sounds like someone needs to go back to Sex Ed 101."

Hearing Rhi's voice, Chandra froze, looking like he was about to have a coronary. Then he tried to explain himself. It was pitifully typical of him.

"It's—it's—it's not what it looks like, Rhi."

Rhi almost enjoyed his discomfort. "I'm sure there's a very good explanation and I'm so looking forward to hearing it."

There was silence, apart from the sound of Victoria sliding back into her underwear. Too late for modesty now, Rhi thought. She'd seen Victoria in a new light, namely the lovely lamp she'd recently bought from House and Home. She'd never be able to turn it on again. She must remember to return it.

"I was helping Vic with a new yoga position." Chandra looked pleased with himself.

"That position isn't new," Rhi said.

Victoria stood and shimmied back into her skirt. "I'd better go."

"Yes, thanks so much for *coming*," Rhi snapped.

"We'll talk about this when you calm down."

"Great. Let's book in a lunch for twenty-fifty."

Victoria actually looked upset. "I understand that you feel the need to hurt me right now, Rhi."

"As far as I can see, Victoria, you got the pleasure while I've been handed the pain."

Victoria gave Rhi a conspiratorial grin. "Not that much pleasure. I think I anticlimaxed."

Rhi resisted the urge to claw her eyes out.

"Pleasure and pain are both intertwined, Rhi," offered Chandra, his yoga-perfected body glistening with sweat. He placed his long slim fingers together in his *I'm a guru* way and spoke in the same tone that he used with his yoga devotees. "This is the perfect example of the yin and yang in a relationship."

The sight of his yang made Rhi want to yin. But at least they'd had safe sex. "Put some clothes on, Chandra."

"It's symbolic, Rhi. I'm standing here exposed. I love you."

"Flowers would've been a more appropriate way of letting me know."

Chandra put on his pleading face. "We've been disconnected for months, Rhi. You're so obsessed with your career. Every audition, every failed casting...you never have time for me."

"Thank god Vic was here to comfort you." She turned to Victoria, her heartbreak finally evident. "Why? *Why*, Vic?"

"It doesn't mean anything."

"That makes it worse. You were my oldest friend."

"What do you mean *were*?" slurred Victoria. Rhi realized she'd been drinking, which wasn't unusual nowadays, but 11am was early even for Victoria.

"You told me you didn't love him any more," Vic said.

"That doesn't give you the right to do this."

"What do you mean you don't love me?" Chandra had the nerve to look devastated.

"It's true," Rhi admitted. "I don't love you any more."

"And it's not like I like him. So this shouldn't be a problem."

"I don't even recognize you right now, Vic."

"He's been hitting on me for months." Victoria was grasping at straws now. "You can't tell me you didn't see this coming."

Rhi glared at her now ex-best friend. "The only thing I've seen coming is something that will haunt me forever."

Victoria began to cry. "You of all people should have predicted this and kept us away from each other."

"So this is my fault?"

"I didn't mean it like that. I'm sorry."

"We're at a fork in the road," Chandra offered. "We need to choose which road to take."

Rhi took a calm breath, which appeared to comfort the other two. "You're right, Chandra, this is a fork in the road. So here's what's going to happen. You two go left, I'll go right, and I'll never be forked by you again."

Rhi walked out the door without a backward glance.

Chapter 2

"My life is crap!"

"No, your day has been crap. Your life is quite enviable."

Rhi stared at her brother like he'd grown an extra head. "Who would envy my life?"

"Oh I don't know." Finn ruffled her hair. "Syrian and Sudanese refugees?"

"Okay, apart from them?" Rhi said as he sat on the lounge beside her. "Listen, I'm allowed to feel sorry for myself today."

"Yes, you are, but let's keep it in perspective."

"Perspective? I saw my best friend with her foof in my boyfriend's face today."

"Who says 'foof'?" Finn grabbed Rhi's wine glass off her. "You need to stop drinking immediately."

Rhi took the wine glass back. "*Vajayjay*...is that better?"

"A much better visual." Finn pulled a face.

Rhi put the glass down and curled up next to her brother. She always felt safe with Finn. "Can I stay here for a while?"

"Need you ask? Take the spare room."

"I might never leave it."

"You can't be a hermit forever," Finn said.

"I can try." Rhi stretched her legs across the lounge. She was more than happy hiding out here. "Or perhaps I should leave New York."

"Why would you do that? You're a born and bred New Yorker, Rhi."

"I might have a better chance somewhere else."

Finn's kind eyes searched her distraught ones. "What do you mean?"

"Wouldn't you love to escape the whole Dee legacy?"

Finn glanced across the room at the framed photo of their parents. He hated being disloyal to anyone. "Sure, there have been times," he admitted.

"My career sucks because of them." Rhi pointed at the photo and it shook slightly.

"Rhi, you're an excellent actress."

"I'm an out-of-work actress. *Constantly!* They are so famous that I never have a chance when I walk into a casting. People still remember me from the TV show."

"Really? I get the occasional 'Have we met before?' But other than that I rarely get recognized." Finn poured Rhi some more wine. "I guess I can thank Taran for pulling the plug on our appearances earlier than you managed to."

"I wish I had a difficult twin."

"No, you don't."

They laughed, both understanding the truth of that.

"Why does it affect your career? Doesn't being recognized help?"

"Not at all." Rhi sat up. "It's different for you and Taran. With your music, and his art, neither of you ask the audience to suspend belief. As an actress, I do—but how can they imagine me as any character when first and foremost I'm *the Witchlet*—the daughter of Brigid and Lugh Dee? They grew up watching me, wearing my clothing line."

"We were hardly the Kardashians."

"We paved the way for the Kardashians," Rhi pointed out. "We should be ashamed."

"Too true."

Long before reality TV was even a genre, cameras followed Brigid and Lugh around to show America how normal witches were. Thing was, they were anything but normal. The show was a hit and it turned Brigid and Lugh and their three children into celebrities. Taran was the first to jump ship. He'd hired a savvy lawyer who also got Finn out of his contract on the basis that being Taran's almost identical twin meant Taran would still be recognized if Finn continued working. So Rhi became the sole focus for three years, until she turned eighteen and refused to appear on any more shows. Rhi had distanced herself as much as possible, but she was still recognized, especially within the industry.

Brigid knew that change was necessary, so she revamped the Dee brand and pitched a chat show to the network. They loved it and she scored herself and her husband a mighty deal. Nearly a decade later, their chat show, *Afternoon Dee-light* was still a success.

Finn wrapped his arms around Rhi. "I didn't realize how bad it was, sis."

"One director joked that he'd get in touch if he was ever casting the witches in *Macbeth*. My agent called last week and told me that there was a small role in *Sabrina: the Next Reunion*." Rhi began to cry. "My career is a wasteland. My last show was so off Broadway it was closer to the Jersey Turnpike."

"Don't knock Jersey."

"Maybe I should give it up. I could teach. I have my degree. I love teaching those summer workshops."

"You'd be a great teacher, Rhi." Finn would support her if she said she wanted to rob banks. He allowed his little sister time to cry and then passed her a tissue. "It could be worse."

"How?"

"You have money. To every negative is a positive. So many people struggle just to survive, Rhi. Be grateful you don't have to."

"Yes, I've got such first-world problems." Rhi sighed. "I need to carve a path for myself. I'd give it all up today, Finn, just to have a life of my own."

"What does that even mean, Rhi?"

"I'll let you know once I've worked it out."

*

Rhi moved out of Chandra's apartment and into Finn's spare room. She ignored the constant calls from both Chandra and Victoria, and the other friends who had "Oh my god! Heard about what happened." She didn't go anywhere and didn't see anyone apart from Finn. She took time out to think.

Rhi quickly realized that she didn't miss Chandra. He could be charming and entertaining and they'd had some great times together, but for months she'd been bored by his narcissism.

They'd met at his yoga studio in the village, just as a yoga DVD he'd released was going global. He'd been genuinely surprised by his sudden success, but thrilled at the opportunity to share his yoga message with more people. That humble, sexy, yoga teacher had been missing for some time and in his place was a self-absorbed man who thought he was way more important than he actually was. As Rhi had recently snapped at him, "You teach rich New Yorkers to stretch, Chandra, it's hardly brain surgery."

Rhi had taken up kickboxing instead. Yoga, she discovered, wasn't her thing. But still, it had taken another six months and a very painful betrayal to realize that the yoga teacher wasn't her thing either. Yes, it hurt, but she was also relieved to be rid of him.

She'd recover from Chandra. It was Victoria's betrayal that cut her to the core. They'd been inseparable since elementary school. Victoria was insecure, superficial and as self-absorbed as Chandra, but she was also funny, smart and generous. They'd had their ups and downs, but they'd always been fiercely loyal to each other. Until now. Rhi couldn't fathom how Victoria could betray her.

"How long do you think it will take me to get over this?" Rhi was perched on a kitchen stool while Finn cooked.

"You were with him for two years."

"Not Chandra. I mean Vic."

Finn stopped stirring his pasta sauce and looked at Rhi. "Maybe never."

"I was googling—"

"Ah, the great oracle."

"Yes...and a lot's been written on the pain of losing a lover, but not much about losing a friend. And this is worse than any breakup. Some mornings I wake up and realize I'm in your spare room, remember why and for a moment think, 'I can't face the day.'"

"It will pass."

"I know. But right now...I miss her, which makes me furious. Why would I miss someone who did that to me?"

"Why indeed."

"I just miss her."

"That might not pass."

"I know that too."

Finn passed Rhi a spoon of his pasta sauce. "Taste that."

She did as she was told, blowing on the spoon first to cool it. "Delicious," she said, watching as Finn turned the flame on the stove off. "What about you, Finn? You've had some pretty horrendous betrayals. How did you forgive?"

"He's my brother. I had no choice."

"Forgiveness is always a choice."

Finn thought about it for a moment. "Those women weren't as important as my relationship with Taran. And I understand why he did it."

"I understand why Victoria did it too—she's been out of control since her dad died. But does that mean I forgive her?"

"Maybe you will forgive but not forget?"

"It would take amnesia to forget that." Rhi screwed her face up. "Oh god, on my coffee table!"

"And I always thought Chandra was more a taker than a giver."

"I'm giving him the coffee table."

"One day you might look back at this and realize it was the best thing that ever happened to you."

"I might," Rhi said. "Or it might break my heart every time I think of it."

Chapter 3

A week after she discovered Chandra helping Victoria with her kundalini, Rhi drove to Boston to attend a friend's wedding. The bride was an old friend from school. She was also the friend who had originally introduced Rhi to Chandra at the yoga studio.

"I hear you and Chandra broke up." The bride looked surprised, although that was from an overzealous Botox shot rather than any real emotion regarding Rhi's relationship woes.

"He was screwing Victoria behind my back."

The bride seemed confused. "Really? I thought he was doing Minnelle."

That was how Rhi discovered Chandra was sleeping with a number of her friends. And why she decided against driving straight back to New York after the wedding. She was in no hurry to return. She needed to do something about the pain in her chest; needed time to think, to plan and to work out where to go from here. So she hit the gas pedal and headed north.

She flew along the freeway. The more distance she put between herself and New York, the better she felt. She wound down the window and let the wind play wild in her hair. She turned on some music, and sang loudly. Cars, towns, the world passed her by. She could've driven like that forever, only she noticed her gas light was on and her tank was hovering on empty.

She scanned the road for a place to fill up, saw a sign for a town called Hamlet, and took the turnoff. Rhi marveled at the gorgeous houses and neat gardens as she drove into town; it was like something out of a picture book. She took a left turn and found herself at the beach. Her gas tank could wait. This was what *she* needed, to fill up her own tank. She parked and gazed out at endless white sand. It was empty, gloriously so, apart from a handful of people jogging along the boardwalk. She grabbed her coat and scarf and locked the car behind her then headed down onto the beach. There was an icy chill but the sky was a vibrant blue. Rhi took a deep breath of fresh air. It filled her lungs and her soul. She could smell, taste the salt. How long had it been since she'd taken time to breathe deeply? She couldn't remember.

She sat on the sand and watched the ocean heave into shore. What the hell was she going to do? Perhaps she could stay right where she was forever.

"What do I want?" she whispered.

For the first time in a long time, her head cleared, and she knew.

"I want to work...and I want it to be meaningful." She took a breath.

"I want to step away from my parents' version of the craft."

She gave a slight nod and continued softly, so only the waves would hear her.

"I want to carve out a space, a life for myself. I want to find me."

A gull cried its approval.

"I want to be happy—"

Something caught her eye. She noticed a jogger nearby, moving toward her.

"Holy crap."

Rhi watched as the guy ran by, oblivious to her. He made the men in the J. Crew catalogue look plain. Tall, dark hair, athletic build and a face that deserved its own billboard.

"And I want one of those." She giggled to herself. Hey, she might as well put it out there while she had the universe on the line.

Rhi stood and dusted the sand off, and then returned to the car. What was she going to do now? She really felt lost. Geographically, she didn't mind. Internally was a major problem.

She found a gas station and filled her car up and then drove along the beachfront, past a lovely set of restaurants and cafes on a wharf, and into the center of town. She parked her car and wandered down the main street. There were a handful of restaurants, grocery stores and cafes, a mouthwatering confectionery shop, a bookshop, an Irish bar and a travel agent. It seemed like a town that knew how to relax.

Further along were a fruit shop, a health food shop and a bakery. The pavement was neat and lined with trees. The storefronts were well kept and quaintly decorated.

She bought some chocolate and bottled water from the supermarket and some pastries from the bakery, eating one as she continued to walk. She turned left into First Avenue. The business district petered off and Rhi passed a library, a daycare center and a swimming pool, closed until summer.

A woman pushing a pram passed her and smiled. A teenage boy on a bike rode by. Hamlet looked like a nice place to live. She almost wished she lived somewhere like it. Chandra and Victoria who?

And then she saw it. Heard it. It almost screamed out at her. The Hamlet Majestic Theater, boarded up and desperately run down, conspicuous in its decay. While the rest of Hamlet was shiny and well kept, the theater was dilapidated and heart-breakingly shabby.

Rhi stood still. One endless moment where the Fates met to discuss what path she should take. Rhi knew. She sensed their silent conversation. She could turn around and keep walking. It was her choice.

Instead, she chose to step forward onto the broken pavement and the theater steps. The overgrown lawn sprouted through the cracks in the pathway. The Majestic sign was faded and the paint peeling, like huge sad tears dripping from boarded-up eyes.

Rhi reached for a window and tried to see through a gap in the boards. She had a view of a cobweb and little else. She did a full circle around the crumbling theater. She didn't see the rats, or the weeds, or the broken glass and peeling paint. She saw possibilities, and plays and people milling around laughing. She saw the future of the old theater. She saw her own future. She saw a life, a normal life, unfold before her eyes.

Rhi stepped back and took the old building in. Beautiful. She smiled and silently thanked Chandra and Victoria for being such assholes. Their betrayal had led her here. Rhi knew, without a doubt, that she was meant to bring the Majestic back to life. And with it, find her own.

Chapter 4

Rhi headed back to Main Street, her head buzzing. First things first, she needed to find out more about her theater. As delightful as the town was, it was a Sunday afternoon, so most of the shops were closed. She could ask in the supermarket or the deli, which were open. She stood for a moment and looked around, rubbing her hands together. There was an icy wind and she was freezing. She noticed a shop called Crystal's Balls. The window display was filled with tarot cards and self-help books. It was everything she wanted to escape in New York, but it was also open and the sign in the window said, *I predict you'll love our coffee.* She could get a coffee, warm up and find out some information.

The door jangled a welcome as she entered. Inside was a jumble of bookshelves on one side of the room and tables on the other. Framed vintage movie posters lined the walls: *Bell, Book and Candle* and *I Married a Witch* and Vincent Price's *The Witchfinder General.* There was a sign that said, *Feel free to read our books while you try our coffee.* In one corner was a spiral staircase, with a sign shaped like a pointed finger aiming upward: *Tarot readings this way.*

The whole place was a welcoming mess of delicious smells, unusual artwork and books. Rhi felt at home and annoyed all at once. She'd grown up around all this. If she was going to make a normal life for herself, places like these were out of the question.

"Can I help you?" A woman was watching her from behind the counter.

"I didn't see you there."

"I blend in when I want to."

Rhi doubted this woman ever blended in anywhere. She was tall with an athletic build and a closely shaved blond head. Although androgynous, her beauty hit you like a sledgehammer. Her haircut added to her stunning looks by making sure nothing detracted from her gorgeous face. She was a strange mix of ethereal beauty and rock'n'roll. She was decked out in cargo pants and a tight sweater with a green pea on the front, *Give peas a chance* written underneath. The rest of her was incredibly and elegantly bare: no shoes, no jewelry and not one scrap of makeup.

Rhi tried not to stare. "Do you own this place?"

"Half of it. I'm Tye."

"Who's Crystal?" asked Rhi.

"My mom. She owns the other half. And she's the one with the balls."

"Crystal ones?"

"So they say."

Rhi laughed. "Can I have a coffee?"

"You sure can. Take a seat."

Rhi took her jacket off and sat at a table close to the counter. Perhaps Tye could give her the rundown on the theater. "It's a nice town. What's it like to live here?"

Tye worked the coffee machine while she spoke. "I love it. We're from New York, but we used to spend our holidays here. About five years ago, Mom got it in her head to move here. I came along to help her settle in. I had no intention of staying...but I did. You couldn't kick me out if you tried."

"Don't you miss New York?"

Tye shrugged. "What's to miss? It's only a few hours away."

Tye placed the coffee in front of Rhi and slid into the seat opposite. She moved like a cat.

Rhi took a sip of the coffee and sighed. "Perfect."

"I came here and couldn't find a decent brew, so rather than leave, I decided to provide one myself."

"You take coffee very seriously."

"It is serious," Tye said with a smile.

Rhi placed her cup on the table. "Do you know anything about the theater up the road?"

The smile faded. "The old Majestic?"

Rhi nodded. "Is it still in use?"

"Not since I moved here. There was an accident there in the late eighties."

"And it's been closed since then?"

"It's been reopened a couple of times—a community center and a dance school, but they didn't last long."

"Why not?"

Tye leaned forward and her voice dropped to a melodramatic whisper. "Local legend says it's haunted."

Rhi laughed. "No theater is complete without a ghost. Do you know who could give me more information about it?"

Tye gave Rhi a calculating stare. It wasn't threatening; it was as though she was trying to protect something. "The owner wants it left alone, so you're wasting your time."

Rhi matched Tye's stare. "That's okay. I have some time to waste."

There was a long moment, and then Tye seemed to relax again. "I'd try Annie Anderson at Captain's Realty. She has the rundown on everything in town, even if it's not on her books."

"How do I get hold of her on a Sunday?"

"There was an auction this morning and she's still in her office, a few doors up. I just took a coffee to her." Tye peered at Rhi in interest. She had the eyes of a sage. "You're going to move here."

Rhi chose to ignore Tye's predictive abilities. Instead, she tossed back the last of the coffee and placed the empty cup on the table.

"I've just discovered a gorgeous abandoned theater and the perfect cup of coffee. I'm left with no choice."

*

Rhi stepped into the cold, pausing to wrap her scarf and button her jacket. What was she thinking? So she liked that old theater? So what? She liked the Lyceum Theater as well but she'd never once asked about renting it. Opening her very own theater was a completely unrealistic dream. She needed to harden up, get back to New York and keep trying to crack it. She wasn't the only actor there who was struggling.

She felt her phone ringing in her pocket. She checked the number: Melanie from EUA, her agent. Timing! She turned and headed toward her car as she answered.

"Hi Melanie. Working weekends now?"

"I'm going on vacation next week so need to catch up on a few things. There's a job if you're available."

Rhi pumped her fist. It paid to be positive. "What is it?" *A film? A series?*

"It's a series of ads for Joe's Car Yard. They've asked especially for you."

Rhi stopped walking as her heart hit the sidewalk.

"The ads will be funny, with you predicting sale prices." Melanie waited for a response but when there was none, she continued. "I know you want to step away from the witch thing, but you still need to earn money. One of these days you might have to accept that that's your niche."

Rhi turned on her heel. "I appreciate the call, Mel, but I'm out of town for a while. I'll let you know when I'm ready to work again." She spotted the real estate and switched her phone off.

Captain's Realty was a bright, airy office filled with potted plants and framed black-and-white photos of the town over the years. Annie Anderson was perched on top of her desk with her back to the door, chatting animatedly on the phone.

"Listen, Sam, there's no way I'm going to date you...Because I've known you forever, that's why. It'd be like dating my own brother...Of course I like you, but not like *that*...No, you can tell Jake I'm not going to date him either...Because he's your brother, you big buffoon. If I can't date one, I can't date the other. It wouldn't be right."

Rhi gave an embarrassed cough and Annie jumped.

"I got to go. Now stop moping and I'll see you soon. Actually, I've been having problems with my washing machine. Would you be a sweetie and swing by and check it out? Thanks, Sam. Bye." Annie hung up the phone and made her way over to Rhi.

Annie Anderson was a five-foot-two powerhouse. She had dark eyes, a mass of black curls and long, manicured fingernails. She was also savvy. She gave Rhi the once over and concluded, correctly, that she was a New Yorker, with money, who was passing through.

"Can I help you?"

"I hope so. I want some information about the Old Majestic."

Annie's eyes squinted slightly. "Why?"

"I'd like to rent it, or buy it—anything really. I want to bring it back to life."

"That's like resurrecting Elvis. Impossible." Annie shifted uncomfortably.

"Nothing is impossible."

"You tell that to Elvis."

"I will next time I'm in Vegas."

Annie raised one eyebrow. "The Majestic has been closed for twenty-eight years. And the owner wants to keep it that way."

"I heard someone once opened a community center there."

"For three days."

"And a dance school."

Annie folded her arms and sighed. "You've done your homework. But since then the owner decided to just leave it be. I know it sounds crazy, but folks round here think the theater wants to be left alone."

Rhi mirrored Annie and folded her arms. She was becoming more determined by the second. "That doesn't sound crazy to me at all. Therefore this won't sound crazy to you: The theater called to me. It wants to be a theater, not a community center, not a decrepit pile of wood that scares the neighborhood kids. A theater. And I intend to see that it happens. Now, whom do I speak to about opening it?"

"You would move here, to renovate the Majestic?"

"Yes." Rhi realized she actually wanted to. "Which means I'll need to hire locals to help."

"Who's doing the selling here?"

"I feel like I need to persuade you."

"You're persuasive." Annie grinned. "It's a massive project. How do you intend to pull it off?"

"No idea yet."

"How do you even know you'll like this town?"

"I thought I might stay the night and see."

"Yes, one night will clarify everything." Annie sighed and took a flyer from a pile on her desk. "Stay here. Tell Hilary I sent you."

"Would it be possible to see inside the theater while I'm here?"

"I've got the keys." Annie pursed her lips. "You're not going to take no for an answer are you?"

"No."

"What's your name?"

"Rhi. Rhiannon...Wall." Rhi flinched at her lie but there was no way she could use her real surname here.

Annie clasped her hand and shook it. "I'm Annie. You from New York, Rhi?"

Rhi nodded.

"Then you'll need somewhere to live around here as well. Why don't we look in to that while I see what I can do about the Majestic?"

Chapter 5

"Fancy just driving into town and deciding you like it so much you want to stay the night." Hilary Chapman had obviously never heard such a thing before, despite being the proprietor of Hamlet's best B&B—so said the flyer. She was clearly suspicious.

"Well that just goes to show what a lovely town it is." Rhi decided that if Hilary thought staying the night was a fly-by-the-seat-of-your-pants decision, then it was best to not mention her spontaneous plans to move here and rent the theater.

Rhi followed Hilary's ample bottom up the stairs.

"Checkout is at eleven," Hilary said over her shoulder. "We let our guests stay a little longer during the winter months."

"That's very nice of you."

"We know."

The stairs opened out onto a landing lined with Oriental rugs and lit by large windows.

Hilary led Rhi to a door at the end. "We ask that there's no smoking."

"I don't smoke."

"And no casual overnight visitors."

"I doubt I'd be that lucky," Rhi joked.

Hilary shot her a look as she opened the door. "Here we are."

The Ocean View room was exactly that. Rhi walked over to the window and stared out at the Atlantic, stretching as far as the eye could see.

"How lovely," she said.

Hilary seemed appeased by Rhi's approval and gave her a much friendlier smile. "Anything else you need?"

"Do you have internet?"

"We do. The password is 'Ten Commandments.'"

"The phrase, or the actual commandments?" Rhi meant it as a joke but Hilary clearly thought she was serious.

"Ten. Commandments."

"Ten the word or the number?"

"The word."

"Excellent."

Hilary clasped her pudgy fingers in front of her. With her graying short hair and caramel-colored cardigan, she looked like she was in her seventies, but Rhi guessed she was actually much younger than that.

"Thank you for accommodating me at such short notice," Rhi said.

Hilary nodded her approval. "Let me know if there's anything you need. If it's to do with Hamlet, we can help you out."

"You and...?"

Hilary looked confused. "It's only me."

"Oh...okay, then I'll ask you."

"We serve breakfast from seven." And with that, Hilary and her ample bottom disappeared back down the hall.

Rhi took a moment to check out the room. The four-poster bed was covered in a beautiful patchwork quilt. The striped wallpaper looked new but gave the room a vintage feel. In one corner was an oversized velvet armchair, placed in front of a small gas log fireplace. Pillows and throws, some interesting framed sketches and a vase of crème roses and white Asiatic lilies finished the room off. And the view was nothing short of sublime.

"Perhaps I could live here," Rhi said to herself.

She pulled her iPad out of her bag, switched it on, and typed in "Ten Commandments," then spent half an hour asking Google questions, searching the history of Hamlet, and anything she could find regarding the Majestic.

She discovered that Hamlet had a population of just over twenty thousand and had been established in 1654. The most recent census showed that due to an influx of Boston residents in the eighties, nearly thirty percent of the residents claimed Irish ancestry. It was the largest Irish population north of Boston.

Now families flocked to the area due to the laid-back lifestyle and good schools. Real estate prices were booming. American classic literature was embraced, and the town boasted a number of literary organizations and an annual literature festival. The Hamlet Historical Society had recently formed a popular historical reenactment organization whose main focus was the pioneer settlers of the area and the American Revolution. There was a burgeoning art scene, with two galleries in town and a monthly artisans market on the beach where artists from all over Massachusetts came to sell. There was an annual Children's Day, telling Rhi there were enough kids, and enough interest in kids, to start some acting classes. There was a lively restaurant and bar scene and one of New York's top chefs had recently opened a restaurant on the wharf. The local newspaper said it was a sign of things to come.

Hamlet really did seem like a lovely town with lots to offer. And yet, there was no theater company. Rhi did a little dance around the room.

She jotted down the addresses for the chamber of commerce and the library, which she had seen earlier, and then, armed with a list of questions, she went and found Hilary, who was listening to a Maeve Binchy audiobook while she knitted.

"Everything okay, dear?" Hilary asked as she paused her CD.

"Absolutely. I love the room."

"The house has been in my family for four generations. Apparently Thoreau wrote *Life in the Woods* here."

"I thought he wrote that while he lived in the woods at Walden Pond."

"Yes, well, my great-grandmother said he used to get away for weekends." Hilary placed her knitting to one side. "Can I help you with something?"

Rhi perched herself on the sofa opposite Hilary. "What can you remember about the Majestic?"

Rhi's question clearly threw her hostess. "That's been closed for many years. No one goes near it. People say it's haunted, although I don't believe that, do you?"

"Sounds like gossip to me," Rhi said.

Hilary seemed to approve, because she opened up further. "I remember the theater as a child. It was a vibrant place. My parents would get dressed up to go to the Majestic on Friday nights. They had dances there, and movie nights. Vaudeville shows often came to town. Ethel Barrymore once performed there, you know."

"What happened?"

"The theater was built by Alfred Knox in the early twenties. His son took over, but he never really had the same passion for it. By the time Alfred's grandson inherited the place, it was well past its glory days." Hilary thought about this for a moment. "It closed in the mid seventies. The community still used it for meetings. It was used a lot for rallies during the Vietnam War."

"It's been closed since then?"

Hilary looked wary. "In the eighties a young theater actor from New York came to town and restored the Majestic. He planned to reopen, but it didn't work out. You sure do ask a lot of questions."

Rhi decided to change tack. "I've read that Hamlet holds some wonderful reenactment events."

"Well now, I'm a member of the Hamlet Historical Society and we organize the annual reenactment of a little-known battle during the Civil War. It's only been running for three years, but it's become quite an event."

"Hamlet sounds like it has a proud history."

"We're certainly proud of it." Hilary gave her an appraising stare. "Why are you so interested?"

Rhi glanced at the clock on the wall. She'd arranged to meet Annie and needed to get a move on. "Because I'm going to move here and reopen the theater."

Chapter 6

Annie was waiting for Rhi outside the theater, and shook a set of keys as she approached. "I only have fifteen minutes until I need to be somewhere, so I'm going the take you in, but then leave you to look around and lock up. If that's okay with you?"

Rhi nodded. It suited her. "What will I do with the keys?"

"Drop them back into the office before you leave town tomorrow."

"You're trusting."

Annie tossed Rhi a look. "Honey, this isn't New York."

"I know. That's what appeals to me," Rhi said with a sigh.

It took Annie a couple of minutes to unbolt the doors. Once inside the foyer, they both stood still for a moment to give their eyes time to adjust to the dim light. Something was scratching in one corner.

"Rats?" asked Rhi.

"Sounds more like a bear," Annie said.

Rhi jumped as a flapping sound came from above.

"You really are a city girl." Annie pointed to a bird's nest.

Rhi was relieved. Birds she could handle, bats not.

"I haven't been in here for years," Annie whispered. She seemed a little nervous too, but put on a brave face, flicking her curls back and marching across the foyer. "As you can see, it's run down but not a complete write-off. Some locals were concerned about the state of the theater, so the owner had a structural engineering firm in about eight months ago. Everything meets current Massachusetts codes. So any work that needs to be done is superficial."

Rhi made a quick circle of the foyer and stuck her head into the box office. Annie opened the doors of another office and a studio space. They were all in relatively good condition, with just some basic repairs and redecoration needed.

"I'll take you upstairs before I race off."

Annie led Rhi upstairs to two rehearsal studios and a storage room packed with old costumes and props.

"There's some water damage on a few floorboards, otherwise she's in pretty good condition." Annie looked around the room. "It's a great space. And apart from the Catholic Hall and the council chambers, there really is a shortage of leasable rooms in town. These rooms would definitely generate an income for you."

Rhi could see it too. The space was fantastic. There was a lot of junk lying around, but overall it was a gem and Rhi was thrilled with it.

Next, Annie led Rhi into the tech box.

"I'm afraid this isn't my area of expertise, but I called Annabelle, who opened the dance school here a couple of years ago." Annie pulled a piece of paper out of her pocket and read from it. "She said she had the theater wiring checked and it's fine. Lights are good. She updated the sound system, but closed the school before she could put in a new phase board." Annie looked back up at Rhi. "Does that make sense?"

Rhi nodded. "Why did she close?"

"Her husband ran off and left her in a mound of debt. She couldn't afford to go ahead with this." Annie glanced at her watch. "Let's have a peek at the bathrooms."

The two women returned downstairs and stuck their heads into the foyer bathroom.

"Might needed to be remodeled," Annie said. "Or you could just make sure the plumbing is fine and go for the retro look."

Rhi didn't say a word. She was starting to feel over-whelmed. Perhaps this was a crazy idea.

"Let's check out the theater," Annie suggested.

The minute Rhi stepped into the actual auditorium all thoughts of bathroom remodeling and tech box refitting disappeared. To her, the place was heaven. The theater seated an audience of two hundred on row after row of red velvet seats. The seats and hall were in excellent condition.

"I have to go, but take your time. Check out the backstage area. See what you think."

"Thanks, Annie. I'll drop the keys back in."

Annie put her hands on her hips. "I have no idea why I'm even doing this. I can guarantee the owner won't want a bar of it."

"Then at least I tried," Rhi said.

Annie disappeared out the door and Rhi was alone. She *felt* alone. There was a weight to the silence that made it easy to believe nothing else existed outside the theater, that this was it; the whole universe, tucked away inside a 1920s theater. There was no place she'd rather be.

She wandered up to the stage. It was a good size with spacious wings. The acoustics were great. There was a strange patch on the roof but that could be fixed. She pushed her way through the curtains and wandered around backstage. There was a small green room and one dressing room, which was one more than most of the theaters she'd worked in. She ran her fingers along part of an old set and noticed it was propped against a door. She pushed it to one side and realized that the door led to a second dressing room. There was a faded star tacked on the door, roughly cut from silver paper.

Rhi opened the door and stepped inside, but just as she did she felt a heave against her chest, as if she'd been pushed. She jerked back and knocked her head against the doorframe as an icy blast of wind caught her by surprise.

"Ow. Damn." Her fingers touched the bump.

"What are you doing here?" echoed a deep voice.

Rhi screamed, stumbled back over the old set and sprawled across the floor. She watched as a piece of a set shook above her, threatening to collapse on her. She scrambled out of the way just as it fell.

Her eyes darted over to the side of the room—a figure was standing there, in no hurry to help her, obviously. Rhi's eyes flickered toward the back door and gauged how quickly she could make a run for it.

"I mean you no harm. Are you okay?"

The man...a gorgeous man...an absolutely *breathtaking* man, stepped out of the shadows.

It was the guy she'd seen running on the beach.

They locked eyes for a moment and Rhi felt the world tilt off balance. She was falling again, only this time it was internally. Yes, this man was dangerous, but not in a psycho-attacker type way. He was so sexy he should wear a warning sign.

"I didn't mean to frighten you. Or injure you. I just want to know what you're doing here."

"Why?"

"Because I own this monstrosity."

She stared at him for a moment. Hot-man-from-the-beach owned *her* theater? And she'd made a total idiot of herself in front of him.

"Did you hit your head?" He sounded concerned.

She rubbed it in answer.

He waited for her to say something. "Do you need medical assistance?"

Rhi shook her head.

"Are you stuck?" He took one step toward her, his hand out as if trying to pacify a frightened animal.

Pull it together! Rhi clambered to her feet and dusted herself off. She decided against shaking his hand, mainly because she didn't trust herself to walk across the room to him without tripping again. In fact, she looked at his hand like it was a live wire, aware that if she actually touched it, she'd be done for.

"I have keys. Annie the real estate agent let me in." She tried to sound professional. Hard to do when the most stunning man on the planet has just witnessed you falling head over ass.

"Annie? A real estate agent?" He chuckled, as if that amused him.

Rhi realized that this moment could make or break it for her. It was a stroke of luck really, running into the owner. "I'd like to lease the theater."

"Whatever for?"

"The town needs a theater."

"That's what I've always said." He watched her for a moment. "What makes you the right person though?"

"I have the right...qualifications." God, her head was throbbing and everything that came out her mouth sounded ridiculous.

"Qualifications? To rent an abandoned theater? What are your qualifications?"

"I have a theater degree from Columbia and a master's in failure from the New York school of life," Rhi said, challenging him.

He clapped his hands together. "The theater has been waiting for you."

Rhi let out a relieved laugh. "I know it sounds weird, but that's how I feel."

"Believe me, not much sounds weird from where I stand."

"I could fix her up to her former glory."

The man smiled, his incredible face lighting up like a Christmas tree. "She was beautiful."

Good lord, so are you, thought Rhi. He wasn't much older than her, probably early thirties. He had thick black hair, smooth olive skin and flashing gray eyes. He had a three-day shadow that gave him an air of devil-may-care. His lips were full and his nose and jaw strong. At well over six foot, he towered above her. He was wearing dark pants and a loose white shirt that emphasized what seemed to be a truly magnificent chest.

He was, without a doubt, the most mesmerizing member of the male species she'd ever met. Rhi had to stop herself from staring. And drooling.

He grinned at her, amused, as though he could read her mind. Not that it would have been a riveting read. There was only one basic thought going through it: *Blah der blah—hot man alert—blah.*

He stared at her intently. "What a suprise you ending up here."

Rhi wasn't quite sure what he meant. It was a strange thing to say, and yet he was right. "It certainly is," she said. For a moment all she could do was lock eyes with him. His stare sucked the air from the space between them and she was left feeling quite dizzy.

"Are you okay? Perhaps when you bumped your head?"

Rhi waved away his concerns. "I'm fine. It's been a big day."

"I'll get out of your way. Take your time to look around." He turned to go.

"So you'll lease the theater to me?"

"I'll see what I can do." He pushed the dark waves back off his face. "Don't mention me being here. We'll let your application go through the normal channels."

"Okay, sure."

"Nice to meet you, though."

Rhi reached into her purse to get out a business card, but when she looked up, he was gone.

Chapter 7

Back in New York, Rhi set about preparing to move. She was surprised to hear that Annie was having problems getting the owner to agree to lease the Majestic; after all, he'd seemed perfectly fine with it when they'd met. But she didn't mention this to Annie. She didn't really know why, she just felt she shouldn't.

"He's stubborn," Annie said. "So we won't give up just yet."

"What's his name?" asked Rhi.

"William," Annie said evasively. She didn't offer his surname. "I'll let you know when I hear more."

"Thanks, Annie."

Rhi got on with making plans. She knew it was a crazy thing to do: to move to a town she'd spent one night in and rent an old theater she'd seen once. Yet it felt right, in every cell, every atom of her being. She tried not to think about what would happen if William decided he didn't want to lease it to her.

She also tried to not think about his dark, brooding eyes and full lips. His broad chest had nothing to do with her growing desire to move to Hamlet. Sure, he was sexy, and there had been some undeniable chemistry between them, but that had nothing to do with her feelings for the theater. She was excited about the idea of reopening the theater and of creating work for like-minded people.

She met an old friend for lunch. John had been working his way through the ranks for years, until he finally cracked it when he was named artistic director of the Carousel Theater, one of the most successful venues Off-Broadway. She needed to pick his brains. She'd trained as an actress and she had her degree and years of experience working in theater, but she was still making her way through foreign territory.

"I wanted to run some ideas past you. Let me know if you think I'm nuts," Rhi said.

John gave his beanie a tug and pushed his glasses up the bridge of his nose. "Okay, deal."

"I'm going to rent a theater in Massachusetts."

"You're nuts."

"Okay, now I want you to tell me I can do it."

"You're nuts."

"Love the support."

"Give me the rundown."

"I found an amazing abandoned theater. Great building, wonderful theater space, two rehearsal studios, the whole place has been vacant for thirty years so needs some renovations, but the basics are solid."

She had his attention. "Keep going."

"I want to form a theater company, and I've been looking at traditional non-profit models, but I'm thinking of trying something different." She sipped her coffee. "I need to create a viable business first. The space is the business. It can generate an income. I can lease that and I'll open a drama school—"

"For adults?"

"Kids. I've taught those summer drama camps for the past few years and I love it. I really enjoy teaching children."

"Each to their own." It was clear he'd rather pass kidney stones. "How else can the space generate income?"

"I'll lease out the studios, the hall...other companies can perform there."

"And your company? The one this theater will house?"

"I'm working it out."

"Community or professional?

"Professional."

"Profit or non-profit?"

"Profit, for now. I can change to non-profit later. From what I understand there's so much paperwork, and I wouldn't be in a position for any grants yet."

"You need to make sure the mission statement for any theater company is clear. A lot will depend on that. What type of plays you intend to produce. How collaborative the structure is." John leaned across the table. He was clearly interested. "How will it pay for itself initially?"

"I'll make a personal loan to the theater. I'll also look into local funding opportunities."

"So basically, you start a business?"

"The theater. Correct."

"Then using your own business, you house a professional theater company?"

"Right, and while I'm not yet sure of the structure, I do know it needs to start small. Two shows in the first twelve months. But everyone gets paid properly."

John slapped the table. "I'm jealous."

"Get out of here. You've got a great job."

"I do. But I answer to a lot of people. This is exciting, Rhi—big, but exciting."

"Thank you. I really appreciate your support."

"Hopefully I can support in other ways too. I'd love to come up and see the place. Perhaps I can do a residency there once you're up and running? Or the Carousel can bring a show to you. I can certainly send good designers and directors up to work."

"That's wonderful. Thank you."

"What are friends for?"

Rhi paid the check and they said their farewells on the sidewalk.

"I'm proud of you, Rhi. I know it hasn't always been easy for you to get work."

"That will change now." Rhi gave him a cheeky grin. "I'll cast myself in everything."

John gave her a hug. "Why else own a theater, deary!"

Rhi watched as he walked off. In her heartbreak over Victoria and Chandra she'd forgotten that she actually had some very good friends in New York she could always rely on.

She turned and headed in the opposite direction, walking the four blocks home to Finn's along 8th Street, past Tompkins Square Park. It was a cold day, but the sun was shining and the piles of snow still on the ground were melting fast. There were certain things she'd miss about New York. Central Park in summer—well, all year round, but mainly summer. The bagel guy at Union Square. Baxter's on Ludlow Street where Taran and Finn met her for drinks each month. Her brothers. She would miss her brothers.

She'd crossed the street and was heading up the stairs of Finn's brownstone when she heard the voice.

"Rhiannon."

Rhi paused, turning slowly. Victoria stood at the foot of Finn's stairs. Her normally beautiful brunette hair was unwashed. She was wearing expensive clothes and a Burberry jacket but everything looked slightly disheveled.

"You haven't returned my calls."

Rhi didn't say anything, her mouth set in a line that spoke volumes instead.

Victoria shrugged. "You have to forgive me at some stage."

"That stage is not now, Victoria."

Victoria started to cry. "Don't cut me off like this."

Rhi braced herself and prayed that Victoria wouldn't cause a scene. She hated that she felt sorry for her old friend, despite the betrayal. She wanted to give in and erase the past few weeks, but she couldn't. Doing so would be enabling Victoria's recent behavior: not only hurting Rhi, but also the drinking and partying and her careless attitude toward everything of any meaning. She needed to take responsibility for herself. Until that moment, Rhi didn't want to see her. She wanted to forgive her. More than that, she wanted to forget what she'd done. But that was impossible.

"Vic, you've broken my heart. Everything has changed. I don't know what the future holds—"

"Of course you do. You're a witch."

"I'm not ready for this."

"When will you be?"

"I don't know." Rhi felt her phone buzz. She pulled it from her pocket to read the text: *The Majestic is yours. Call me when you can. Annie. xo*

The whole world, in that instant, changed. Rhi looked up.

Victoria wiped the tears and smudged mascara from under her eyes. "Perhaps we can meet for lunch in a few weeks once things have settled down?"

Rhi was so elated that she almost threw her arms around Victoria. Victoria seemed to sense the shift, and it surprised her.

"You'll meet me for lunch?"

"I can't," Rhi said. "I'm moving."

"You've found a new apartment?"

"No. I found a new life."

Chapter 8

Brigid and Lugh Dee sat at each end of the table like the lord and lady they fashioned themselves after. Their children—their most loyal subjects—ate in silence as they listened to their parents relate fantastic tales of who they'd met and what they'd done recently. Autograph hunters, fans and the occasional evangelical regularly interrupted the meal. Brigid and Lugh treated everyone who approached with equal friendliness and respect.

"Turn away from the devil," hissed one woman, her hand tightly clasped around her frightened daughter's arm.

Brigid sighed. "He's one of yours. Witches don't believe in the devil."

"You worship Satan."

"My wife only worships George Clooney," Lugh said gently, as if talking to a child.

"May God save your souls," the woman muttered as she scurried away.

"I'm sure she will. Thanks for dropping by," Brigid called after her and then turning to her husband. "What a formative experience for her daughter."

"She'll smoke dope and study Buddhism later in life," Lugh assured his wife.

Rhi pushed her plate away, her appetite ruined. Eating out with her parents was the best way to control her weight.

Brigid leaned back in her chair and stared at her. "Chandra wasn't able to join us tonight?"

"No."

"Is he working?"

"I have no idea. We broke up."

Her mother raised her perfectly shaped eyebrows. "I see. Well...he'd become a real asshole, hadn't he." It was a statement not a question.

"I guess so."

"But an important pit-stop for you," offered her father. "What have you learned from it, darling?"

"That I prefer Pilates."

"He's actually a very good yoga teacher. Just a shitty boyfriend," Finn said.

Taran rolled his eyes at his twin. "He's such a tool, he belongs at Home Depot."

Rhi looked at her brothers and, not for the first time, marveled at the sheer sight of them. Finn and Taran were three years older. Their faces, their features, their soulful blue eyes, were the impossible to tell apart, but while Finn was as blond and bright as a sunny day, Taran had jet black hair and moods to match. Finn was like their father and drew people in with kindness and compassion while Taran was like their mother, cynical and wild, a human bug zapper, impossible to resist but watch out if you got too close. Finn saw the good in everyone, even his difficult twin. Taran roared through life like the thunder god he was named after. While Finn was always willing to forgive, Rhi knew that Taran would run Chandra down if he had half a chance.

Taran leaned back in his chair. "I always thought he was gay."

"I can assure you, I caught him in a position that would prove otherwise."

Taran's eye narrowed. "You caught him with someone else?"

Rhi nodded. "Victoria."

"Vicky De Whittaker?" Lugh looked horrified. "She's your best friend."

"Apparently she didn't get that memo." Rhi took a sip of Cristal, her parent's staple drink.

"She's got the loyalty of a stray dog." Taran looked thunderous. "I can't believe she did that to you."

"Imagine hurting someone like that," Finn said, casually pouring another drink.

Taran glanced at his brother, a shadow crossing his face before he turned his attention back to Rhi. "You are so much better than both of them."

"Well, darling, out with the old, in with the new," announced Brigid, holding her glass high.

Lugh lifted his own glass and winked at his wife. "Miss one bus, catch the next."

They smiled at each other, silently acknowledging how relieved they were that they would never again have to take public transport.

Brigid turned her attention back to her daughter. "So what are your plans now?"

Rhi thought about the contracts she had signed just two days earlier. "You owe me a drink when you move here," Annie had said when Rhi phoned after receiving her text.

"I owe you more than one drink. I really appreciate the effort, Annie."

"You've got me all caught up in this hare-brained idea of yours. Besides, we need some new young blood in town. So the Majestic is yours to rent. Any renovations are yours. He's agreed on a five-year contract. At the end of the five years, if all goes well, he will *consider* selling."

"But what if I renovate and he sells to someone else?"

"Won't happen. You have first option to buy in the contract."

Rhi felt breathless. There was no turning back now. "How did you talk him into it? I thought it was impossible."

"As you said, nothing is impossible...except that Elvis thing. Anyway, can you come up next week and sign the contracts? I'll also show you a house then."

"How's Monday?"

"Perfect. I'll see you when you get here."

"Okay. And Annie...thank you."

Rhi tossed the rest of her Champagne back for courage and smiled first at her mother, then her father. This wasn't going to be easy. Her mother hated people making plans without her involvement—her approval. She was the ultimate control freak. Rhi glanced at Finn for support and he gave her a gentle nod.

"I've decided to leave New York for a while."

Brigid clapped her bejeweled hands together. "Oh, lovely! Travel always heals the heart, doesn't it, Lugh? Where will you go, sweetheart? Paris, London? Berlin is always fun." She tapped a cigarette out of her pack and waited for Lugh to light it.

"I'm going to Hamlet."

Lugh pulled a vintage Cartier lighter out of his pocket and fired up the cigarette, the only thing he disliked about his wife. "Excellent! I didn't realize it was back on Broadway."

"No, Hamlet, Massachusetts."

Silence fell over the table as Brigid stared at Rhi. She took a deep drag on her cigarette and then stubbed it out. She never had more than one or two puffs. Then she deftly patted her hair down. She never went into an argument looking anything but immaculate. "Weren't you up that way for a wedding recently?"

"Yes. And on the way home I stumbled across a charming little town called Hamlet and have decided to move there," explained Rhi.

Finn motioned for another bottle of Cristal, figuring his parents would need it. "I think this calls for a celebration." He didn't let on that he'd been privy to his sister's plans. "It's wonderful news, Rhi."

"Yes, fabulous." Taran chuckled. He relaxed back with a grin on his face and prepared to watch the show. For once it wasn't him shaking things up.

Brigid smiled and spoke to Rhi as one would a child. "You can't possibly move there."

Rhi didn't take her eyes off her mother's. She was determined not to back down. "Why not?"

"Because...it's a small town."

"Do you know it?"

Brigid looked uncomfortable. "Why would I?"

"Then what's the problem?"

"It wasn't that long ago they were killing our kind in small towns," Brigid snapped.

Rhi laughed. "Mom, I appreciate the concern, but the burning times ended a while ago."

"Not in small towns, Rhiannon."

"I promise I'll leave quickly if they start building a pyre."

"I was burnt at the stake three times and let me tell you, it's nothing to joke about."

Rhi rolled her eyes. "You wouldn't even know about that if you hadn't done past-life therapy."

"Rubbish. I always sensed it. Just talking about this makes my feet burn."

"It's not common practice in modern-day America."

"Obviously you've never been to Mississippi."

"Mom!"

"You are a witch, Rhiannon. You can't escape that."

Rhi felt like she was about to cry, which would be embarrassing in the middle of the restaurant. "I can try."

"You'll never fit in. And surely you don't want to, there."

"Actually, I do. People won't know me, Mom. For once I will fit in. I'll just be me, rather than the lord and lady's daughter."

Brigid reeled back slightly. "Are you ashamed of us?"

"Ashamed? No."

"You'll be there five minutes before someone finds out who you are," Brigid said. "Unless they don't have the internet there."

Rhi prepared for battle. "I changed my name."

"You what?" Brigid looked thunderous.

"I'm using Dad's surname."

"Ours is a matrilineal line."

Rhi was unmoved. "You decided that, Mom. It's not like I'm breaking with generations of tradition." She glanced at her father, who actually looked proud of her. "Please understand, Mom, I need this."

Lugh reached out a hand to calm his wife. "Now, now, Brigid, we know that it's been tough for Rhi to find work. This might be what she needs. She won't be recognized."

"And what is wrong with being recognized?" Brigid gripped the edge of the table. "We've worked our asses off so as she can have this life she's rejecting."

"I'm not rejecting it, Mom."

"Be reasonable, love, she wants to work. She's a gifted actress but is often overlooked because of us." Lugh pushed a tendril of hair off his wife's face. "Let her go somewhere where she can work this out. It's what she wants."

"Thank you, Dad. And this is exactly what I want."

Brigid refused to believe it. "Tonight perhaps, but given a week you'll have forgotten all about it."

"Given a week, I'll be gone. I've already rented a house…I've rented a theater. My stuff is packed. I leave next Tuesday."

Chapter 9

Rhiannon parked her overloaded car in front of the Callahan cottage and stared at it for a moment. It was a blue, two-story bungalow with a front porch, surrounded by large trees. Most of the homes on Maple Drive were tucked away, at least partially out of sight, which gave the road a deserted feel.

She was glad she was alone. She'd dropped in to Captain's Realty to pick up the keys and Annie initially insisted she'd bring her over to the house.

"Don't put yourself out, Annie."

"It's not a problem."

How would she put this? "It's just...I need to do this alone."

Annie gave a nod and handed Rhi the mound of keys. "They're all labeled. The red one is for the front door. Let me know if there's anything you want moved from the house."

"Do you think the owner would mind if I got rid of one of the couches?"

"Which one?"

"The hideous one that looks like a fruit bowl. Everything else is perfect, but that just makes me want to scream." Rhi widened her eyes for comedic effect.

"I'll organize someone to pick it up."

"Should you check with the owner first?"

Annie was obviously trying not to laugh. "I'm the owner."

"I'd apologize but I don't want to choke on my foot."

Annie brushed her off with a laugh. "Don't worry about it, Rhi."

"You rented me your house?"

"One of them. I thought you'd be happy there."

"I will be. I love the house." Rhi was embarrassed now and tried to backtrack. "And the lounge isn't too bad."

"It's hideous. It was fine for summer rentals, but asking you to live with it is cruel. I'll get Dan West to pick it up. He's a good option for helping clear the debris at the theater too. He can rent you a dumpster."

"I thought I'd go in tomorrow and make a list of what needs to be done. I'll start the dirty work on the weekend."

"Great." Annie guided Rhi toward the door. "Come, I'll walk you to your car." Annie ushered her out the door and down the street, pointing out stores and people along the way.

"There are two grocery stores in town and I try to buy from both. Although Sweeney's has a better selection of cheese." Annie gave an attractive woman a wave. "That's Annabelle Hampton. She was a dancer in New York, if you ever need a dance teacher or choreographer at the theater." Annie placed her hand on Rhi's arm and guided her to one side of the pavement as she nodded to a guy who was approaching. "Morning, Keith." Once he'd passed she whispered, "It's pretty much a given that he'll try to hit on you within a month. He hits on everyone except his wife." She led Rhi past Crystal's Balls.

"The coffee here is excellent, much better than at Cafe Max," said Annie.

"I've already tried it. It was one of the things that sent me into your agency in the first place."

"Oh, so you've met Tye? She's my dearest friend."

Rhi thought of Victoria, and felt a wave of grief. There was a huge gap in Rhi's life for one of those. "This is my car."

Annie turned to Rhi and gave her a warm but evaluating stare. "So 'fess up, why did you decide to move here?"

"Why not?"

"Why open a theater so far from New York?"

Rhi paused and stared out the window. What could she say? That New York had chipped away at her spirit until she was afraid there was so little left she would dissolve? That her boyfriend and best friend had betrayed her? That her parents were infamous in New York and had dragged her along for the ride? That her mother was so overbearing that sometimes Rhi felt she couldn't breathe? She decided less was best.

"I need some time out."

"You're an actress?"

"Yeah."

"Have I seen you in anything?" Annie's eyes narrowed slightly. "You look kind of familiar."

Kind of familiar! How many times had Rhi heard that? "I've done a couple of commercials. You've probably seen those," said Rhi.

That seemed to satisfy Annie's curiosity. "Well, I'm glad you're here. Let's have a drink once you've settled in."

"I'd love to."

Annie gave Rhi a hug. "Welcome to Hamlet. And enjoy my cottage. That house has a lovely heart."

Standing before it now, Rhi had to agree. She grabbed the bags of groceries she'd bought and carried them over to the front door, where she fumbled for the keys. All three locks were bolted which, although probably unnecessary here, calmed her New York–bred mind. She stepped into the entrance and put the shopping on the floor.

Annie had taken her through once, on the trip she'd made to Hamlet to sign the contracts, but this time the house was hers. She stood for a moment and absorbed the silence. She was alone. She'd never lived alone. She'd moved from her parents' house to various share houses with friends, and then in with Chandra. This was the first time she'd had her own place, and the realization petrified and thrilled her all at once.

She wandered from room to room. There was a large combined living and dining room, a kitchen and a small sitting room at the back with windows overlooking the garden. Upstairs there were two large bedrooms, a bathroom and one small room she'd use as an office.

Rhi opened the windows and then the blue shutters in the bedroom she'd chosen for her own and let the afternoon sun in. There was plenty of cupboard space. The ceiling was high, and the windows large. The bed frame was vintage mahogany, but the mattress looked brand new and was firm.

She took mental notes of what needed doing. There wasn't a lot. The cottage had been freshly painted, and new curtains hung. The colors were warm, the rooms bright and the hardwood floors shone beneath the freshly shampooed rugs. Apart from one hideous sofa, she would keep all the furniture that came with the house. The place had character, but it would be up to Rhi to make it feel like home with her own belongings. The few she had. She'd walked out of the apartment she'd shared with Chandra with only her personal belongings. Despite buying furniture and art with him, she'd left it all behind; she didn't want any reminders of him here. Anything that was important to her was in her car. She headed out there now and started unloading her bags and boxes and carrying them inside.

Box by box she unpacked. Her suitcases, bathroom box and linen went upstairs. Hours passed as she unwrapped each item and found a place for it in the cottage. There were throws and pillows, candles and photo frames for the living room. She shoved her books into the bookcase, promising herself that she'd arrange them properly later. The kitchen was well stocked with the basics, but she added her small but sentimental collection of fine bone china cups and saucers. She hung a quirky little sign that said, *Dinner is ready when you hear the smoke alarm*, then slapped a bunch of magnets on the fridge.

You had me at Merlot.

I only have a kitchen because it came with the house.

If you think I'm a bitch you should meet my mother. A gift from Taran.

She stalled as she held a photo of her parents that she usually attached to her fridge. Her mother was stunning, even at nearly sixty. Especially at nearly sixty. She was one of those genetically blessed women who started out beautiful and got better with age. But she was also one of those women who had used those looks to get her own way constantly, so she wasn't used to hearing no. Rhi thought about the conversation she'd had with her mother just yesterday.

"If you leave New York, I'll disown you."

"Don't be ridiculous, Mom," said Rhi. "I'd like you to visit me."

"I know you don't mean that."

Her mother was right. She didn't. "Would you feel the same way if I said I was moving to Paris for a while?"

"Paris I could understand." There was a catch in Brigid's voice. "Stay in New York. We can work on our relationship with each other."

"Mom, I need to work on my relationship with myself first."

And her mother hung up.

Rhi took the photo and shoved it in a drawer.

Next she leaned Taran's artwork against various walls, deciding on where best to display them. Annie had given her permission to hammer hooks into the walls, so she hung them one by one. She adored Taran's work. He was supremely gifted, and his work spoke directly to her soul. Each piece was a tale, but never an obvious one. Each painting had layers and layers of stories to observe and understand. Hanging each piece now meant she felt immediately at home. The house looked like a home. Her home. And Rhi loved it.

She opened a bottle of wine and poured herself a glass, and then stepped out onto the back terrace. The garden was a mass of tangles and weeds that ended at a huge old oak tree. Rhi stared up at the moon that was already rising in the late afternoon sky. She breathed her in and silently apologized for rejecting her in any way. It wasn't so much her faith that she needed to escape, but her parents. They had become symbols for witchcraft and had done a lot of good for followers of the old ways by bringing the religion out of the broom closet. They had educated people on a mass scale. Yet most still missed the essence of the craft, and instead concentrated on the eccentricity of Brigid and Lugh Dee and their wacky ways. Rhi would never miss the notoriety, or the way her faith had been packaged and marketed for a modern American audience. But she did yearn, constantly, for that connection to the Goddess. It was as essential to her as the air she breathed.

It *was* the air she breathed.

She turned to go back inside but something caught her eye near the old oak tree. The trunk seemed to be shimmering, glowing. She paused, afraid to move, when suddenly a woman stepped out of the tree. She was tall and radiant, with glistening green skin and long flowing hair. She appeared as though underwater, her hair drifting around her, her body gently undulating. She stared straight at Rhi, tilting her head to one side as she watched her.

"Who are you?"

Rhi stepped back, startled. "I'm Rhi."

The dryad didn't respond, so finally Rhi spoke again. "And your name is?"

"Pip," the nymph said. "This garden needs some care."

"I can do that."

"You're not like the others."

"No, I've signed a long-term lease."

"I mean you can see me."

Rhi wished that weren't true. "Yes, I can."

"You're a witch."

Rhi felt uncomfortable. "Not really...now."

"It's not a light switch, Rhiiiiiiiii. Can't just turn it on and off."

Wow, an annoying dryad. "I can try."

"You are what you are. I can't just turn around and go, 'Oh, I want to be an elf, or a human.'" Pip shimmered brightly. "Wouldn't want to anyway."

"Good for you." Rhi didn't mean to snap.

Pip put her hands on her hips. "I liked Ishbel better."

Rhi had no idea what the dryad was talking about, and wasn't given time to ask. Pip looked like a pouty teenager as she flicked her hair. "Remember the garden." And in a rush of glittering green, she flowed back into the tree.

Great! So much for escaping the supernatural. But Rhi was determined to claim this place as her own. She wasn't going to be bossed around by a moody dryad.

Behind the garden were the woods that led to the beach. Rhi placed her wine glass on a step and headed for them now. The wooded area wasn't large, but it still sang of spirits found in untouched environments. She heard the ocean before she saw it, but then, running up over an embankment, the beach...her beach. Empty as far as the eye could see.

She ran down to the water's edge, tossed her shoes off and dipped her toes in the icy water. She felt free. She was free.

And with that, she sat down in the sand and began to cry, as the waves washed up around her.

Chapter 10

Rhi pushed open the door of the Majestic. It was cool inside, and smelled musty. She actually felt quite ill. There was no going back now. It was hers. The Majestic was hers. And so was the work that needed to be done to it.

She'd been inside before, but with the knowledge that the theater now belonged to her, it took on a special radiance. She saw beyond the work and the rubbish and the dank smell. She heard laughter, and applause and the camaraderie of late-night rehearsals.

She walked into the hall and sat on the edge of the stage. She would set up an office eventually, but this would be where it all began. On the stage. And as overwhelming as the job in front of her appeared right now, she needed to start immediately, one step at a time.

She pulled her iPad out of her bag and started writing lists: things to buy; things to do; people to find. She intended to be hands-on, but would never manage it all alone. She'd already received a phone call from Dan West. He'd agreed to provide a couple of dumpsters and collect them later. She also needed a plumber, a builder and an electrician. The gardens needed to be cleaned up, and the front repaved. Opening a theater was going to be a bigger challenge than she'd ever imagined, but she was up for that challenge…and then some. Every new note she made on her growing list fed the fire in her belly. She couldn't contain her excitement at the thought of forming the Hamlet Players, but to begin with she needed to turn this space into a viable business. When had she last been this motivated and excited about anything? Had she ever?

"Congratulations," boomed a voice from the back of the auditorium.

Rhi screamed.

"Sorry, sorry, I've done it again. I keep scaring you."

Rhi had her hand on her chest and could feel her heart beating wildly beneath. "It's fine. I just drift off into my own little world when I'm here. Any interruption makes me jump."

"You've just scored yourself some back-breaking work."

Rhi smiled. She was actually extremely pleased to see her new landlord. She put her iPad back into her bag and walked over to him. "Thanks for agreeing to lease the theater to me." She didn't mention the long wait before he'd agreed to it.

"Nothing to do with me," he said. "Your persistence paid off."

"I've got a long way to go," Rhi said, looking around.

"This is all minor. Moving here was the big step. What do you think of Hamlet?"

"I like it."

"Small, isn't it?" He seemed to be fishing for something although Rhi wasn't sure what. "What's the population nowadays?"

"Twenty thousand."

"Christ, you're kidding?"

"I know it's not large, but there are also nearby communities that would access this theater." Rhi didn't want him being negative. She already had enough negativity to battle from her mother. Not to mention her own fears. "The town is small, but it needs this."

"Oh, I agree. Was it Olivier who said, 'I believe that in a great city, or even in a small city or a village, a great theater is the outward and visible sign of an inward and probable culture'?" He moved onto the stage, a position in the theater that suited him. He clearly knew it too, and grinned down at Rhi, his audience of one. "Did you leave behind family in New York?"

Rhi felt like a bumbling teenager in the company of a rock star. "Yep. Parents. Brothers. They'll survive."

"Pity."

"Excuse me?"

"Pity you left them behind. Your mother must've been upset about losing you."

"I'm hardly lost." She should be so lucky.

"Are you close to you mother?"

"Do you work for the CIA?"

He looked confused.

"All the questions," she clarified.

"I'm like Magnum P.I. I always wanted a role on that show."

Rhi had no idea who that was, but she enjoyed watching him laugh at his own joke.

They stared at each other for a moment, his eyes more intense than she was comfortable with. He seemed to sense that. "I'm sorry, it's just you remind me of someone."

"Someone fabulous, I hope," Rhi said.

He didn't answer. Instead, he leaned against a piece of an old set. "Have you thought about what play you'll open with?"

"I'm focusing on getting the theater up and running first." Rhi flipped one of the theater seats down and perched on the edge of it.

He moved to the front of the stage. "Surely you've thought about it."

"I have a few ideas." But it was difficult to think when you didn't have a brain. Why did she feel like such an idiot around him? *Pull it together!* "My main priority is to reopen the theater so it can generate an income."

"But you need a play. The town needs a show." He lifted his arms to the sky, as if by doing so, one would magically appear.

"True. And I'm certainly planning to—"

"How about *Hamlet*?"

"*Hamlet*? That's an option."

"I think it would be perfect."

Rhi felt like she was in a dream. Work brain, work! "Yes, you're right. The Hamlet Majestic...*Hamlet*." It wasn't a bad idea. A tricky play to stage. She'd research the demographics more first. From what she'd read about the town she was leaning toward an American classic, something that would be popular with everyone, such as *You Can't Take it With You*, or *Our Town*, or something by Sam Shepard.

"I'll think about *Hamlet*. Thanks for the suggestion," she said evasively.

"Rhi, are you here?" Annie's voice rang out through the foyer.

Rhi spun around. "Annie?"

"I've got to go. I'll see you soon, Rhiannon."

Rhi turned. "How did you know my name?" But he was gone. Rhi shook her head then laughed. Of course he knew her name, from the contracts.

"Rhi?" Annie's voice bounced off the walls.

"I'm in here, Annie."

Annie and Tye entered the hall. Once again, Tye was wearing cargo pants and a tight sweater, which said, *An eye for an eye leaves the whole world blind.*

Annie gave Rhi a hug. "How does it feel to be a local?"

"A little daunting today."

"And you've met Tye?" Annie asked.

"Yes, of course. Fabulous coffee." Rhi's eyes flickered down to Tye's bare feet. "No shoes."

"We wanted to let you know we've organized a posse of helpers for Saturday," Tye explained.

Rhi was lost. "What for?"

"To help clean this place up," Annie explained. "You can't do it alone."

"Oh Annie, that's really lovely but I couldn't possibly put you all out."

Tye sat on the stage and stretched her long legs. She exuded laid back. "It's the way things are done round here, Rhi."

Rhi sat in one of the front-row seats. She was feeling a little strange.

"Are you okay? You look pale," said Annie.

"The owner just scared the hell out of me. Turned up to say hi."

"Who? Tad?"

"I thought his name was William." Rhi couldn't remember Tad on the contract.

"William Daniels...everyone calls him Tad. You positive it was him?"

"Tall, dark...um, rather nice looking?" Rhi blushed again and silently cursed herself for being so obvious. How typical to fall for a pretty face—and broad chest.

Annie and Tye glanced at each other and burst out laughing.

"Sounds like Tad to me," said Tye. "Makes Joe Manganiello look ordinary."

"Don't be embarrassed, Rhi, Tad has that effect on every woman he meets...well, except me, of course," chuckled Annie.

"Why not you?" asked Rhi. "Are you blind?"

"Tad's my cousin."

"Your cousin owns this theater?"

Annie looked sheepish. "Yes."

"Does your family own everything in town?"

"Not yet."

"No wonder you got him to sign it over to me."

"Are you serious? When I asked him if he wanted to rent this place to you, his exact words were, 'When hell freezes over.' So I got Tye to speak to him. He listens to her."

Rhi felt an annoying tug of envy in her gut. "Are you and Tad...?"

"Together? Doing the wild thang? Good god, no," laughed Tye. "We grew up together. And we're in a band together. He's like my brother."

"Sounds like one big family," Rhi said.

Annie drifted off to the side of the stage. "I'm surprised he came here."

"He wanted to make sure he'd rented it to the right person," said Rhi.

"I guess there's a first time for everything."

"First time?" Rhi looked from Annie to Tye.

"Tad hasn't set foot in this place for over twenty-five years," explained Annie. "There's a history here."

"What sort of history?"

Annie and Tye gazed at the patch in the ceiling. Tye turned away, silent.

Then Annie sat back down on the edge of the stage. "Tad's father, my uncle, died here. The ceiling collapsed. I was only three and I can't remember it—or him. Tad was five. He was standing in the wings and saw everything. His mother closed the theater down and kept it for him. When he turned twenty-one, she gave him the keys and told him to sell it.

He couldn't sell. He hasn't been able to let go...but he hasn't been back here either. So we thought."

"What about you?" asked Rhi, horrified.

Annie's black curls bounced as she shook her head. "No. I'm fine. As I said, I can't remember the accident or my uncle. It only affects me because I love Tad. I would never have suggested that he reopen the place, but then you bounded into my office, full of life and enthusiasm, and I figured it was just what the old Majestic needed. It needs to come back to life."

"Are you sure this is okay? I feel like I'm stirring up the past."

Tye looked Rhi straight in the eye. "Sometimes you have no choice."

Chapter 11

Annie and Tye arrived as promised, bright and early on Saturday morning. Annie was decked out in overalls, her hair pulled back in a baseball cap. Tye was in old patched jeans and her usual 'statement' sweater. This one said *Fur is Dead*. The woman was a walking Greenpeace billboard. They were carrying coffee, cake and two bottles of red wine.

"The coffee is for before two o'clock, the wine is for after two and the cake is for any time," explained Tye.

"Or was it the wine is for any time?" Annie asked in mock confusion.

Tye looked around at the theater. "Perhaps we should crack open a bottle now, to help with the job ahead."

Rhi laughed. "It would take more than two bottles."

"So what do you want done?" asked Annie.

Rhi led Annie and Tye into the front office and pointed out a huge mound of hardware supplies.

"My, what a lot of tools you have," Annie said.

"Elijah down at Henderson Hardware delivered for me."

"You obviously made an impact. He doesn't deliver for his mother."

"His mother never spends that much money at his shop," Tye pointed out.

"He sure liked me more once he knew what I was buying." Rhi had forked out a small fortune on tools and cleaning equipment. She'd also got a quote on some paints. It wouldn't be cheap but she didn't care. "It's about time I spent money on something worthwhile, rather than purses and shoes."

"We hear you, honey," Annie said. "I collect real estate and Tye doesn't even buy shoes."

"I do…I just rarely wear them."

"Don't your feet get cold?" Rhi had to ask.

"Sometimes. And when they do, I put boots on." Tye grinned at Rhi. "I have shoes with me. I don't want a rusty nail in my foot."

Annie marched over to the hardware and started looking through it. "You have everything you need here."

"How do you know that?"

"I've renovated four places now."

"So I'll just leave this to you?" Rhi said.

Annie laughed. "No thanks. All yours. Just means I have an idea of what you're in for." She flicked on a light switch. "You got the power on."

"And had the wiring checked. Annabelle was right, the wiring is good." Rhi raised her hands to the sky. "And now we have light."

"I notice Dan delivered the dumpsters."

"Yep."

"Then let's get to it. This place needs to be cleared."

Tye and Annie looked at each other and nodded.

Rhi led them back into the theater. "The roof and foundations are rock solid. The craftsmanship is incredible. There are a few areas where the wood has rotted and needs fixing, plus there's the…ceiling above the stage. I'll rebuild it properly."

"Good idea," said Annie.

"We can rip the curtains down. I bought some material in New York and took the measurements to the shop on Lincoln Street here. The lady said she'd have them finished early next week."

Annie nodded approvingly. "Glenda could sew the ear back on Van Gogh. She'll do a good job. What about the windows?"

"The boards need to come off and I'll get Glenda to make black curtains. They'll keep the theater dark when we need it and can be pulled back when we want some light."

Annie walked over to one of the windows. "Who's your contractor?"

"Harris and Sons."

Annie nodded her approval. "Bobby Harris will check to make sure none of the windows need to be completely replaced."

"Why would I do that?"

"Heating bills in winter. If this place is secure, it will be easier to heat it...and if it's warm, people will still come to the theater."

Rhi was impressed. "How do you know so much?"

"Real estate is my thang."

"And she's like the Rainwoman of renovation," Tye added.

Annie turned and looked up at the tech box. "Can't help you with that though."

"I've organized a guy I know from New York to come up and help with the tech box, but that won't be for a few weeks.

"The whole place needs to be checked for lead," Annie said.

"I've already spoken to Bobby and he'll organize that."

Annie smiled. "We've got a big job ahead of us."

"I don't expect you to..."

Tye and Annie shared a look and then beamed at Rhi.

"We want to help," Annie said. "It's going to be fun."

Tye rolled her eyes and scanned the theater. "Let's not exaggerate."

"By the way," said Annie, "I've roped in some help and they'll be here around noon."

"Oh, I'd hate to put anyone else out," said Rhi.

Tye gave a snort. "It's only Sam and Jake Knight and they'll do anything to be near Annie."

"I grew up with them both. Jake was in my year at school, Sam a year above us."

"And both have been mooning over her since back then," Tye said.

"That's only because there is a tragic lack of available women in Hamlet. Perhaps Rhi might be interested in one of them."

"Or both."

Rhi shook her head. "No, thanks. I've just left one relationship and have no desire for another. What about you, Tye?"

"Single and intending to stay that way."

"Rubbish," Annie said. "You're just waiting for that guy you dream about."

"You dream about someone?" Rhi asked.

"Yeah, and I figure I'll know it when I meet him."

"*If* you meet him. I dream about Johnny Depp and he's yet to visit town," Annie said.

Rhi laughed. "These Knight brothers are all yours, Annie."

Sam and Jake Knight rocked up right on the dot of twelve. They were similar in looks and character: tall, broad shouldered, blond and partial to clowning around. Sam was a couple of years older and seemed slightly more laid back than his rambunctious younger brother. Rhi liked them both immediately, but she wasn't attracted to either of them. Besides, it was immediately obvious that they both only had eyes for Annie.

"You just tell us what to do, Rhi," Sam said as he shook her hand.

"Because they like being bossed around," Tye said.

"Only by a pretty lady," said Jake.

Annie turned her head and picked up some pliers.

The five of them barely drew breath all day. They carried debris out to the dumpsters, tore old boards away from windows, cleaned vents and swept floors. Jake and Sam kept the women entertained, and were always on hand to lift something heavy.

Rhi watched as they joked and teased Annie. There didn't seem to be an ounce of rivalry between the brothers, despite their obvious affection for the same girl. She flirted and deflected their attentions with ease. It was obviously a pattern of behavior perfected over the years. Rhi was tempted to tune in and find out which one of these men would end up with Annie. She felt fate, or perhaps Annie had already made a choice. But before she could, she felt someone staring at her. She turned and locked eyes with Tye, who gave her a small nod before turning back to her work.

By five o'clock they had only begun to scrape the surface of what needed to be done, yet already the theater seemed different. Everyone agreed a drink was in order so Tye did the honors and opened a bottle of red. She poured the wine into plastic cups then everyone lifted their cups for a toast.

"To Rhi, for moving to town," Annie added.

"To Rhi," said Tye.

They clinked cups and Rhi surreptitiously blinked tears back.

"To the old Majestic and the new Majestic," Sam said. "We'll help out whatever way we can."

"Because there's nothing I enjoy more than back-breaking work on my day off," Jake finished.

"Hear, hear," Tye said.

"What do you guys do?" Rhi asked.

"We own Knight and Day Music," Sam said.

"The music shop on Main Street?"

"That's right—you want a big instrument, you come to us," Jake joked.

"Yeah, yeah, and we give lessons too."

Tye turned to Rhi. "These guys are in my band. We've got a gig tonight. You should come."

Annie clapped her hands together. "Yes, Rhi, please come."

Rhi was so tired she was tempted to just go home to bed but she was also excited by the prospect of spending more time with these people. They had a long history together, yet they were willing to fling open the doors of friendship and welcome her into their lives. It was an odd feeling. There was no reserve with them, no pretence. They were take it or leave it and from what Rhi had seen so far, she wanted to take it.

Rhi liked Annie. She was a compact ball of energy topped with a mop of curls. Her immaculate clothes, nails and makeup screamed high maintenance, but in reality she was relaxed and fun, with a quick wit and an open mind.

And then there was Tye, with the body of a Greek war goddess and the eyes of a mystic. She had the gift. Rhi recognized it in her, and Tye had seen it in Rhi. But she hadn't said anything and Rhi trusted she wouldn't.

Rhi felt an immediate connection to both these women. She wanted to know them more. She was fascinated by, and even a little envious of, their ease and affection with each other. It was a reminder of Victoria's betrayal, but also had her questioning how close she'd actually been to the woman she'd called her best friend. They'd gone through the motions of friendship for years, but watching Annie and Tye together, Rhi realized she and Victoria had lacked that genuine warmth. These women, and their friendship, left her feeling slightly on the outer, wanting to join in. She felt like she was in high school, without the bitching and padded bras.

Hamlet, the theater, and these people had switched on a light. Rhi was no longer simply going through the motions. She was actually excited by the moment and the prospect of what tomorrow would bring. Or tonight, for that matter.

Rhi poured herself another wine. "What time does this gig start?"

Chapter 12

Rhi and Annie pushed their way through the crowd to the bar.

"Is it always like this on the weekend?" Rhi asked.

"Oh no! In the summer it gets really packed," Annie called over her shoulder. "O'Reilly's is a local favorite. And when Ceridwen plays, everyone comes to listen."

"Are they that good?"

"Jake and Sam are decent musicians and could charm a snake, but Tad and Tye are the main event." Annie waved her manicured hand at the barman. "Stan, has there ever been a barman as handsome as thee?"

The bartender spotted Annie and headed straight to her. He was huge and red: his shirt was red, his skin had a reddish tint, his large nose was deep red and he had a mop of red hair. "The gorgeous Annie! What would you like?"

"I'll have a couple of glasses of that Californian Merlot I like so much."

Stan grabbed a bottle of wine and began to uncork it. As he did, he turned to two men slouched against the bar and barked, "Dom, Erich, where are your manners? Off those stools and let the ladies sit down."

Dom and Erich didn't argue. It was obvious that no one argued with Stan.

"By the way, Stan, this is Rhi." Annie raised her voice over the noise. "She's a local now so you'd better get used to her face."

Stan grinned and thrust his hand over the bar. "A face that pretty, won't take much getting used to. Are you the New Yorker who's opening up the old Majestic?"

Rhi nodded and Stan leaned across the bar. "You know, I've got a voice that puts Sinatra's to shame. Not sure if you've ever thought of putting on a musical, but if you do, think of Stan, 'cause I'm your man." Stan plunked the bottle of wine on the counter. "On the house," he said, with a wink, before wandering off singing, "The Surrey with the Fringe on Top."

Annie gave a chuckle as she poured the wine. "That's a first. Stan Knight charges his own mother."

"Knight? As is Jake and Sam?"

"Yep. He's responsible for those boys. And their mother sells Avon, so beware." Annie lifted her glass. "I'm glad you moved here, Rhi."

Rhi lifted her glass and clinked Annie's. "Me too."

Rhi scanned the room. O'Reilly's was large, with deep green walls above wood paneling and floorboards. There were tables and chairs in the center of the room, with higher tables and stools against the walls. There was a jukebox and two pool tables to one side, but the attention tonight was focused on a small stage. The decor was sedate and stylish. The clientele were anything but. They were loud, casually dressed and, without exception, appeared to be having fun. Rhi relaxed and took another sip of her wine.

"I finally get to meet you!"

Rhi was suddenly enveloped in a huge set of bosoms before they stepped back and she could breathe again. It took her a moment to recover and take in that the bosoms were attached to a rather large woman with an ornate blond updo and a fabulous smile.

"I'm Crystal," she said, before leaning over and giving Annie a similar hug. Unlike Rhi, Annie was prepared, and kept her head on an angle that meant she could breathe.

"Don't you look gorgeous?" Annie said.

"Thanks, honey. I've got a hot date." Crystal waved two fingers at Stan and he immediately started pouring her two Guinness. Then she turned back to Rhi and gave her an appraising stare. Rhi matched her and realized Annie was right. Crystal was gorgeous. She had lovely skin, high cheekbones, full lips and curves in all the right places...even if they were extra large.

"You obviously like a challenge. Taking on that pile of bricks."

"I'm giving it a shot."

"You'll succeed." Crystal's incredible blue eyes searched Rhi's. For a fleeting second she looked quite sad, but then she smiled again. "I'm so pleased you've moved to town."

Rhi was thrown by her warmth and familiarity.

Annie butted in before she had time to respond. "Who's your hot date, Crystal?"

"Larry Embers." She waved her head toward the corner where a good-looking man sat.

"God, Crystal, you're an inspiration. Every single woman in town over forty has been after him for years."

Crystal gave a chuckle. "Says she who's been leading two of the hottest men in town along for about that long."

Annie gave her a playful slap. "Rubbish. Now go get him."

Crystal gave them both a wink and sauntered off toward Larry, ample hips swaying sexily. Annie leaned toward Rhi.

"You should get Crystal to read your tarot cards, Rhi. She's amazing."

"Do you believe in all that?"

"Of course. She told me I'm going to be rich, happily married and have two gorgeous kids. What's not to believe?"

The two women laughed. Rhi noticed a poster advertising St Patrick's Day celebrations in town. She turned to Annie. "I read that there are a lot of Irish in Hamlet."

"A lot with Irish heritage. Irish is a state of mind 'round here. What's your background?"

"My parents are both English but met in New York and decided to call it home."

"Any siblings?"

"Twin older brothers. What about you?"

"One sister. Married, lives in Chicago and has four kids. My parents moved out there to be near the grandkids." Annie ran a red nail around the rim of her glass. "So how hot are your brothers?"

Rhi burst out laughing and was about to describe Taran and Finn when she saw Tad Daniels enter the bar and her mind went blank. Annie followed Rhi's gaze and gave a chuckle.

"Speaking of hot." She raised her arm and gave Tad a wave. He smiled and waved back, before his eyes rested on Rhi. His stare was like a Sahara summer. She nodded a hello. His eyes narrowed briefly, as though trying to recall her, and then he disappeared through the backstage door.

"Is he blind?"

Annie poured them both another wine. "Probably nervous before the gig."

"Either he needs glasses or he doesn't remember me." Embarrassed, Rhi took a long swig of pride salve. "Obviously I didn't make much of an impression."

"That's just Tad. He's reserved."

"He didn't seem reserved when I met him," said Rhi, remembering his amused gray eyes and knowing grin. And they'd met not once, but twice. Surely he recognized her? She stared at the backstage door, silently willing him to come back out.

As though on cue he appeared, followed closely behind by Tye, Sam and finally Jake. O'Reilly's erupted into cheers. The band ignored the crowd. Sam moved in behind the drums and picked up his drumsticks, twirling them around a few times. Jake slung a guitar around his neck and Tad sat at the keyboard. Tye kept her back to the crowd. Her voice rang through the cheers.

"One, two three, four."

And suddenly she turned and sprang to life, a fiddle at her chin, a look of intense concentration on her face. She was decked out in her usual barefooted garb, this time her top—touting *Peace by example*—was smaller than usual, displaying her flat, toned abs. The crowd went ballistic.

Rhi watched as Sam scanned the others, his drum the beating heart of the group. His blond hair kept flopping in his face and his mouth would twist into a pucker as he blew it back. Jake's fingers slid across the guitar strings, while he locked eyes with girl after girl, rewarding them with a grin or a wink.

"Look at the fool, flirting with all the girls," Annie called over the music. "He'll lose track of where he's at."

"He seems to know what he's doing."

"With the guitar...or with Sophia Copeland down the front?"

Rhi watched a pretty brunette smile up at Jake. "Does that bother you?"

"No, why would it?" Annie straightened her skirt. "We're just friends."

"And Sam?"

"Same. Just friends. Mind you, that man concentrates on his instrument."

Rhi gave Annie a look and the two started laughing.

"You know what I mean! They're good, aren't they?

"They are."

But it was Tad and Tye who stole Rhi's breath. Tad poured himself into the keyboard, his eyes closed, occasionally lifting his head to sing harmony to Tye's spell-binding voice. Rhi watched him, fascinated by the way he moved as he played, occasionally closing his eyes as though it helped him feel the music more intensely. He was wearing dark blue jeans and a white T-shirt with a chambray shirt over the top but left unbuttoned. He dressed like he didn't have a care in the world, but he played like he carried everyone's. He was alone with his band and his music. Nothing else existed.

Tye, on the other hand, switched from punk to pixie and back again. She connected with people. She sang to them. She gazed into them, glamoring them, then snap—she was off again, leaving whoever it was looking rather bewildered. She bounded around the stage, playing the fiddle with fierce intensity, and then she'd stop still and her angelic voice would ring through the night like an otherworldly echo.

The music was a mix of Celtic punk, funk and rock. It contained whispers of centuries lost while paving the way to something new, something fresh and completely unique.

Annie leaned in and yelled in Rhi's ear: "Tye and Tad write all the music."

"I'm not sure whether to be completely impressed or wildly jealous—they're so talented."

Annie nodded. "I usually settle for a mix of both."

Ceridwen played for well over an hour, including three encores. By the end of their set, Tye's long, sexy limbs glistened with sweat. They finished with a ballad, which Tye and Tad sang *acapella*. They sang of love and magic and a world hidden in the hills. The way they sang, they sounded like they were from another realm; nothing human could sound so perfect. Rhi looked at the crowd: mesmerized, moved, a scattered few let tears flow unashamedly.

And then it was over, and the roar was louder than ever. This time Tye and the boys acknowledged everyone. They bowed, grinned and waved, and then, placing their instruments to one side, left the stage and headed toward the bar. The crowd gathered round, hugging them, slapping their backs, handing them drinks. Tye made her way over to Rhi and Annie. Rhi noticed a small tattoo of a pentagram poking over the top of her cargo pants.

Annie threw her arms around Tye and gave her a loud kiss on the cheek. "You rocked, darling."

Tye laughed and gave Rhi a grin. "What did you think?"

"I didn't think. I felt. You are incredibly talented, Tye."

Tye nodded and thrust her hands in her pockets. Praise obviously made her squirm, even though she knew she was talented. "We all have our gifts, Rhi."

Rhi glanced at Tye's pentagram and then back up at her face. A look passed between them, an unspoken understanding. Rhi broke the gaze first. She couldn't escape what she'd been born in to.

Annie thrust a wine at Tye. "You have some catching up to do."

Rhi watched Tad as he talked to a couple of women. He shifted, as though aware he was being watched, and turned his gaze toward Rhi. Their eyes locked and she felt a crack, like the space between them was charged. She turned her head and pretended to be interested in a game of darts.

The guy was leg-meltingly good looking. He was obviously talented, and judging by the gaggle of panting women who now surrounded him, he was highly sought after. Three excellent reasons to stay away from him.

"Hi...have we met?"

The color sprang back into Rhi's cheeks again as Tad stepped in front of her. Perched on her stool she had a perfect view of his insanely well-built chest.

Once again, she was rendered speechless. What did he mean?

"Er...yes...we..." *And the award for most highly articulate goes to...?*

Annie, used to her cousin's effect on women, came to Rhi's rescue. "You know Rhi—she's your new tenant."

Tad raised his eyebrows. "Of course."

Rhi was completely confused. Was he messing with her? Was he pretending they hadn't met for Annie's benefit?

"Don't worry," Rhi said. "I almost didn't recognize you either. Your hair is different." He'd decided to go for the let-it-fall-all-over-your-face look tonight. It suited him. Unfortunately.

Tad narrowed his eyes slightly, as though he was trying to work her out. Rhi matched his stare. She searched for recognition, but there was none. He wasn't pretending he hadn't met her—he actually thought he hadn't. The guy was either completely self-centered, an alcoholic or had the IQ of a plank of wood. Rhi decided he was all three and gave him a forced smile.

"Thanks again for agreeing to rent it to me."

"I got the feeling you weren't going to take no for an answer. Nice to put a face to the name though."

Annie snuggled up under Tad's armpit and pouted at him like a small child. "Can you drop us home tonight? I've been hitting the vino all night and am too drunk to drive."

Tad ruffled her hair. "Sure, I'll just go grab my things."

After he walked off, Annie settled back up on her stool. "Local law number one, Rhi, Tad can always be relied upon for a lift home. He doesn't drink."

Rhi mentally crossed out "alcoholic" and inserted "drug user" in its place.

Chapter 13

Rhi sat in the front passenger seat of Tad's car and watched with amusement as Annie tripped up the steps as she gave them a wave goodnight.

"I'm okay," she called, opening her front door and disappearing inside.

"Do women always trip in front of you?" asked Rhi, remembering her own fall.

Tad obviously didn't follow her. "What do you mean?"

"When I fell head over ass?"

He gave her a sympathetic smile. "Tonight? Did you? Oh no, I missed that."

She gave him a look that pretty much said *asshole* and then turned and stared out the window.

"You're at Annie's place near the beach, right?"

"The Callahan cottage."

Tad put the car in drive and headed back down the street. "I hope witches don't scare you?"

Only my mother. "Why would they?"

"The original owner, Ishbel Callahan was a *witch*." He whispered the word "witch" like one would "murderer" or "One Direction fan."

"Do you believe in that stuff?" Rhi asked.

"I know some witches. Good people. A bit mad." He smiled at her and Rhi was once again floored by his looks. "I don't mean to scare you, just when you've moved in."

"You're not. I feel at home there." *And now I know why.*

"Ishbel used to dance naked under each full moon, rain hail or shine, right up to the night she died at ninety-eight."

"Was that under a full moon?"

"Was what under a full moon?"

"Did she die naked, dancing under the moon? Wonderful way to go."

"Er...no..." Tad scratched his chin. "She passed away in bed after a particularly intense lovemaking session with her seventy-five-year-old neighbor."

"Not Douglas McNeil?"

Tad shot her an amused grin. "So the story goes."

Rhi chuckled. "She sounds like she was quite a character. Did you know her?"

"I apparently met her a couple of times, but can't remember her."

Rhi's smile faded. "Do you do that a lot? Forget people you've met?"

"How would I know if I can't remember them?" Tad clearly thought he was being funny, but when he saw the look on Rhi's face, he turned his full attention back to the road.

They fell into a self-conscious silence. Rhi really had nothing to say to him. He didn't remember her, and she wasn't going to bother reminding him. He didn't remember Ishbel either. There was something a bit wrong with him. He wasn't worth her time. Case closed.

If only he didn't smell so fantastic. She had the overwhelming urge to slide across to his seat and nuzzle his neck. Rhi breathed deeply.

Tad took one of his hands off the steering wheel and pushed his hair back off his face. Rhi noticed the shape of his fingers—long, strong—and wondered what it would be like to have them running through her hair.

Goddess, how much longer till I'm home?

She watched him from the corner of her eye. He seemed different, calmer, than when they'd met at the theater. There he was a little intense. Perhaps he did secretly drink, and it was during those sessions that he went to the theater. It would explain why he didn't remember her. And why he seemed to have more bravado during those meetings.

She had to ask. "Is it true you don't drink?"

"I'm not a teetotaler."

Ha! She knew it.

"I'll have the occasional wine at a wedding or something."

Or when you visit your theater, thought Rhi.

The silence shifted toward uncomfortable.

"So, do you like Hamlet?"

His voice was deep and calming. She wanted to like him, but her pride was hurting too much.

"So far, yes."

Pause.

"Did you like O'Reilly's tonight?"

"Yes, very much."

"Looks like we might get some rain."

She had to give him ten points for at least trying to converse, despite the inane territory they were now covering.

"Looks like."

Highly awkward silence. Tad pulled the car into Rhi's driveway.

"Have I offended you?" Tad asked.

"Why would you think that?"

"You seem to be angry at me." He grinned, teasing her. "Or perhaps you're angry with everyone?"

Rhi opened the door. "I have a huge problem with people forgetting that they've ever met me before. Call it egotistical, but I like to think I'm not completely forgettable. Thanks for the lift." Rhi got out of the car and slammed the door shut. She was acutely aware of him waiting until she got inside the house and refused to look back until she closed the door behind her. That is what peepholes are for. And that's where she stood and watched his car back out of her driveway and disappear.

*

Tad headed for home. His mind ticked over while he tried to remember where he'd met her before; obviously he had, or she wouldn't be so furious.

He came up blank.

Perhaps it was while he was living in New York. God knows there'd been a few women whose names and faces he'd never remember. Never knew at the time. There were a rough couple of years before his old friend Crystal intervened and suggested he come back to Hamlet for a while. To clear his head, she'd said.

He'd initially come for a week, which was the amount of time he'd spent in Hamlet each holidays with Crystal and Tye. He could handle a week, but always thought actually living in the same town as the theatre would haunt him as much as his father's death always had. Instead, he'd found solace. He reconnected with Annie. He played music with Tye. He eventually bought himself a place on the edge of town, where he locked himself away to write music. Then, when he emerged, he had his circle of friends and family. He'd built Hamlet up in his mind as a place of shadows, but instead, it was where he let the light back in. He loved it now. Apart from the theater, which he steered clear of. Renting it out to Rhi was really digging up the past. His problem was he found it impossible to say no to either Annie or Tye. And when they'd ambushed him together one day, he'd crumbled.

"It's a piece of history I don't want to dredge up," he'd said.

"You let Annabelle rent it."

"And what a shambles that turned out to be. It's better off left alone."

"But it's prime real estate just sitting there rotting." Annie was an estate agent to the core.

"Dad died there."

"I know honey, but 'died' is the key word. He's not there. I think it's time to let it go." Annie had given him a hug. "Have you ever thought that he'd like this?"

Tad looked at Tye, who shrugged. "It's exactly what he tried to do, Tad. He came to town to do this. Let this woman complete his dream."

"His dream? She might be opening a burlesque theater, for all I know."

Annie burst out laughing. "From what I've heard, Uncle Kip would've loved that. But I can assure you, that's not her thing. She really does want to open a theater here. Just like he did."

He thought about this for a moment. "Fine, do it. Rent it cheap. It's not about the money. And leave me out of it."

"I'm telling you, this woman Rhi is perfect," Annie said. "You'll love her."

Tad squirmed at the memory. Love her? Rhi seemed to be ten cents short of a dollar. But hell, he was attracted to her. He'd seen her across the bar and it had been like a punch to the guts. He'd never felt that before. Talking to her made him feel like an inarticulate fool. Her scent! Damn, he could still smell the faint vanilla in his car. And those flashing eyes as she slammed the car door. What a woman.

A confused one admittedly. She must have him mixed up with someone else. One thing was for certain, if he had ever met Rhiannon Dee before, he'd have remembered her.

Chapter 14

Brigid Dee looked composed, but inside she was a wound coil. She glanced at the clock on the wall. The audience would be seated now.

Her assistant Kenneth entered the room and pulled up a stool beside her. "Your publisher called and asked where the first draft is."

"Did you tell him I have more pressing matters to deal with right now than chasing up my ghost writer?"

"I'll do it for you." He looked a little apprehensive, and then pulled a folder out of his bag and handed it to Brigid. "The report you wanted."

Brigid looked surprised. "That was quick."

"It's called the internet." Kenneth gave Brigid a peck on the cheek and headed out of the room. "I'll call you in fifteen."

Brigid opened the report in front of her, hands shaking. Her heart was in her throat. No turning back now. She read through it. It wasn't long, but Kenneth had detailed everything she'd asked for.

Tad Daniels, a composer, owned the Hamlet Majestic but recently leased it to one Rhiannon Wall. Tad spent some of his early childhood in Hamlet, until his father's death, when he returned to New York to live with his mother, actress Collette Kelly. Growing up, he lived with family friend Crystal Hemmingway for chunks of time. When Crystal and her daughter Tye moved back to Hamlet five years ago, Tad also returned to the area.

The report turned her insides to ice. Brigid looked into the mirror. Her face was a picture of calm, but inside she was screaming. She wouldn't allow this. She couldn't. She had to find a way to bring Rhiannon home.

*

Brigid Dee ran up the four flights of stairs to her apartment two at a time. She clutched the New York Times in one hand and her key in the other. This was it, the moment everything was going to change. And she'd never been so excited in her life.

It was the 80s and New York City was the center of the world. At least it seemed that way to Brigid. She'd moved here from London knowing that this was the city where she would make a name for herself. In London she was simply one of a long line of witches, most who practiced the craft in private. She felt stifled there. But in New York her big dreams and aspirations would come to fruition.

Brigid wasn't particularly good at anything except self-promotion, which of course worked to her advantage in New York. Londoners hated that shit, but here, you were admired for it. People supported a go-getter. Especially a beautiful one. She was gorgeous, with intense violet eyes, endless golden limbs and waves of chestnut curls. She was a showstopper, a fact she used to her advantage daily.

She modeled, which paid the rent.

She said yes to a lot of dates. That kept her fed.

But it wasn't enough to make her famous. She was determined to make a name for herself, but so were countless other stunning girls out there. She needed to stand out from the pack. She needed to be different. And with no real education, talents, or gifts (she couldn't sing or dance) she decided to use the one thing that did set her apart from everyone else.

Brigid was a witch.

Not a hideous Disney-style witch, but a sexy, smart Samantha Montgomery–type witch. It was time witchcraft came out of the broom closet. So she wrote a piece for the New York Times…and they published it.

"My Life as a Witch: the Truth about Witchcraft," by Brigid Dee.

Brigid fumbled the key and opened the door. The apartment was silent. A dump, filled with revamped second-hand furniture. Colorful rugs covered broken floorboards. Movie posters disguised peeling paint. There was nothing redeeming about this Lower East Side walk-up, and yet it was home, and had been for two years. The apartment was spotless too. Not her doing. Housework had never been her thing. The lovely décor and squeaky clean rooms were all thanks to her roommate.

Brigid decided then and there that when she upgraded to a more suitable apartment, she'd take her roomie with her. Not just to clean, although that was certainly a bonus, but because she was actually a good friend. Her only friend, really.

"Anyone home?"

Perhaps she'd gone to work.

Brigid laid the newspaper flat on the kitchen table and looked at her photo again. She ran her finger across a crease, where she'd folded the paper. Even with a big line down her forehead she looked fabulous.

The phone rang and she pounced on it. "Brigid speaking."

"Brigid…Gregory Goldberg here from Ladies who Lunch."

Brigid's whole body tensed. She knew the show well. This was it.

"I got your number from the Times. Hope you don't mind."

"Not at all." Brigid lowered her voice enough to make it sound like it was being poured from a jar of maple syrup.

"I've got an offer for you."

Brigid listened to his pitch. It wasn't quite what she'd expected, but it was her break.

"I'll have to speak to my roommate and get back to you," Brigid finally said.

Gregory gave her his number and Brigid hung up.

"What do you need to speak to me about?"

Brigid swung around to find her roommate wearing nothing but a bed sheet and tousled hair.

"You scared the crap out of me! I thought you were at work."

"Took the day off." She gave Brigid a wicked grin.

"That's three times this week," Brigid said. "Careful, you'll fall for him."

"Too late...unfortunately. Who was that on the phone?"

Brigid pulled a chair out. "Sit down and I'll make us a tea. I have something I need to ask you, Crystal."

*

"Brigid? Darling?"

Brigid plummeted back to the present day. Lugh was standing in the doorway watching her. "You're not dressed."

"I'll only be a minute."

Brigid walked over to her clothes rack and removed her dress for the show, a vibrant turquoise number with batwing sleeves in her favorite empire style.

She needed to pull it together, and quickly. She could feel Lugh's inquisitive stare burning into her. And she never lied to him. Perhaps he was the only man she'd never lied to. Theirs had been an unexpected love. For her anyway. He'd been keen right from the start, but she'd been through so much by the time she fell into his arms; he was a safe harbor rather than a grand passion. Surprisingly, the passion had grown over the years. She often wondered if, early on, Lugh had tired of her aloof ways and had cast a little spell on her. It wasn't really his style, but how else would she explain that one day she looked at him and had a sudden and overwhelming wave of desire engulf her? She'd been floating in it ever since.

Perhaps she simply fell in love. Stranger things had happened. She looked at him now, handsome in his cravat and beard. She really did love him and felt fortunate that he'd persisted for so long.

She had to be honest. "I just spoke to Rhi."

"How's life in the boondocks?"

"I'm worried for her."

"Why? What's happened?"

"Crystal Hemmingway lives there."

Lugh locked eyes with his wife and, as they so often did, held a complete conversation in the beat of a look.

"Did you know?"

"I suspected. Kenneth checked it out for me. You know how useless I am with the internet. I had no idea where she was."

It was true. Brigid had tried to find Crystal a few times. Not because she wanted to catch up, but because she wanted—needed—to know she had a safe distance from her. Crystal had always been impossible to find—no trace of her online. She indeed flew under the radar, just like she always said she would. Brigid had lived in hope that their paths wouldn't cross again. And yet there had always been this gnawing dread that they would. So this didn't surprise. It simply filled her with fear.

Rhiannon had moved to the same town as Crystal. She'd rented a theater from a man Crystal had a hand in raising.

Brigid didn't believe in coincidence. There were no coinciden-
ces in life. She didn't know whether the Fates or Crystal had
manipulated all of this into place, but either way, she wasn't
having it.

"It's a coincidence."

"You know there's no such thing."

"You need to let it go." Lugh was calm but firm. "It was a
long time ago."

"Obviously not long enough."

"She's a very powerful witch, Brigid. I'm sure she'll do the
right thing. Promise me you'll let it go."

Brigid took a deep breath and patted her dress down.
"Come on, we have a show to do." She gave her husband a
kiss and swept from the room. She never lied to Lugh. But
that didn't mean she told him everything.

Chapter 15

Rhi held her phone to her ear and half hoped her mother wouldn't answer. This was a confrontation she really didn't need right now, but was unfortunately necessary. She glanced at her computer screen, willing it to change. She didn't want to have this conversation with her mother. But there was no denying it, she was running out of money. It was there on her bank statement.

"Rhiannon, what a nice surprise. To what do I owe the pleasure of this call?"

"I'm just wondering why I haven't received my check this month?"

"You haven't?"

She goddamn knows I haven't, thought Rhi. "I'm looking at my accounts now."

"Oh yes, that…We've gone biannual. We sent the details to your accountant."

"She's on leave, so perhaps you can explain what this means?"

"We've restructured the trust. You'll get your checks twice a year rather than monthly."

"A few months' warning would have been nice."

"Goddess, Rhi, you're not going to argue about money with me are you? You really have had it too easy."

"Easy? I was exploited for years."

"I'm not a money tree." Brigid was using her wounded voice.

"That's unfair, Mom. It's my money. I earn it."

"I'm not sure if you've realized this, Rhiannon, but you haven't worked for the Dee brand for a decade."

"No, but most of my dividends are from the Witchlet line. I created it. And while it exists, I earn from it."

"I was going to talk to you about that. We're thinking we might pull it."

"But it makes a fortune."

A mower started up outside so Rhi closed the window. She watched as Warren, the local landscaper, cut the lawn near Pip's tree. That would appease the dryad, but now she had no idea how she'd pay him. She gave him a wave and walked into the living room, where it was quieter. Her mother was still trying to justify her abhorrent behavior.

"The Witchlet line seems a bit outdated."

"You know that's not true." Rhi was furious. It's not like they were still selling her original clothing and accessory lines. They were redesigned annually, but she owned the IP and still got a percentage of the profits. "I know what you're up to. You want me to fail here in Hamlet."

Rhi could almost hear her mother roll her eyes. "Oh please, simply being in Hamlet is a failure."

Rhi felt the blow to her guts. "You think I'm a failure, Mom?"

"I didn't mean it like that. But if you want to be an actress, then it's either LA or New York."

"Success isn't just about fame."

"In this business, that's exactly what success is, Rhi."

Rhi could feel the tears welling up. Her mother obviously sensed it too, but clearly didn't want to deal with it.

"I need to go, Rhi. Now don't be melodramatic about this money. You haven't been cut off. You just won't receive a check until July."

"But I need to pay the plumber—" Rhi said. But her mother had gone.

Rhi jumped in the car and headed for the theater. She'd be okay. She'd manage. She'd set up an account for the theater and had pumped personal money into that as a loan, and she had a bit of money left she could move, but she was relying on her income to pay the smaller jobs. How could she be so cash-strapped a month into her move?

Successful. Her mother's words still stung. Rhi had always defined success by her mother's standards. By New York standards. Success meant being visible. But that visibility came with a price tag. Rhi knew that from the show. People thought they knew you, when they only knew one very shallow version of you. She'd experienced that time of visibility. Success. But it wasn't fulfilling because it wasn't hers. So she tried everything she could to distance herself from that and to achieve something of her own.

It was only now she realized she'd been trying to recreate something she'd already experienced. Sure it would be packaged differently—any fame would be due to great acting in stellar roles, not some cheesy television series. But she'd never thought about the other aspects of a successful life. Not really. She was so focused on her destination that she never once stopped to ask herself if the journey itself was worthwhile. Was she happy? Were her relationships rewarding? Did she go to bed each night satisfied with how she'd spent the day?

She'd only started asking these questions in Hamlet.

She drove the now familiar route to the theater. She weaved along the beachfront until she came to Main Street, where she turned right. She took a left down Maple and passed Sam driving in the opposite direction. He honked his horn and she laughed.

She stopped at the crossing for Vaniqua Boyken and her twin daughters Tirrell and Terri. Vaniqua gave her a wave. She'd already cornered Rhi at the deli, asking when the drama classes were going to start. Her twins and at least five of their friends all wanted to sign up. In fact in the past few weeks, Rhi had had calls from a number of local parents expressing interest in the children's classes. She'd taken names and told them all the same thing: once the theater was safe, classes would begin.

She parked outside the theater and sat a moment to take it all in. The dumpsters were filling fast. The garden had been cleared and the branches that had been pushing at windows and guttering from a couple of nearby trees pruned.

She headed up the path, which still needed to be repaved; it was an insurance claim waiting to happen. And one of the steps had to be fixed. But the windows shone, and thankfully didn't need replacing. She entered *her* theater—because it felt like hers now—and stood for a moment in the entrance. The carpet had been pulled up and underneath she'd found flawless mosaic tiles. She'd stood in absolute amazement with Tye and Annie.

"You've just hit the jackpot," Tye said.

Looking at them now, she couldn't agree more. The treasures they found as they peeled back each layer. Not for one moment would she ever regret taking this on. Her mother was wrong about success—Rhi knew she was already a success, even if this venture failed, simply because she'd tried. And had loved every minute of doing so.

She moved into the auditorium. It looked so different from that first day. It was light and everything had been cleared. She stared at the stage for a moment and then turned and looked at the tech box. Would it be possible to project old movies onto a screen? Perhaps Majestic movie nights could be another money-spinner? If she could get the theater earning an income as quickly as possible, she'd never need to rely on those dividend checks again.

The tears she'd held back during the phone call with her mother suddenly erupted. Brigid was so frustrating. Was it too much to expect her to support her daughter? Not financially, but emotionally. She was determined to trip Rhi up so she'd return to New York.

"Are you okay?"

Rhi jumped. She realized Tad was standing in the wings watching her, just visible behind the curtain. He must've come through the back.

"You should take up haunting houses," Rhi said, pulse racing. She wasn't sure if that was from the fright or just seeing him again.

He laughed. "Rather than just this theater."

"Did you come to apologize?" Rhi's pride was still stinging from the lift home.

"Did I hurt your feelings?" He looked a little surprised. "I certainly never meant to. I do find with women, though, it often can't be helped. Sensitive creatures."

"Wow, could you be any more patronizing?" Tears were welling up in Rhi's eyes again. She really wasn't in any frame of mind for this.

"I don't mean to be patronizing. I feel nothing but adoration and admiration for women—collectively I mean."

"How New Age of you."

"Did I interrupt something?" He sounded genuinely concerned.

"Only me having a howl."

"Did someone die?"

"No...I wish..."

"Oh, harsh. Boyfriend troubles?"

"Mother issues."

"Well, she's a bitch." His voice echoed through the auditorium.

"Excuse me?"

"I said that's a bitch. Parental conflict—it's always difficult." He moved toward the center of the stage.

Rhi wiped her eyes with the corner of her sleeve. "I just needed to let off some steam."

"Don't let the old witch get you down."

They stared at each other for a moment too long. "What did you call her?"

"I apologize, I was just joking…trying to make you feel better about your mother."

"Oh."

"She might be perfectly nice for all I know."

"She has her moments. She had one in 1974 apparently." Her voice cracked as she erupted into tears again.

"Oh, the tears!" Without warning, he broke into song, his powerful voice belting out "Cry Me a River". He sang a verse of that and then with a spin and a transition only a seriously talented performer could make, he began tap dancing to "Singing in the Rain."

Rhi laughed and clapped. He certainly knew how to break the tension.

He stopped, placed his hands out flat to show they were empty, and then one clap and he produced a handkerchief, with a rose on it. He tossed it to her and it fluttered through the air until she placed her hands under it and caught it.

"A rose for a rose. Wipe your tears." And then with a dramatic roll of his eyes. "And women aren't sensitive?"

She dabbed her eyes. "Perhaps you could clap again and produce someone who knows what the hell they're doing, because I sure don't."

He wiggled an imaginary cigar and sounded like WC Fields. "If at first you don't succeed, try, try again. Then quit. There's no point being a damn fool about it."

Rhi was doubled over laughing as he finished with an elaborate little bow.

"Oh god, you think I should quit?"

He crouched down on the edge of the stage. "No way. I think you're doing a marvelous job." He paused, watching to see that she was listening. "I think you're very smart and utterly gorgeous."

Holy hell. He thinks I'm gorgeous? "I bet you say that to all the girls."

He rolled his eyes. "Not for a helluva long time, believe me."

He turned and looked around the theater. He seemed entranced, staring beyond her, drinking in the changes she'd made. Finally his eyes drifted to the ceiling above the stage, which had been repaired. It looked brand new, the old damage impossible to see. He strode out to the edge of the stage, his presence filling it.

Rhi watched, captivated. He was sexy and unpredictable. Very different to how he'd been the other night, although admittedly that version of him seemed more reliable. Right now, she had no idea what he'd do next. It both excited and unnerved her.

He didn't disappoint.

"To be or not to be: that is the question."

Rhi's heart beat wildly in her chest. Hamlet's soliloquy?

"Whether 'tis nobler in the mind…"

She moved forward, almost unaware that she did so. He filled the character, became the character and expressed him in a way that sent waves of pure emotion rippling around the theater.

"To die, to sleep. To sleep, perchance to dream."

Rhi was rooted to the spot. She couldn't think, couldn't respond. All she could do was watch and feel. He was not only a talented musician, but he could act. Really act.

He finished and turned to her, their eyes connecting in a blaze of heat.

Rhi nodded and sat down on the edge of the stage. She gazed out at the phantom audience, the one she longed to mesmerize, the way he'd just mesmerized her.

"Was that an audition?" she asked.

"When do rehearsals start?"

"When I decide what play will open the season and hold auditions."

"C'mon, Rhiannon. I thought we'd already discussed this. The play will be *Hamlet*."

"You suggested it. I said it was an interesting option."

"Great! Then that's settled."

Rhi sat with her mouth hanging open. She couldn't believe his nerve. He really knew how to get under her skin. "What's it to you which play I choose?"

He shot her a look as if he was a little tired of her acting like an annoying child. "Because I will be the lead."

Rhi added arrogant beyond belief to the list of reasons why she should steer clear of him. Yes he was entertaining, and fun, and too damn sexy. But he also seemed to have a multiple personality disorder.

She strode toward the stage. "Just because I got this place off you doesn't mean you have any say in how it's run."

Tad sighed impatiently and folded his arms. "Didn't you like my Hamlet?"

"That's beside the point."

"Aha! So you did like it? Well, why begin with mediocrity?"

Rhi had to agree with him on that, but was boiling inside at his attitude and nerve. She didn't need to put up with this.

He was in her theater now. She had a contract. She paid rent. She had restored the place herself. With her bare hands and all of her money. She was the boss and it was time he understood that.

But his performance was sublime.

"Okay," she whispered.

"Okay?"

"Yes, I said okay."

He leaped up into the air. "Yes!"

"We'll do *Hamlet* first. But I remain in charge. And I'm directing."

"That's fine by me. I just want to act." He looked like he'd won the lottery.

Rhi stood and thrust her hands into her pockets. "I need to get to work, but I appreciate you dropping by and...showing me your Hamlet."

He grinned, sexy as all hell and he knew it. "Go on, say it...I'm the best you've had..."

She had to put a stop to this flirting. "The best what?"

He pretended to be horrified. "The best Hamlet. What did you think I meant? God, Rhiannon, you're my director. You need to stop flirting with me."

Rhi turned and walked toward the entrance.

"I ask that you stop sexually harassing me while we're in rehearsals."

"You'd better watch yourself or I might cast you as Yorrick," Rhi shot back over her shoulder.

Chapter 16

Despite the effortless rhythm of Annie and Tye's friendship, which Rhi had initially envied, both women welcomed her into the fold with surprising ease. She spent a lot of time with them, hanging out at each other's houses. It was an unexpected bonus of moving to Hamlet.

Tonight they were at Annie's, drinking wine in her hot tub. Annie's house was a small, two-bedroom cottage only steps away from the beach. She'd retained the quirky exterior, but inside she'd completely gutted the place and made it simple and modern. The bedrooms—upstairs under a sloped roof—were the only segregated rooms. Downstairs was one large room, all white and eggshell blue, flowing beautifully to a small garden with a hot tub at the back and a terrace overlooking the ocean at the front.

"Your turn with the talking stick, Rhi," Annie said, passing Rhi a fresh wine instead. "How are things?"

Rhi was still slightly surprised that anyone was genuinely interested. Spending time with Tye and Annie, seeing how they both offloaded and listened to each other's day, was something of a novelty. It brought to light just how one-sided her relationship with Vic had been: their regular lunches were usually a chance for Victoria to offload all her shit. Rhi couldn't remember the last time Vic took an interest in her.

"How are things with me?" She relaxed back in the hot, bubbling water and looked up at the stars. "Truthfully, I've hit a bit of a wall with the renovations. With money."

"You've run out of money?" Annie was surprised. She thought Rhi was loaded, and she usually had a nose for this type of thing.

"Not run out exactly." Rhi took a swig of wine. She felt like she could share everything with these women. "I came into some money when I was younger, and I've budgeted most of that for the big jobs and rent. However I also get an income from a trust fund that my mother runs. I'm paying all the smaller jobs with my monthly checks. At least, that was what I planned. My mother, who I have numerous issues with, doesn't want me living here, so she changed the structure of the trust, which means I don't get paid for three months. So for the next three months, I'm broke."

"What sort of mother does that?" Tye exclaimed.

"The sort who eats her young," Rhi said. "Sometimes she makes Joan Crawford look like Mother Theresa."

"What are you going to do?" Annie asked.

"I'll slow down. I'll reschedule a lot of the smaller jobs. And I'll hold off painting the theater until I can afford it. And I'll do what I can myself."

"But that will put you so far behind schedule."

"Can't be helped."

"Don't worry about a thing, Rhi. We look after our own in Hamlet." Annie glanced at Tye across the rising steam from the water. "We'll do what we can, won't we, Tye?"

"Of course we will. And Annie's boyfriends."

"They're not my boyfriends."

"Okay, your pets." Tye grinned.

Rhi laughed as Annie flicked water at Tye.

"At least I'm not pining over some dream man." Annie turned to Rhi. "Tye is totally saving herself for this guy."

Tye rested her head back on the side of the tub. "You make me sound like a virgin."

"Virgin on the ridiculous."

Tye laughed. "I love how you always change the subject when we talk about Jake and Sam."

"There's nothing to talk about," Annie said.

"Rubbish," said Tye. "So who is it? The older more sensitive Sam, or the younger, sexy Jake?"

"You don't think Sam is sexy?" Annie looked surprised.

"So it's Sam?"

"I never said that."

"When are you going to choose, Annie?" Rhi asked.

Annie stared at them both, mouth open, as if she'd never even considered it. "That's ridiculous. We're friends. That's all."

Rhi and Tye give her a mutual *oh really?* look.

"I could never choose." Annie looked like she was about to cry.

"Haven't you thought about this before?" Rhi asked, surprised.

"No! I mean, people tease us, but I've never seriously thought that anyone expects me to choose. That I should choose."

"Why not?" Tye asked. "Put them out of their misery."

Annie looked mortified. "You think they're both miserable?"

"I think they're hanging around, hoping you'll choose." Tye ran her hand over her shaved head. "Everyone expects you to choose. Including them."

"You can't keep both on a string forever," Rhi reasoned.

The doorbell rang and Annie placed her glass on the table next to the hot tub.

"Saved by the bell." She grabbed her towel and stepped out of the water. "Damn, it's cold." She grabbed two fluffy guest robes and held them out for Rhi and Tye.

Rhi stepped out of the tub and into the robe. She knew the routine at Annie's now. Tye followed, but she wasn't going to let up, just because Annie was trying to give them the slip.

"Annie, are you in love with both of them? Is that why you won't talk about this?"

Annie waved a hand in front of her face, as if to say stop. "I've got to work this out myself. Now the pizza's here—where's my wallet?"

"I thought friends were meant to help."

Annie looked up at Tye. "Normally, I would agree. And of course I'd speak to you...and to Rhi now too. I feel like I've known Rhi for years."

Rhi was unexpectedly moved. She felt the same.

"But Sam and Jake have been my friends my whole life. *My whole life.* Every memory of every birthday party, every school event, every major life event includes both of them. *Both!* They've both been there for me. And vice versa, I'd like to think. I might not tell them the things I tell you—it's a different type of friendship—but it's real and rich and I can't imagine life without them. So if I were in love with one, or god forbid, both, and we changed that dynamic...what would be left?"

"You might find something even more important," Tye said.

Annie headed toward the front door. "True. Or I might lose them both. And I'm not willing to take that chance."

Chapter 17

The following Saturday, Rhi arrived to find the theater surrounded by people. She saw Hank, the drama teacher from the high school, talking to a group of teenagers. She noticed Jake carrying a ladder around the side, and then Dan throwing something into one of his dumpsters. Were people working on her theater? She hadn't organized this. She didn't have the money to pay anyone at the moment, and had postponed all work. She quickly parked the car and jumped out.

"Morning, Rhi." Annie was standing at the doors of the Majestic, which were open. She was in old jeans and had a scarf tied around her head. In her hands was a paint scraper.

Rhi stalked over to her. "What the hell is going on, Annie?"

"It's a bee."

"I can't afford this."

"The very nature of *this* is that locals get together and work for free. It's for the community."

"Oh Annie, I can't ask everyone to do this for me."

"You didn't. I did." Annie put her hands on her hips. "Honey, this is just Hamlet. It's how things work around here. If you're going to call yourself a local, then you need to get used to it."

Rhi bit back her tears. "Geez, people are doing this to help me?"

"It's not a big deal," Annie whispered. "Don't cry. Smile and give them all a job to do."

Rhi smiled, but still her chin quivered.

"Great," said Annie, "now you look like something about to eat its prey."

"Everyone knows about my money problems?"

"No. I just threw the invite out there. These are the folk who turned up. I certainly didn't relay our conversation in the hot tub."

"You two were in a hot tub together?" Jake appeared and gave Rhi a kiss on the cheek.

"Yes we were, Jake," Annie said, teasingly. "And Tye was with us."

"Why don't I ever get invited to these evenings?" he said, pretending to be wounded.

"Because you're not very interesting."

Vaniqua Boyken interrupted at that moment and enveloped Rhi in a hug and a cloud of musk perfume. "Can I just say, this is the most exciting thing that's happened to this town since Denzel Washington was seen on the beach with his family two years back."

"I remember that," Annie said. "Built like a god."

"Mmm hmm." Vaniqua fanned herself to emphasize the point.

"Many locals said at the time that we have a similar build," Jake said, flexing his arm.

Annie rolled her eyes. "C'mon, muscles, Sam is lugging stuff himself and needs some help." She grabbed Jake's hand and dragged him toward his brother.

Rhi smiled at Vaniqua. She was such a nice woman, and had been very supportive of her upcoming classes. "I can't believe the turnout."

"People care. There are a few theater folk in town too. Give the place a knock and they'll crawl out of the woodwork. I was a founding member of the Singing Shakespeare Company."

Rhi was impressed. "Seriously? I love their work. I've seen all their shows. What was that first one?"

"*Othello in D Minor?*"

Rhi suddenly twigged. "Oh my god, you were Desdemona."

"That was me."

"*Midsummer Night's in B*...and *Romeo and Juliet Rap.*"

Vaniqua nodded. "My life, before I fell in love with a banker and moved up here. I also taught singing and voice for years, so if there's anything I can do to help you, just let me know."

"Thank you so much, Vaniqua. I will." Rhi was excited now. Vaniqua would be perfect for the company. "Would you be interested in some work?"

"Hell, yes. The twins are older now and I'm going a bit stir crazy with playing the perfect mother role. I need something for me. Count me in."

Vaniqua walked off and Rhi made her way into the auditorium. Both Jake and Sam were now heading up teams of people who were scraping paint from the walls. Tye was perched on top of a ladder cleaning a vent. Stan and a stout blond with a cheery face and big blue eyes were placing paint covers over the auditorium seats.

"Rhi, meet the missus," Stan called.

The woman gave Rhi a warm hug. "I'm Jules. I've heard a lot about you from the boys."

"You two have more than enough work with O'Reilly's without doing this," Rhi said.

"It's give and take in Hamlet," Jules said. "Oh by the way, I've popped an Avon catalogue on the desk for you. You might need a hand cream after all this manual labor."

Rhi looked down at her dirty hands and chipped nails. "You might be right, Jules."

One after another, Rhi met the locals. Hank, the drama teacher at the school, called out to her. "Rhi, come and meet these guys."

She was introduced to six senior drama students: Indy, Raffy, Oscar, Tadhg, Quinn and Ren. They were thrilled that a theater was opening in Hamlet, and enthusiastically promised to do everything from stage managing to ushering.

"Treat us like interns," Ren suggested.

Rhi watched as the people of Hamlet hammered and scraped and painted and cleaned her theater. Being a tight-knit community, this type of support wasn't unusual, and Rhi knew that. And yet to be the one they were supporting was a humbling experience.

She went outside and it was more of the same. Crystal and Hilary were on their knees, planting some flowers around the newly dug flower beds, chatting to each other. Rhi was amused to find the buttoned-up Hilary was friends with Crystal.

Crystal let out a throaty laugh. "Not many people I get down on my knees for, Rhi."

"You're naughty, Crystal," Hilary tittered.

"And Hilary usually only gets on her knees to pray," Crystal said to Rhi.

Another titter from Hilary.

"How's it looking inside?" Crystal asked.

"Come and have a look."

Crystal wiped a wrist across her forehead. "I'm fine, love. I haven't been in there for years. Perhaps once it's finished."

Rhi noticed Hilary give Crystal a sideways look.

Everyone was working so hard that they didn't even realize it was lunch time until Sal Sanderson and her sister Beck from the Wharf Restaurant rolled up with baskets of sandwiches and soft drinks in their van. With their almost white-blond hair, tan skin and pretty faces, they looked like your typical beach babes, but they were also amazing chefs and their restaurant was one of the most popular in town.

"We've been swamped with some functions, Rhi, and haven't been able to help out. So we're feeding you instead."

"You didn't have to do this!" Rhi was stunned by their generosity. By everyone's.

"Beck is just hoping for a role in one of your plays," Sal said.

"She can have the lead in all of them after this feast," said Rhi.

"She went to drama school and has never given up the dream."

Beck laughed. "I channel my creativity into food now. But I'll do anything to support this place."

"Did you bring food?" Jake walked across the grounds. "You girls are awesome."

Sam and Annie joined them and Rhi noticed as Sal gave Sam a shy smile.

"I just realized how hungry I am," Annie said, giving both Beck and Sal a kiss. She took one of the baskets. "I'll start handing these out."

Jake picked up another basket and headed for the theater entrance. "I'll eat these," he called over his shoulder.

"We'd better get back to the restaurant," said Beck. "Leave the baskets out the front. We'll pick them up later."

Sal gave Sam a little wave over her shoulder as she walked to the car. Rhi turned to see if anyone else had noticed. Crystal had, and gave her a wink.

"Finally, things are about to get interesting."

Chapter 18

Brigid puffed away at her third cigarette of the evening, ignoring Lugh's glares and Taran's fake coughing. She was in no mood for dinner tonight. She wanted to be alone. Cutting off Rhi's money hadn't sent her running home. Brigid needed to think of something that would.

"So tell me about this new album, Finn," Lugh said, trying to gloss over his wife's foul mood.

"I go into the studio next week."

Lugh nodded his head "It will be marvelous, I'm sure."

"I'm trying some different things with it. I don't know...I need a change musically, but not sure what that means yet."

"As long as you don't buy a theater in Bumblefuck, Idaho, I'm sure it will mean positive things," Brigid snapped.

Taran bit back a yawn. "She's renting it, Mom."

Brigid shot him a look. "And you, Taran? How was your week?"

"Fine."

"Surely you can give us more information than just 'fine.'"

Taran looked intently at his mother. Lugh often put his foot down about things, but he certainly didn't challenge her like Taran did. Taran's very presence riled her at times. He treated her with derision. She simply didn't intimidate him at all. While one glare from her could wither the strongest men, Taran always matched her stare and indicated that he was bored. He found her amusing, annoying and certainly petty. It drove her crazy.

"What have you done this week? Broken any hearts? Stolen any girlfriends?"

"D, all of the above."

"What about work?"

"There's a gallery in Boston that is interested in my work. I'll drive up there in a couple of weeks and meet with them."

"You should visit Rhiannon while you're up that way," Lugh suggested.

"I might." Taran couldn't bear committing to anything. He even abhorred committing to a phone plan, let alone real plans in advance or, horror, a relationship. "I'll think about it closer to the time."

"When are you going up, Mom?" Finn asked.

"When hell freezes over and women embrace cellulite."

Taran let out a laugh. "You really are in a charming mood tonight, Mom."

"Taran, I'm tired from work, that's all."

A woman tentatively approached the table. "You need to know—"

"Oh just fuck off will you," snapped Brigid. "What do we need to know? That we'll burn in hell? That your vengeful bloody god will strike us down?"

The woman looked like she was about to burst into tears. "I'm so sorry, I was going to tell you that your show saved me.'"

Brigid looked shocked. "Oh. I don't mind knowing that."

Lugh reached out a hand to the woman. "How did it save you, dear?"

"I followed your instructions to get out of a real bad relationship. I disconnected energetically from it. Saved my life. Thank you."

"No, thank *you*. We appreciate you sharing that with us, don't we, Brigid?"

"I do, honey," she said plastering a smile across her face. "I thought you were one of those god-botherers."

The woman looked relieved. "Oh no, I haven't been to church since Jesus wore sandals."

"I apologize for snapping," Brigid said, clearly not.

"Don't you worry. Enjoy your dinner." The woman gave them all a nod and scurried away.

Brigid let out a weary sigh. "Since Jesus wore sandals? We really need to find a new local. The clientele here has gone to the dogs."

Lugh gave his wife a look that said zip it, and turned his attention to his sons. Brigid actually did as she was told, which was rare. But she wasn't in the mood to challenge Lugh. He might normally be extremely patient and even-tempered, but watch out if you crossed the line. He had great respect for their fans. While she admired this about her husband, she really had no idea why. Most of them looked like rejects from a Renaissance faire. Her own respect was faked, although only she knew that.

Brigid lit another cigarette and stared into space. Her thoughts drifted to the only thing she'd been able to think of for weeks.

*

Brigid was reeling. This was not part of her plan. Just when she was being offered the opportunity to make something of herself, her dearest friend was going to stand in the way.

"Please understand, Bridge." Crystal was pleading now, still in her bed sheet. *"I don't want to be famous, like you do. I don't want to be in the public eye."*

"So you're ruining my chance because of that?"

"That's unfair."

"The producer was clear...he wants two witches for this show. Two!"

"That's your fault for writing about me in the article without my permission." Crystal pulled the sheet tight.

"I didn't use your name, just the details of our life together. Of you and I being best friends."

"Don't pull that card on me, Brigid. I am your best friend. And if you were mine, you would understand why I can't do this."

"Well, I don't," Brigid snapped.

"You need to find someone else for this."

"Oh yeah, witches are a dime a dozen."

"They are in New York." Crystal was trying to lighten the mood, but it didn't work. *"How about Lugh Wall? He's a very powerful witch, and has had a huge crush on you for months."*

Brigid rolled her eyes. *"Not my type."* She sat in front of Crystal so they were eye to eye now. *"Please, Crystal. Be a friend."*

Crystal was immovable. *"I am your friend. But I can't do this."*

"Is it because of whatshisface in there?" Brigid nodded toward Crystal's bedroom door. *"You're besotted. He's fogging up your brain."*

"Is that so bad?"

"Don't let him get in the way of our friendship."

"I've never felt this way before." Crystal looked at Brigid, begging her to understand. *"But this isn't because of him. It's the craft, Bridge. I don't judge you for wanting to*

commercialize it. I don't. But it's not my path. I'd be more than happy just working from my own shop, and practicing solitary. That's my path."

"This is my moment, Crystal."

Crystal nodded. "It might be. But it's yours. Not mine."

"So you'll destroy our friendship over this?"

"I don't believe it's so flimsy."

Brigid smiled at Crystal. She always had been naïve.

Chapter 19

By the time St Patrick's Day rolled around, Rhi felt as if she'd been living in Hamlet for years. She was enjoying her work, her theater, her new friends and the little town. So far there wasn't a single thing she missed about New York, except for her father and brothers.

Rhi spent the day cleaning all the light fittings. Some were simple brass and glass ones while fothers were fiddly glass chandeliers. Her brain was ready to explode by the time she was finished, but she was happy knowing one more job could be crossed off the list. She locked up and headed into the center of town.

Hamlet was decked out in green. There were shamrocks and streamers everywhere. The town was throwing a huge party, with various events planned for the weekend.

Annie was waiting outside Crystal's with Sam and Jake. She was wearing blue jeans and an emerald blazer with emerald stones at her ears and throat. Her hair was pulled into a chignon to show them off.

"Am I Irish enough?" she said as she kissed Rhi hello.

"Perhaps you'd prefer a pint of Guinness to this," came Tye's voice behind them. She thrust a tray of takeaway coffees at her friends. "Sorry they're not green," she said. "But they'll warm you up."

"Exactly what I need," Rhi said.

Tye propped the tray against the shop, and then the five of them made their way to the edge of the pavement. It was crowded by Hamlet's standards, but there was still plenty of room to move.

"So Rhi, what do you think of Hamlet today?" asked Annie.

"Very...green," Rhi said.

"Looks like a leprechaun threw up," Sam said.

"A giant leprechaun...and he exploded all over town," Jake added. "Attack of the killer leprechaun zombies."

"And you wonder why you can't get a date," Annie said.

Sam gave her a wry smile and moved over to Rhi. "This parade has been the same since we were kids. I think they use the same float."

"Don't build it up too much, Sam," Jake called. "Let Rhi be pleasantly surprised."

Annie pointed at the end of the road. "They're coming."

They heard the music first as the procession made its way toward Main Street and then finally turned the corner.

"Don't blink," quipped Tye. "Or you might miss it."

It certainly didn't compare to New York's St Patrick's parade, but what it lacked in size it made up for in enthusiasm. There were music and balloons and streamers. The dance ensemble from the local school gave an Irish jig their best shot. Michael Flatley would have cried but the rest of the town lined the streets and cheered. Tim McCartney wheeled his three-year-old triplets in a green wheelbarrow with *McCartney Clan* painted on the side. There was also a float with the head of the Irish Heritage Society waving atop it, the high school marching band, three firefighters and two police, a James Joyce Readers' Association, and a dyke on a bike.

Everyone felt she had the wrong parade but gave her a warm cheer anyhow.

Afterward, Annie turned to the others. "That was seventeen seconds I'll never get back."

"Don't be bitchy," Sam teased. "I remember you used to head that parade up each year, dancing that jig."

"I know, and I've apologized to everyone in town since."

"Give us a little jig now," Sam teased.

"In your dreams."

Tye threw an arm around Jake and Sam. "We've gotta love you and leave you. We need to set up for tonight. Let's go, you two."

"See you at O'Reilly's," Annie called after them, as Rhi gave them a wave.

"What now?" she asked.

"I think we should head back to yours, crack open a wine, and find you a decent outfit for tonight."

Rhi looked down at her jeans, covered in dust. "I happen to like this look."

"I'm not adverse to it myself, but tonight you need to dress for Paddy. Ceridwen is playing and the whole town will be turning out with their best Irish face."

"You guys sure do take it seriously." Rhi slipped her arm through Annie's. "C'mon then."

Back at the cottage, Rhi headed straight upstairs. "Make yourself at home, Annie."

"I will...seeing I own it."

Rhi showered and then rifled through her wardrobe. She'd lived in nothing but jeans and sweatshirts since arriving in Hamlet. She dug out an old favorite from the back of her wardrobe: a belted emerald green jersey dress that clung in all the right places. It had long sleeves but a short hem, so she paired it with brown boots with sky-high heels. She let her freshly washed hair hang loose, threw on a couple of bangles, and was ready to party.

Annie whistled as Rhi walked down the stairs. "I sure hope you have a permit for that."

"You told me to dress up." Rhi shrugged, taking the glass of wine Annie offered.

"I didn't mean for you to look that hot. Now no one will look at me."

Rhi laughed. "Rubbish. Sam and Jake can't take their eyes off you."

Annie flicked at one of her fingernails, as though she was cleaning something under it. "I've been thinking about what you and Tye said over at my place, about choosing. And I think I should encourage them to…date other women."

Rh nodded. "That's up to you, but one of you will have to move on first. You can't keep this up forever."

"No. It's unsustainable."

But Rhi still didn't believe Annie was convinced.

*

O'Reilly's was already packed when they arrived.

Rhi signaled Stan. "Do you have a red with my name on it, Stan?"

"One look at you, Rhi, and I have more than a red with your name on it," Stan called, as he grabbed a bottle and an opener. "You'll like this one. A playful Pinot."

Annie's face lit up and she motioned for someone to join them. Rhi turned to see Crystal making her way across the room. The woman moved with sexy grace, greeting everyone she knew, and many she didn't know, along the way. Dressed in head-to-toe fluorescent green she looked like a huge leprechaun with expensive jewelry. Only Crystal could get away with such an outfit without looking ridiculous.

"Don't you look bright?" said Annie.

"I love green. It's very healing." She gave Rhi and Annie a kiss each. "Looking lovely, ladies."

"Do you have any Irish in you?" Rhi asked her.

"I haven't for many years," Crystal said cheekily. She perched herself on the barstool and ordered a Guinness. "Excellent source of iron," she explained to Rhi. "I find the good in all my guilty pleasures. That's the secret to a guilt-free life."

"Give us an example," Rhi asked.

"Chocolate is full of antioxidants, as is red wine. The occasional cigarette is the perfect antidote to a constant habit. Casual sex with Larry is good for my blood flow and skin. Live without an ounce of regret, and no harm will come to you."

"So you have no regrets?"

"None I'm sharing."

A large man in his seventies wearing a bowler hat and a cravat walked past and gave Crystal a wave.

Crystal leaned in to Rhi and chuckled. "Apart from him. He's a regret." And she threw her head back and laughed, and Rhi joined in. She thought Crystal was nothing short of fabulous.

The bar filled up quickly. Many faces were familiar but there were a lot of out-of-towners as well. O'Reilly's and Ceridwen were famous for their St Patrick's Day celebrations. Stan had some extra staff on, including Jules, who gave Rhi a wave. In return for helping out at the theater, Rhi had bought a bunch of Avon products that she would probably never use.

"How's that lip plumper, Rhi?" Jules called over the noise.

"Better than collagen, Jules. Very Angelina Jolie," shouted Rhi, trying to make her lips look fuller as she spoke.

"I popped one of those cuticle moisturizers aside for you. Just let me know when you need it."

Rhi gave her a nod and silently wondered if her cuticles needed their own moisturizer.

A murmur rippled around the room and Rhi noticed that the band had made their way to the stage. Her eyes flickered over Tye in a white shirt with a dark green shamrock across the front, but rested on Tad. Why oh why did the man have to be so good looking?

Tad settled into his seat and raised his head, locking eyes with Rhi across the crowd for a brief moment. Then, rocking to a silent rhythm, he began to play a haunting melody. After a moment Sam joined in on the guitar, followed by Jake on the whistle. Finally Tye's voice rang out across the room and time was lost in the lilting sounds of Ceridwen. Their music, perfect and glorious, took over Rhi's body and seeped into her soul.

Ten minutes; thirty; one hour passed and then it was over and all Rhi was left with was gratitude. She cheered along with everyone else, the spell broken by doing so. The band had played some of their familiar tunes but had mainly stuck to Irish folk ballads in honor of St Patrick. It had stirred deep memories in Rhi, of long forgotten lives in lands forever altered. She turned and looked at Annie, who was dabbing her eyes and trying not to ruin her makeup. They locked eyes and then burst into uncontrollable giggles.

"I'm glad I'm not the only soppy mess around here," said Annie.

"I've never been so deeply affected by music before."

Annie leaned over and whispered in Rhi's ear: "It's magic, Rhi."

The evening wore on. Stan got up and, accompanied by Ceridwen, sang some old Irish songs. He hadn't lied when he told Rhi he could sing. He had a deep, rich baritone voice that suited the old drinking songs he chose to entertain everyone with. Then he finished with a heartbreaking rendition of "Danny Boy" to loud applause and the sound system took over with some more upbeat music, which got everyone up dancing.

Rhi leaned against the bar and watched as Annie wiggled and grooved in between Sam and Jake. So much for encouraging them to date other women. She was tossing wine back as if it were water. Before long they'd have to carry her off the dance floor.

Beside them were Tye and Crystal. Rhi could see where Tye got her sex appeal. Despite the fact that Crystal was probably fifty pounds overweight, her moves were sexy and graceful. She had an easy rhythm and swayed her hips seductively. Tye and Crystal were chatting loudly as they danced and looked so comfortable, so right together. Rhi could never imagine getting dirty on the dance floor with her own mother—Brigid was more a good bottle of bubbly at a top restaurant kind of woman. Not that her mother was *uptight*. Rhi had walked in on her parents and ten of their friends playing Spin the Bottle once. Rather than be embarrassed, they had invited her to join in. Rhi declined, but it had been the beginning of her understanding how truly liberal her parents were. Nudity at home was nothing new, and certainly nothing to be ashamed of. Her parents often performed rituals and spells skyclad. But when you walk into a topless tea and scones affair on a Sunday afternoon, and find your mother entertaining a famous actress, a number of witches and a well-known politician with her tits hanging out, the reality of your home life begins to sink in.

As a result, Rhi was slightly reserved regarding sex and nudity. She wasn't self-conscious, but it was private. Her body was for the Goddess and the man she loved. Or would love. For a moment Rhi had believed Chandra could be the one, but by the time she had caught him and Victoria in the coffee table *Karma Sutra* position she had already realized that she wasn't—and had never been—in love with him. Or anyone. She was yet to meet someone who completely swept her away.

"Penny for your thoughts."

With a jolt, Rhi came back to earth and the faint smell of mint and Gucci aftershave.

Tad stared at her in amusement. "You were off with the fairies."

Rhi thought abut the dryad in her garden.

"Can we start again? I don't like getting off on the wrong foot."

Rhi waved his concerns away. He'd already apologized at the theater, and certainly made up for any rudeness by entertaining her to cheer her up. She still felt like she'd been slightly sideswiped by the whole *Hamlet* thing, but it also made sense creatively for that to be the first play.

"Forget about it. Let's dance," she said.

"I'm not much of a dancer."

"Yeah, right, Gene Kelly. Isn't tap a dance?"

Tad looked like he was trying to work her out. "Okay, I'll give it a shot."

Rhi led him out onto the dance floor and started to dance. "C'mon, twinkle toes, show me some of those moves." She did a little tap dance. "I know, I don't have your finesse."

Tad shook his head and laughed. "You're crazy, Rhi."

"You should talk."

Without warning, he grabbed her and pulled her in close. "Good idea. Let's talk."

"I thought we were dancing." She looked around and noticed people were looking at them, smiling.

"We are dancing...in a swaying kind of way. This way I won't tread on your toes. I'm not big on shaking my booty in public."

"Oh, I get it. You save those dances for private." Rhi relaxed a little. She had to admit it was nice being in his arms. His body was strong, carved from rock. She could feel the contours under her hands. Her palms began to sweat.

"Feeling Irish enough?"

"Feeling something," Rhi said.

Tad's hand pressed against the small of her back and sent a charge of electricity straight between her legs. She concentrated on taking a few breaths. This was ridiculous. She wasn't at her first high school dance.

"How about you?" she said. "Any Irish in the gene pool?"

"I get a bit from both sides, especially my mother."

"Does she live around here?"

"New York."

"Do you see her often?"

"Every weekday at two."

Rhi was obviously confused, which made Tad smile. "My mother is Collette Kelly," he explained.

Rhi never watched soaps but even she knew of the grand dame of daytime soaps. "Wow, I'm quite impressed. That woman has never been out of work."

"Nor has her plastic surgeon."

"Meow. Mother issues?"

"Not at all. I actually like her a lot." Tad turned his head to watch Crystal wiggle her way past them with a loud laugh. "Crystal has been more of a mother to me. Collette is great, just not maternal."

"So you've known Crystal for a while?"

"My whole life. My mother sent me to Crystal's for school vacations. Tye and I grew up together. They were the ones who talked me into moving back here."

"No wonder you and Tye work so well to-gether...musically, I mean."

Tad pulled back slightly, his eyes searching hers. "One eye is slightly darker than the other."

Rhi flushed. Not many people notice that.

"Are you embarrassed?"

"Not by my eyes."

"By me looking into them?"

Rhi realized they'd stopped dancing. There was a space filled with nothing but a gaze. She felt like the rest of the world could disappear in that moment and she wouldn't notice. It was she who broke the spell.

"Tell me more about yourself," she said. "I know that you're quite a performer. What else?"

"I write jingles and show openers. Music for commercials and television shows."

Rhi noticed a very faint freckle on his lip. It took all her willpower to not reach up and kiss it.

"Any commercials I'd know?"

Tad was clearly embarrassed. "Remember the Heartfelt Card Ad?"

Rhi nodded and burst into song, "She was feeling blue, and then that card came from you, a card in the mail, when she was feeling so frail…You made someone happy today."

Tad rolled his eyes, amused. "Nice rendition."

"You really wrote that?" Rhi was laughing now. "I used to cry when that came on."

"You're not the only one. I once had an email from the PMS Society asking for an interview for their monthly magazine."

"Hilarious. Anything else?"

"I don't know. A bunch of things. Mintlip Mouthwash. Air America. Also wrote the theme song for *Manhattan MD*."

"I love that show."

"I write if I'm in the mood, but lately I've been concentrating on Ceridwen."

Rhi had a clear flash in her mind's eye. She saw big things for Tad's band. He seemed to sense the unusual energy shift, but before either of them could say anything, they were interrupted by a crash.

Tad shielded Rhi until the noise stopped, and then both turned to find a drunken guy sprawled out on top of some of the instruments.

"Hamish! You okay?"

"I think I'm gonna puke."

"C'mon, man, not on the instruments." Tad turned to Rhi. "I've got to…"

"Of course."

"How about I drive you home? Take two?"

"I'd like that."

He gave her a smile and then made his way to Hamish, a huge man who had obviously consumed a huge amount of booze. Rhi watched Tad deal with him with kindness and humor, despite Hamish's capricious mood swings.

"Tad, my ol' pal! Man, it's good to see you."

"I'm going to get you into a cab, Hamish." Tad swung an arm around Hamish and hauled him to his feet.

"Get ya fucking hands off me."

Tad disappeared out the door with Hamish and Rhi made her way across the bar to another patron who'd had way too much to drink.

"Annie, grab your things. Tad and I will drive you home."

Chapter 20

It really was take two. Tad agreed to drive Annie home and while she didn't trip this time, she did drop her keys.

"Isaall good guys," she called from her porch. "Jush gotta find 'em."

"Should I help her?" Rhi asked, watching her from Tad's car.

"No."

It took Annie a couple of minutes to find the keys and then unlock her door. She waved as she stumbled inside. "Shanks for the lift."

"Perhaps I should stay with her."

"No need."

"She might be sick."

"I hope so."

Rhi was surprised by his attitude, which could only be described as tough love. "Does she always drink this much?"

"Only recently."

Rhi turned to Tad. "Does that worry you?"

It clearly did. "I'm keeping an eye on it."

Annie's behavior was bringing up all sorts of issues for Rhi. "I just lost my best friend because of her drinking."

Tad reached out and grabbed her hand. "I'm so sorry. That's awful."

"Yes, it's been tough."

"When did she die?"

"Die? Oh god, no, I'm sorry, is that how it sounded?" Rhi burst out laughing. "No, the bitch didn't die. She had sex with my boyfriend. Now ex-boyfriend."

Tad threw his head back and laughed too. "Totally different scenario."

"Totally."

The laughter died down but left an easy comfort in its place that had never been there before.

"It's like a death," Rhi admitted. "I miss her every day. We've been friends most of our lives, so it's a large space she's left behind."

"She's an alcoholic?"

"Her father died a few years ago and she hit the bottle hard. She never really stopped. She was high functioning until recently. But lately she's done some stupid things."

"And your *ex*?"

"That was on the cards. It's her I miss." She stared back up Annie's driveway. "What's going on with Annie?"

"Sam and Jake. It's messing with her head. So whenever we all go out, she gets wasted. She doesn't drink alone, or at home. Just around them."

"Yeah, I've noticed. Perhaps she's looking for the courage to tell them."

"Or to choose."

"Do you think she will?"

Tad started the car and backed down the driveway. "I think she already has. That's the problem."

Rhi watched as Annie's house disappeared. "You obviously keep an eye on her, Tad. That's good."

"I do." He smiled at her sideways. "Who keeps an eye on you, Rhi?"

"No one up here."

He angled his head to one side. "That's no good. You should always have someone looking out for you."

"Who looks out for you?" Rhi asked.

Tad didn't miss a beat. "Crystal. It's always been Crystal."

"Yeah, well I kind of like it this way. I feel like people have kept an eye on me for years." Rhi shrugged, a little embarrassed. "It's nice to blend into the background where no one knows me."

"You hardly blend in." He gave her an appreciative glance. "Especially in that dress."

Rhi was grateful for the dark car, where he couldn't see her blush.

Tad pulled up outside her house. "Home sweet home."

"Where do you live?"

"Not far from here. Up the other end of Cadman's Beach."

"My house backs on to Cadman's. I love it. It's home."

Tad stared at her for a moment. She wanted to reach out and stroke his face. He seemed so different tonight. At the theater, with his quips and routines, he was entertaining, but here and now she felt she could rely on him. He was grounded, and she liked that.

"I never really knew what home was until Crystal dragged me back up here."

"I know what you mean. I feel like I'm carving something out for myself that's both unexpected and just right. I couldn't find that in New York, even though I was born and raised there." Rhi turned her whole body toward him. "There was this moment when I saw the theater...I just knew I had to be here. Did you have a moment like that?"

Tad stared out the darkened windows. "I guess for me that moment occurred after I'd spent a couple of weeks here, hanging out with Tye and Annie. Getting to know Jake and Sam. I was composing, something I hadn't done for a while. And one day...I had a moment. I realized I was happy and wanted to stay. I realized that being here didn't make me miss my father more than when I was in New York." He searched her face. "I'm guessing you know how he died?"

"I do now, yes."

"I was only five when he died, but my memories of him are as clear as if I'd seen him yesterday. I spent holidays here, but I thought coming back to live would be too difficult. It was the opposite."

"Perhaps in some ways you're closer to him here."

"I'm certainly closer to the good memories, but if you're suggesting some sort of spiritual connection, I don't really believe that."

"You don't believe in life after death."

"Now you sound like Tye. I wish I did. I don't know."

"But what is death?"

"No idea. The lights go out. The power gets switched off. That's it probably."

"What if there's more to it? Do you believe in spirits?"

"I was pretty fond of vodka for a few years there."

"Is that the reason Crystal talked you into coming up here?"

"I'd had a few years of clichés. Made a shitload of money from some jingles, had a nasty heartbreak, hung out with the wrong crew, kept making money from jingles even though I wanted to be a serious musician. I went off the rails a bit." Tad grinned. "I sound like a pompous idiot when I tell that story. So many people struggling for any type of success and here I was rolling in it, but it wasn't the type I wanted."

"I understand more than you realize."

He waved his hands in the air. "Bought me my house. Home and security. I have more gratitude now. The jingles pay the way and I get to make music with Tye." He stared her straight in the eye. "Are you going to stay?"

"I'd have to bring a toothbrush."

Tad threw his head back and laughed. "I meant in Hamlet, but I'm more than happy to follow through on that conversation instead."

Rhi went a hundred shades of red. "We'll have that conversation once I've extracted my foot from my mouth."

They stared at each other, the car crackling with heat, and yet neither of them reached out. And then, much to Rhi's horror, she realized she was going to sneeze. She turned her head and tried to stop it—but too late.

"Gesundheit."

"Thanks."

"I hope you're not allergic to me."

"I think it's seasonal. Spring is coming." She tried to hide her embarrassment. "I cry, I sneeze. But at least I can always ask you for a handkerchief."

"Have I missed something?" Tad clearly had no idea what she was talking about.

Great, he was playing at that again. "Thanks for the lift home, Tad." And with that, Rhi slipped from the car and ran into her house.

*

Tad watched Rhi close the door behind her and then turned the headlights on and drove down the road. He had no idea what had happened. He'd come so close to kissing her. He probably should've—just get it out of the way, right? That sort of chemistry didn't come along very often. But he also knew what chemistry mixed with crazy was like. He'd had a couple of relationships with gorgeous women who stood all his hairs on end, but once they were in a relationship, they turned into Medusa. The signs had been there from the start, but he'd chosen to ignore them.

But not this time.

He had sworn off women with issues and as much as it pained him, Rhi fell into that category. She said the weirdest things. Like just then, and that whole thing about him being a tap dancer. Yes, she was flirty and quirky, but there was something about the familiarity with which she'd said it that unnerved him. It didn't matter that she was already under his skin. Or that she was also gorgeous and smart and interesting. And had the most incredible eyes. For a moment tonight he'd seen his future mapped out in them. But the only thing that really mattered was keeping her at arm's length.

Kissing her would only lead to trouble.

Chapter 21

Rhi was restless. She was a creature of habit, always wanting to build a strong base for herself. But tonight, the edgy energy consumed her. She wanted to soar. She knew there was only one way to satisfy it, to calm it. But she couldn't. She'd moved away from New York, away from her parents, to start anew. She wanted to be known as Rhi who ran the theater.

She didn't want to be known as the town witch.

She ran around the house and closed all the curtains. Still, the moon called her. She flicked on the TV. Fox News...she flicked it off. She wasn't that desperate.

She went into the kitchen and yanked an old recipe book off the shelf. Perhaps it was time to learn how to cook. But still, like a whisper, the Goddess followed.

The doorbell rang and she jumped, startled. She still wasn't used to people just dropping by. Rhi opened the door and found Tye wearing a deep emerald green monk's cape and hood. She put a finger to her lips. "Let me in."

Tye stepped into the light of the hallway and closed the door behind her. She clicked the lock shut and turned back to Rhi, who stared at her, speechless.

The monk's cape was made out of the softest velvet and seemed to skim every sinewy angle of Tye's body. Around her wrists and ankles were silver bracelets. Bejeweled stars dripped off her ears and fingers. She pushed the hood back and Rhi saw she was wearing makeup. Her eyes had been lined, her lips painted the color of blood. Her face shone with shimmering glitter. In the center of her forehead was a moon. Tye was the most beautiful woman she had ever seen.

"Spring Equinox," Tye said. "Get dressed."

Rhi didn't argue. She ran upstairs and tore through her drawers. She found what she was looking for and threw it on. The night-blue empire dress fit her body like a second skin, caressed it like an old lover. Then she raced to her mirror and applied some color to her cheeks and lips. She scattered gold across her brow, and fastened her amber and jet amulet around her neck. She was quick. She had done it all before, countless times.

Finally, she pulled a small trunk out from under the bed. She stalled. This was what she'd said she wouldn't do. She'd decided she wouldn't practice any more. Oh sure, she would believe. How could she not believe the truth? Her truth. But what if someone saw her? The jokes would start, followed by the fear. People would point, whisper, avoid her even.

What if Tad saw her?

"To hell with them," she muttered. "Just tonight. I owe the Goddess this. Tonight. And then...no more."

Rhi opened the lid and burrowed to the bottom of the trunk. There she found her athame. To a non-initiate it would look ominous with its carved black hilt and silver blade. To Rhi, it was anything but. It was an instrument of magic. The athame had never known blood. It had never known darkness. The average kitchen steak knife had seen more murder than this ornate dagger.

She slid a garter on, up to her thigh, and slipped the athame securely in. Then she grabbed her cape from the trunk and closed the lid. She tied the cape around her shoulders and made her way back down the stairs. She didn't need to check herself in the mirror, she knew how she looked. There was no one to impress. She was dressed for something much greater.

Tye nodded when she saw Rhi. "Perfect. Let's go."

She took Rhi's hand and led her out the back door, through the garden, past Pip's oak and into the forest. Rhi could feel the earth beneath her feet. Even when the path was rocky it seemed to caress her soles. They ran further into the darkness. Branches scraped at Rhi's cheeks, spirits nipped at her heels. Tye ducked between two rocks and disappeared. Rhi followed and came out in a clearing, lit, almost violently, by the full moon.

Crystal was waiting, sitting in the center of a ring naturally charred into the earth. Candles were placed in the four quarters of the circle, in the east, south, north and west. The flames flickered and danced even though the night was deathly still. A flat rock formed a natural altar, covered in tools and spring flowers and facing the east.

Rhi could hear the waves crashing on the nearby beach but the space was protected from prying eyes by a circle of trees and rocks. Rhi smiled. Mother Nature had provided a grove.

Crystal rose and welcomed Rhi with a hug. "Tye and I have been looking forward to tonight."

"I wasn't sure you knew."

Tye laughed. "I knew from the moment you first walked into the shop."

"I knew before then," said Crystal. "I dreamed you would come."

Rhi shifted uncomfortably. She couldn't even escape it here. Tye understood and took her hand.

"No one else knows, Rhi. They don't even know about us. Sure they come to us for readings and stuff, but they don't truly understand. We're eccentrics to them, psychics. Not witches."

"I came here to get away from all this," Rhi explained.

Crystal smiled gently. "You didn't come here to get away from it. You came here to find it."

"You know my parents?"

"I know who they are." Crystal drifted back over to the altar and picked up a beautiful wooden pentacle.

"Then you understand why I need a break from all this."

"Their television show has helped destroy many of the myths and preconceptions about the Pagan religions. They are two of the most powerful witches alive. Despite the hype, they are true followers. They know their craft. Now you must discover yours. That is the beauty of the Old Way. Every Way is different. You've come here to find yours."

Crystal handed Rhi the pentacle. Its energy shot up her arms like warm liquid gold. Rhi knew Crystal was right. Her belief was energy, like this wood, this symbol: pure, real and wondrous. But she had misplaced the joy and the innocence somewhere inside a television studio.

Crystal was right. She needed to find her own path, and in doing so perhaps understand theirs.

"Let's begin," whispered Crystal.

Rhi had never worked with anyone but family. She had grown up casting spells and working magic with her parents and brothers. There were festivals and celebrations that involved other witches but on those days the children played together while their parents prayed together. Her parents had never been intimately involved with a particular coven; they were both hereditary witches and believed practicing the craft was a family affair. It was fine to educate people, enlighten them on the finer aspects of the craft. It was okay to use your psychic abilities—after all, not all psychics are witches, and not all witches are psychic. It was even acceptable to have a line of merchandise ranging from T-shirts to lunch boxes. But any serious veneration of the Goddess, any acknowledgement of the eight holy days, was done as a family, or alone.

In recent years Rhi had traveled a solitary path. She practiced alone on all days but the holy ones. Those days she spent with her family.

Tye sensed this and embraced her. Crystal began to cleanse and then consecrate the circle. All thoughts of Rhi's family, her past, were lost like petals in the wind. Suddenly these women were familiar. They had been friends, sisters for centuries. All three naturally understood what needed to be done. They worked together silently, their glances, their emotions and their faith louder than any words.

The called upon the guardians, the rulers of the elements. Their request echoed across the astral planes and the elementals took their places. First came the sylphs, who rode in on a wisp of a breeze. Their ethereal forms floated above the eastern candle, their attention drifted and scattered like the wind they dwelled in. Next came the salamanders, bursting forth from their home, the fire. Their ever-watchful yellow eyes assured the women they would protect the south. The undines brought the illusion of water with them as they swam to their post and agreed to keep watch in the west. Finally the gnomes arrived in the north. They were slow, methodical but ever eager to be involved in magic.

The circle was alive, the energy was raised. Rhi could feel the power spiraling around and around until her body too rotated with the force. She was aware, connected, as Tye danced and Crystal rocked. The Lord and the Lady were honored. The darkness of winter cast away and the new beginnings of spring, internally, externally, embraced by mind, body and soul. The power, for a time reined in, was now let loose. It increased, roared through the night, into the point of a cone, spinning, throbbing, creating, until finally, together, they let it go, set it free, into the universe from which it came.

Afterward, they sat in comfortable silence and shared a picnic with the nature spirits and each other. It was Tye who broke the silence.

"I'm yet to find a man who can take me to such heights."

Crystal gave a knowing chuckle. "He'll come along."

"Yeah, yeah." Tye had obviously heard that before.

"Sooner than you realize," Crystal added. "What about you, Rhi? Have you found the one yet?"

Somehow Rhi felt Crystal knew more than she did about her past and future love life—or lack of. "I'm enjoying being on my own at the moment," she admitted. "I ended a relationship a couple of months ago. I'm over it, but I still need some time."

"What was he like?" asked Tye.

"Flexible." Rhi giggled. "He was a yoga instructor." Oh what the hell, she thought. These two women knew more about her than anyone had in years. She may as well 'fess up. "I lived with Chandra."

"The Chandra? The *Yoga Guru* series Chandra?" Tye burst out laughing. "But he's so slimy."

"I can see that now. I met him when he was just starting to make a name for himself." Rhi laughed at Tye's disbelieving stare. "What can I say? For once I paled into the background. It was a nice change."

"I think we carry a coffee table book of his," said Crystal. "*Chandra in India.*"

"Oh yeah," said Tye. "His amazing spiritual journey through India, pose by pose."

Rhi snorted. "That's such a load of lies. He hated India. Took an endless supply of antibacterial wipes and bottled water. Had a full medical when he got home, including a CAT scan."

"Did they find anything?"

"Nada."

"So what happened?"

Rhi fiddled with a twig, drawing pentacles in the sand. "Walked in on him and my best friend having sex."

"How devastating!" gasped Tye, her eyes wide in horror.

"Not really. I didn't really love him."

"I'm not talking about him." Tye playfully punched Rhi's arm. "I'm talking about the friend. How devastating for a friend to do that to you."

A wave of anguish engulfed her. "It has been."

Tye took her hand and looked straight into her eyes. "I can see it still hurts. You'll get over it one day."

Rhi sipped her wine. "It has been healing moving here."

Tye smiled at her, both aware that their friendship was secure now.

"Why are you single, Tye? You're so gorgeous."

"I'm waiting for a man who sees beyond that."

"He's not far off," said Crystal.

"Goddess, Mom, will you zip it!"

"What about Tad? You guys make beautiful music together."

"Only with instruments. He's like a brother to me." Tye watched Rhi carefully over the rim of her goblet. "You think he's cute. Why don't you ask him out?"

Rhi turned her face into a shadow so the others didn't see how flustered the mention of Tad had made her. "I don't think that's a good idea."

"Why not?" Crystal asked. "He's gorgeous, sweet as any man who's ever lived and writes beautiful music."

Tye's eyes gleamed wickedly. "And I'm friends with an old girlfriend of his who says he's amazing in bed."

"Tye! Way too much info." Rhi turned to Crystal for support but found nothing but a knowing smile.

She decided to confide in them both. "I'll admit it, he's extremely attractive...but I often feel like I'm dealing with two different people."

"How do you mean?" Crystal asked.

"When he drove me home the other night, it was so easy being with him. He's smart and funny and, yes, incredibly hot."

Crystal and Tye both nodded. They knew all that.

"But when he auditioned for *Hamlet* for me—"

"He what?"

"He was doing some dances and songs for me and then launched into *Hamlet*."

Tye was obviously dumbfounded. "Tad performed *Hamlet* for you?"

"Yep, center stage at the theater. I'm furious that he's using his position as landlord to manipulate me into staging *Hamlet*, but on the other hand...he was so incredible, I'd be stupid not to."

Crystal stared at Rhi, speechless. Tye waved her hands around, trying to clarify things.

"So Tad has gone into the theater—?"

"A few times."

"And on one of those times...auditioned for you?"

"Am I missing something here?" Rhi asked.

"Yeah! Apart from the fact that it's totally out of character." Tye turned to her mother. "*Hamlet*?"

Crystal looked upset. "I don't know. We know he needs closure. Always has."

"By performing *Hamlet*?"

Rhi was completely confused. "What's going on?"

"*Hamlet* was the last play performed in that theater," Tye explained. "Tad's father was killed during it."

"Are you serious? I knew he was killed during a play but I had no idea it was *Hamlet*. Why would he want to revisit *that*?"

"What do you think, Mom?"

Crystal didn't say a word. She was lost in thought, staring into the darkness.

"I asked you what you think, Mom."

"I think you're right…it's totally out of character."

She lifted her head and the moonlight lit her face. Rhi noticed she had tears in her eyes.

"I've already emailed the ad to *The Examiner*, but I can call and ask then to pull it," Rhi said.

"Things unfold the way they're meant to," Crystal said simply.

Both Rhi and Tye waited for her to say something else. But she was silent.

Chapter 22

Rhi paused outside the theater. Her mother's calls were always inconvenient, but she couldn't ignore all of them.

Brigid seemed to sense that her daughter was distracted. "I'll make it quick. I just wanted to tell you that we missed you at Ostara."

"It was a lovely night here," Rhi said evasively. She was busy looking at the new path that had just been laid. Jake had done a great job.

"Did you celebrate?" Brigid sounded surprised.

Rhi walked along the path, crouching to touch the corner where she'd signed her name and the date before the cement set. "I did. I celebrated with friends."

"And how does one celebrate up in the boondocks? With a keg?"

"With love and respect, mother. I was with my friends Crystal and Tye."

Brigid went silent.

"Are you still there, Mom?"

"You need to be careful when choosing friends, dear."

"I know. I learned that lesson with Victoria. Fortunately I'm meeting some wonderful people here. It has been incredibly healing."

"I thought you weren't going to tell anyone that you're a witch."

"I haven't. Crystal and Tye knew. But I don't want anyone else knowing. I'm too happy here." Rhi stared up at the theater. She'd never tire of looking at it, especially now it was painted a brilliant white. She noticed a car pull up. "I've got to go, Mom. Toby has just arrived."

"Toby Bryant? What's he doing there?"

"He's giving me a quote on the tech box."

"Give him my love." And with that Brigid hung up.

Toby headed up the path and scooped Rhi into a hug. "Gorgeous girl."

"It's so good to see you, Toby." Rhi slipped her phone into her pocket. "That was my mother. Sends her love."

Toby pulled a face. "Oh dear, not sure I want it. It comes with so many strings."

Toby was handsome, with coffee-colored skin and long-lashed eyes. He was of medium height and extra large build. Some would call him fat; Rhi called him cuddly. In fact, a lot of women called him cuddly—he'd never been without a string of panting girlfriends skipping faithfully behind. His latest girlfriend, Darna, had been around longer than most. She was a doll, so Toby was smitten, and a witch, so Toby's rather overbearing mother also approved. Toby's mother was America's leading voodoo practitioner, and often appeared on *Afternoon Dee-light* with Rhi's parents. Their families had long been friends.

Toby spent a couple of hours surveying the theater and the lights. "Finn mentioned your money problems." Toby gave her a squeeze. "You know your mom, all Bs and Ws."

"She's either a witch or a bitch."

"She's either Brigid or Wigid."

They cracked up at the joke they'd shared since they were kids.

"Come here, darling." Toby slung a chubby arm around Rhi's slim shoulders. "You'll be pleased to know this won't cost an arm and a leg."

Rhi breathed a sigh of relief. "Thank Goddess."

"Just a few fingers," he said. "Perhaps an elbow."

"That I can handle."

"The lights are all great but you'll need a new phase board and digital control board. They go here," he said, showing her around the lighting box. "Also, the globes all work. It really is in great condition." He patted one of the spots. "I know they look dated, but they're in top condition. I'm not surprised. Patterns like these last forever."

"That's such great news."

Toby held Rhi at arm's length and scanned her face. It was his way of asking how she really was. He rarely needed to ask the question out loud.

"You're happy, Rhi."

"I am Toby, I really am," Rhi agreed. "All the pieces are coming together. Hamlet, the theater..."

"Love?" Toby had once held a flame for Rhi but that had long burnt down to the warm embers of friendship.

"No time for love. Unless you count this place," she said, gesturing to the theater.

"I have to head back to the city tonight, but I'll call you next week with a price."

"Thanks, Toby."

"I'm doing a show from mid-June in LA so I'll have this done well before then." Toby gave Rhi a long, affectionate hug. "You take care, Rhiannon. Blessed Be, dear one, Blessed Be."

After Toby left, Rhi decided to tackle the second dressing room. The only place that hadn't been cleared during the various community help days. Even big, burley Stan Knight had told her, in no uncertain terms, that he would rather see women play in the major leagues than enter that room himself. But Rhi wasn't frightened—the theater wasn't haunted. Obviously if it were, she—of all people—would know. People were just used to old town tales, that's all.

Rhi flung open the door and clapped her hands together. "Right, prepare for battle."

"Rhiannon!"

"Fabulous," Rhi muttered to herself. "My lord and landlord has arrived."

"There you are," he said as he walked backstage.

Rhi hadn't seen him since he'd dropped her home on Saint Patrick's Day, and that had been quite uncomfortable. "What are you doing here?"

"Just popped by for a chat."

They stared for a moment, drinking each other in. Despite herself, she was pleased to see him.

"Did I interrupt something?" he asked.

"I was going to sort through the second dressing room."

"Can I help?"

Rhi was taken aback. He'd visited, but never offered to help before. "Of course you can."

"After all, it's my dressing room."

Rhi swiveled on her heel and walked back into the dressing room. "If you'll excuse me, I have work to do."

"Did I say something wrong?"

Rhi, eyes flashing and hands on hips, snapped around. "Listen, this is my theater now. My lease. My money renovating it. My hands getting blisters. *My theater*. Get used to it."

"But when I play *Hamlet*, I'll have this dressing room. Wow, you're really uptight."

Rhi had been surrounded by actors long enough to understand their insecurities, as frustrating as they were.

"Yes, you can have this dressing room. Jesus, you'd swear you were Gielgud."

"Then I'll help you get it in order."

He didn't help. Instead he lounged in a chair, his long, muscular legs stretched out before him, and watched her as she cleaned and cleared the room. At first, it made her uncomfortable, his dark, dreamy eyes watching her every move. But before long she forgot about his looks, his languid posture and suggestive grin, and found herself enjoying the conversation.

"Theater comes from the Greeks and the word means *seeing place*. Stella Adler said it's the place people come to see the truth about life...or something like that." He placed his hands behind his head. "So where did you train?"

"Columbia."

"Did you always want to perform?"

"Yes. How about you?"

"My mother once said I was born performing. I had a set of lungs that understood voice projection right at birth. She was horrified."

Rhi laughed. "And you come from a theatrical family."

"No, my parents thought the theater was for vagabonds and thieves."

Rhi didn't understand how this could be, seeing his father died in this very theater and his mother still acted. But she didn't have time to ask; he was off again.

"That's what actors were, you know, during Elizabethan times. We revere Shakespeare today, but his players were considered to be nothing more than rogues. I think actors are still seen like that by their audience, but it's this rejection that has strengthened our bonds, don't you think? It's a tight-knit community."

"There might be some truth in that. I've never thought about it. Though I'm not sure audiences feel that way about actors any more."

"Of course they do. They always will. The general public will always judge the performer. It's the very nature of the audience."

"I think they only judge us when we don't move them."

"Iris Murdoch once said that—and I paraphrase here—that actors regard the audience as their enemy, mainly because the audience sits there night after night in judgment."

"I do often think of the audience as a single entity, a beast to be tamed, but never my enemy."

"One single audience member. I think I was in that play." He roared with laughter. "How many nights have you emoted your guts out, despite the empty seats?"

Rhi had to laugh. She knew exactly what he was talking about. "I'm hoping that will never happen here."

She knew she was on a rollercoaster with this man. One minute she felt like she could curl up in his arms, both sexy and safe. But then he'd drag her up onto her toes with his outrageous wit, his challenging ways. She looked at him now, his eyes piercing into her. He talked like it was a battle to the death sometimes.

Before she knew it, the dressing room was finished. All it needed was a coat of paint, which she would do later. She walked over to the door and was just about to remove the silver star when he jumped up.

"Don't touch that."

"Why not?"

He looked flustered and ran his hand through his hair. "Silly old superstition...let it stay."

He'd lost his composure and was clearly upset. She stepped toward him, to comfort him, but then stalled. She realized she couldn't smell him. That heady scent that made her dizzy when she got close was missing.

Rhi felt a rush of blood to her head, and all of a sudden he seemed hazy. She reached out for him but missed and her hand rested on the doorframe. Was something wrong with her eyes? What was he wearing? Was he wearing the same clothes all the time here?

"Rhiannon," he snapped as he stepped away from her. "Have you eaten today?"

Rhi shook her head and looked at him. The room returned to normal. He returned to normal.

"No, I haven't." She smiled at him. "What were we saying?"

"You need to eat something."

"You're right." Rhi wandered out the door and piled some of the rubbish against the wall. She'd carry it out to the dumpster later. Right now she needed air. "I'm going to call it a day."

Chapter 23

It was finished. The final coat of exterior paint was drying. Inside was done and the curtains had been hung. Everything shone and glistened and beckoned people to enjoy the space. Rhi stood back, her arm slung around Annie's shoulder, her new friends scattered around her, and surveyed the theater. It finally suited its name. It really was majestic.

Jake sniffed. "I think I'm going to cry."

Annie gave him a playful punch. "You always know how to ruin a moment."

"I don't ruin it—I shine a humorous light on it." He clapped his hands together. "This calls for a celebration."

"All in agreement say aye," Tye sang out.

There was a chorus of "Aye", followed by laughter.

"I need to get home and put dinner on for the kids." Vaniqua gave Rhi a kiss and headed for her car.

Hank and his drama students followed suit. "They're too young to attend theater parties," he explained.

Ren pulled a face as they walked off. "All work and no play. I so can't wait until I'm twenty-one."

"I'm sure the next five years will fly by, Ren," Hank said.

"Before you go, Hank, can you take a photo? To mark the moment?" Tye called out.

Tye handed him her phone and then stood on the theater steps with Rhi, Annie, Jake and Sam. Big smiles, easy hugs, a perfect moment captured in time.

She leaped back down and took her phone back as Hank headed off.

"Don't you dare put that on Facebook until we've all approved it," said Annie.

"You can put it on mine," Sam said.

"You don't have a Facebook account," Annie said.

"Oh that's right, because I don't need the whole world to know what I'm doing every minute of my day." Sam turned to the others. "What now?"

"Party time," Tye said.

"We're all covered in paint." Rhi held her paint-spattered arms out straight, to emphasize the point.

"Come over to mine," Annie suggested. "Let's have a clambake."

Jake wrapped his arm around her. "I love your style."

"I'll lock up and meet you there," Rhi said.

As the group headed to Annie's, Rhi went back into the Majestic. She needed this moment, to absorb the enormity of it. She'd done it. She'd actually done it. She lifted her face to the sky and allowed the tears to roll.

"Christ, you cry a lot. I'm afraid I can't offer you another hankie. You never gave the last one back."

Rhi turned to look at Tad standing in the doorway. She hadn't seen him since the day she'd left the theatre early. She'd put that down to exhaustion and hunger, and was pleased to see him now. "Not to worry. These are tears of joy. And relief."

"Ah, your tears fall into categories." He scanned the room. "You deserve a howl. Magnificent job. What now?"

"I'm heading over to Annie's for a clambake."

"The Elvis film turned me off those things forever."

"What on earth are you talking about?"

"*Clambake*. Old Elvis film. He ponced around singing and dancing at a clambake, looking like he was having a marvelous time when really he ought to have been ashamed of himself. Awful film."

"Forget about Elvis, you should come along."

"Yes, I should...but can I? That is the question."

"Listen...um..." She took a deep breath. What the hell! Crystal and Tye thought it was a good idea. And with the theatre complete, she was feeling invincible right now. "Do you want to go out with me sometime?"

"Out...with you?"

"Yes, that's what I said."

"On a date?"

"Yes."

"I'm flattered, but no. I can't."

Rhi felt the heat spring into her cheeks. "Okay. Anyway, I have to go." She turned, picked up a box of old theater papers that she intended to sort through at home, and started up the stairs. Then she felt him, felt his heat, standing so close behind her that they almost touched. Goose bumps prickled all over her skin. Her breathing became shallow.

"There's a woman. We're in limbo right now...or I am," he whispered. "But I love her."

"I didn't realise."

"Otherwise I would because you're wonderful."

"I understand," she murmured without turning.

"What we have, Rhiannon...has surprised me. I do value it."

"Me too."

She closed her eyes and placed her hand on a nearby seat to steady her. Then, drawing on more strength that she ever knew she had, she headed for the door.

"I might see you at the clambake then," she called cheerily. "Make sure you lock up."

*

The others had already set up for the evening on the beach in front of Annie's place. Annie had grabbed them all towels, and threw one Rhi's way when she arrived.

"I've also called a few more friends. Let's make a night of it."

"Sounds good," Rhi said, trying desperately to throw off the sting of humiliation.

"We've made a pit," said Sam.

"Use the rocks I've got at the side of the house from the last fire pit," Annie said.

Beck and Sal arrived with clams and lobsters. Annie's neighbors, David and Mark, brought lemons and enough dessert to feed a football team, which was something they admitted they'd like to do. Vaniqua and her husband Morgan turned up with a case of wine.

"I thought you couldn't party," Rhi said.

"I said I had to feed my kids. Done that, and called the babysitter."

Last to arrive was Tad, with a big bag of corn. "I'm the corny one. I also brought some instruments."

He'd obviously gone home to change as he was now wearing shorts and a casual shirt that clung lightly to his chest. He gave Rhi a friendly wave but there was no indication of their earlier exchange—knowing him, he couldn't remember it. Anyway, she refused to hide in shame. They'd just have to pretend it didn't happen.

Everyone chipped in and began organizing the meal. Tye covered the table in brown paper, so that after their meal they could roll up the mess and throw it away, and placed wet wipes at each end. The others gathered seaweed and prepared the fire pit. And then as the sun set, they all swam in the ocean, Rhi washing the final remnants of theater paint from her skin.

She stood waist deep in the water. The water was cold but she barely felt it as she watched the horizon fade. She drew strength from the ocean. So a guy had rejected her offer to go on a date? Boo hoo. That wasn't a reflection on her. As he'd said, he was involved with someone. Although it was strange that Tye and Crystal hadn't mentioned that. Perhaps he was reeling over some woman who'd hurt him or something. Rhi respected his honesty. It didn't mean they couldn't be friends. Or at least friendly.

"Dinner!" yelled Jake from the beach.

Rhi turned to watch all her friends heading for the fire pit and Annie's back terrace. She noticed Tye and Vaniqua laughing over something. She saw Sal stumble and Sam catch her arm. She smiled up at him, her affection obvious. Annie was organizing everyone, oblivious to it all. And then there was Tad. He was a tough nut to crack. One minute he was the life of the party, mainly their party of two, the next he was more subdued. Yes she was attracted to him, but she also just liked his company. She'd crossed the line by asking him out so now it was up to her to make things comfortable between them.

Rhi made her way up the beach and wrapped a towel around herself. Then, leaving her wet hair dripping down her back, she filled a plate with food and took a seat at the end of the table, next to Tad. Better to face the humiliation head on, and move on.

"I'll sit here with you, in the corn-er," she said to him, tucking into a cob. "That was a joke."

"It was pretty corn-y." Tad ate a clam and then wiped his mouth with a napkin.

"I guess the whole Elvis thing didn't scare you off?"

"Elvis?"

"*Clambake*, the movie."

"Oh right. I remember seeing that on TV as a kid. My father bitched and moaned all the way through it. Hated the film." He smiled. "How does it feel to be celebrating the end of renovations? You've done a mighty job."

"Much of that's due to the entertaining company I've had while I've been working on it." She smiled at him, wanting him to know that what happened earlier didn't matter.

"Yes, I've heard everyone got involved."

Rhi swallowed both her corn and her pride. "Listen, about today, I appreciate the way you handled things. Let's just move on, okay."

He looked at her for a moment too long and then stood up. "Good idea. I might play some music." He walked into the house.

"Good idea. Do you take requests? How about 'All By Myself?'" Rhi tried to hide her embarrassment.

"You talking to yourself?" Annie came and sat down beside her in Tad's place. She was drinking wine like it was water.

"Have you eaten?" Rhi asked.

"I nibbled. Not that hungry."

"You can't drink on an empty stomach." Rhi shoved a baked potato at her.

"Good, you're feeding her," said Tye, joining them.

"Hey, have you noticed Sam and Sal getting all cozy?" Annie said through a mouthful.

"Does that bother you?" Rhi asked.

"Christ, no, why would it?" But Annie's eyes told a different story.

Rhi glanced at Tye. She'd seen it too.

"I think it's time that one of you three finally breaks ranks."

Annie stared across her yard for a moment and then tried to lighten the mood, even though both Rhi and Tye could see her heart wasn't in it. "Things are okay the way they are."

"You know that's not true," Tye said. "Your drinking is out of control because of it."

Rhi raised her eyebrows, amazed that Tye would confront the issue head on like that. Rhi had tried it once with Victoria and she'd gone ballistic.

"I've had a few glasses of wine," Annie said. "So what!"

"The minute Sam and Jake are around, you get drunk, because you can't handle the pressure any more."

"Thanks, Dr Phil." Annie turned to Rhi. "What do you think?"

Rhi was surprised that her opinion counted. "I have noticed that you drink more when they're around."

"Really?"

"Yeah, really." Rhi was worried about where this conversation was heading.

"What can I say, they drive me to drink."

Rhi watched as Jake and Tad started jamming on guitars. So he could play guitar too? The man was supremely talented. Then she noticed Annie's face fall, and she followed her gaze toward the beach, where Sam and Sal were walking away from the house.

"You're both right," Annie said. "Enough is enough. I love them both...and even if I did have feelings for one more than the other, which I don't, how could I choose? Impossible. We all need to move on. And I need to lay off the wine."

And with that, she put her glass down, turned and walked back into the house, leaving Rhi staring after her in amazement.

Chapter 24

Rhi stretched out on a sunlounger in her garden and let the late afternoon sun warm her face. She needed to clear her head. Erase the humiliation she felt every time she thought of Tad. It was the weirdest relationship she'd ever had. Not that she thought of it as a *relationship*. But they knew each other pretty well now, and yet she still couldn't work him out. He ran hot and cold.

She looked around her garden. She'd had it cleared. Not completely—she had no desire to have one of those manicured gardens. She wanted it to be wild, and overgrown, but deliberately so. She'd planted more flowers and placed a small cast-iron table and two chairs under the oak, and the lounger nearby. The garden hadn't changed a great deal but the energy had been shaken up. Spring had brought with it an explosion of warmth and color and Rhi was spending more and more time outdoors. She'd never had a garden before. She'd grown herbs and had a natural affinity to nature, but being a New Yorker hadn't allowed for much gardening. Her parent's brownstone had a small backyard where her mother grew herbs. In Hamlet, her garden began at her back terrace and continued to the edge of the woods, getting lost in the forest that eventually spilled out onto the beach.

The beach. That's where she needed to go to clear her head of Tad Daniels.

Rhi jumped up and headed for the path in the trees. She made her way into the now familiar woods, her pace picking up until she was running. She dodged tree branches and leaves. She soaked in each tree root, each rock and each deviation in the path as she passed. It was becoming as familiar to her as the lines in the palm of her hand. She ran past the half-hidden rock entrance to the secret grove. She ran up over a mound where the trees stopped and the sand began. She breathed deeply as she jogged down the other side of the sand dune and saw the sea before her, stretching into oblivion. She considered it part of her back garden; a garden that ended somewhere in France.

Hamlet's pristine bay and beaches were part of the town's attraction, yet it was rare to see anyone else on this small stretch of sand. She glanced around. Apart from a lone figure in the distance, the beach was all hers. She slid out of her jeans and drew her T-shirt over her head. Clad only in her underwear, she jogged down to the water's edge and waded into the icy water. She forced herself to continue up to her waist and then dived in. The days were warmer now but the water was still cold and it stole her breath as it enveloped her body.

She emerged from a wave with an elated gasp and a laugh. She was determined to never lose this freedom to dive into the sea whenever the urge hit. In New York, things like this had to be preplanned. Here in Hamlet she had license to swim on the spur of the moment. She wanted to appreciate and take advantage of that whenever possible. It made her feel alive.

She felt a sensation that had been missing for a long time spread from her limbs into her chest. She ducked under another wave, and as she reemerged she realized it was happiness.

She was happy. Not constantly. Happiness seemed to be the most fleeting of human emotions. But it was there. It came and went regularly now. It caught her by surprise, not for when it appeared, but rather for how long she'd be feeling it before realizing. It was, to her utter surprise, becoming a habit.

"You must have seal blood running through your veins."

"It's refreshing," she lied. It had been refreshing but was starting to shift toward freezing. "I thought the beach was empty."

"It is...apart from us. That's my house up there," Tad said pointing to a large wood and glass structure.

"I know. I've been there...to Tye's flat underneath."

"And you didn't drop by to say hello?"

"N—next time." Her teeth began to chatter.

"Blue suits you."

"Excuse me?"

"Your skin is turning blue." Tad chuckled. "Do you want to come out or are you working on hyperthermia?"

Rhi felt she didn't need to work on hyperthermia as it had already set in. "I'm too embarrassed to get out. I'm in my underwear."

"Don't you have a swimsuit?"

"This was a spur-of-the-moment swim."

"I'll turn around," Tad called. "I promise not to peek."

He turned his back on Rhi and wandered up to where her clothes were. Rhi made a mad dash for her T-shirt and slid it on over her head. Then, with some difficulty, she scrambled into her jeans.

"Okay, I'm decent now," she said.

Tad turned, and in one slow, sweeping appraisal warmed her shivering body up. "You may be dressed, but you're hardly decent."

Rhi glanced down at herself and realized her T-shirt was clinging suggestively to her wet body. Her hair hung in damp tendrils around her face and neck, spilling onto her shoulders, leaving a trail of transparent fabric. She looked back at Tad, whose eyes were burning hungrily.

"I need to get warm," she whispered.

"Here, let me help you." Tad reached out and gathered her into his arms and then, before she could protest, his mouth crushed down on hers. Her arms slid around his neck and she pressed her body into his while they devoured each other with their lips, their eyes and their hands. She could smell him. Taste him. Feel him. Each sensation swamped her body with complete desire.

Rhi moaned and pulled away. Her tongued flickered over her lips where he lingered. .

"I've wanted to do that from the first moment I laid eyes on you," Tad admitted.

"Why'd you wait so long?" Rhi arched her back to look up at him.

"You confuse me."

He bent down and pressed his forehead against hers. Their breath mingled, and came out misty as it hit the cool evening air. Their gazes were locked. His lips hovered just above hers, lightly pressing and then moving across to her cheek. They stood like this, exploring, dancing, feeling each other, until Tad's hand grabbed the back of her head and his lips landed on hers again.

Rhi felt she could go on kissing him forever.

Finally Tad pulled back. His eyes searched hers. "I was wondering...perhaps we could go out some time?"

Rhi slithered out of his embrace. "I thought you couldn't."

"Couldn't what?"

"Go out with me."

"I don't know what gave you that idea. I'd love to go out with you. How about tomorrow night?"

Rhi felt the anger creep up like a rising thermometer until it hit her throat. "What the hell are you playing at?"

Tad looked confused. "I'm not playing at anything. All I'm suggesting is dinner, perhaps a drink. I certainly wouldn't mind a rerun of that kiss...it's all fairly straightforward."

"Perhaps in your weird little world, but from where I'm standing, you are the least straightforward person I've ever met."

"You should talk. Every time we speak I end up feeling as though I've just killed your grandmother or run over your dog."

"And are you stalking me?"

"You *are* nuts!"

"At least I don't turn up just when you least expect it, like some weirdo."

"I've obviously offended you in some way. I hope you'll forgive me. I'd hate to find my pet rabbit boiling on my stove."

Tad turned and stormed up the beach. Rhi watched his retreating back with an overwhelming urge to run after him. Instead, she turned and sprinted over the sand dune and into the woods. He wasn't worth catching pneumonia for.

She fled through the trees and back up the path to her house. She'd just reached her porch when she heard someone laugh.

Rhi swung around. "Are you laughing at me?"

Pip flicked her hair back. "You're so funny."

And you're a dryad pain in the ass, thought Rhi.

"I cleaned up the garden, Pip. So how about you leave me alone now?"

Pip gave the garden a sweeping stare. "Yes, it's much better."

"A thank you would be nice."

Pip looked genuinely confused. "Why?"

Rhi realized her teeth were chattering. "I need a shower."

"The sexy man didn't warm you up for long?"

"None of your business."

"I was just going to give you some advice, but now why bother?"

Great! A dryad with attitude. Rhi hated herself for it, but she was suddenly very curious. "What advice?"

Pip gave her a wicked smile as she stepped back into the tree. "Look in the box!"

Chapter 25

Life as she knew it was officially over. Rhi sat on her front step as tears streamed freely down her face. She'd loved the morning sun since arriving in Hamlet. Each and every day it symbolized a new start.

Which was exactly what she'd need now. All her hard work, her hopes and her dreams had been destroyed. There, on the front page of the local paper was a photo of her and her mother, and the accompanying article:

MAJESTIC'S ARTISTIC DIRECTOR IS DAUGHTER OF FAMOUS WITCH.

Who knew we had a famous witch living in town?

Certainly no one at The Examiner *suspected a thing when Rhiannon Wall came in to the office and introduced herself as the Majestic's new artistic director. Attractive, friendly and obviously passionate about her craft—theater craft, that is—Rhiannon paid for a series of upcoming ads for drama classes, theater rentals and auditions.*

So imagine our surprise when the infamous Brigid Dee called. Ms Dee is well known for her books, DVDs and television shows on witchcraft. She was more than happy to talk about her daughter's move to Hamlet and her latest project.

As Ms Dee said, "I'm supporting her any way I can, which is why I'm doing this interview. I'm helping drum up some publicity, to bring the support Rhi needs to make her theater project a success."

Rhi couldn't believe what she was reading. She scanned the rest of the story. Brigid was quoted liberally throughout.

"Oh no, Rhi is very proud of being a witch."

"She's using her father's surname now, but she'll always be a Dee."

"Rhi knows that if it doesn't work out for her there, she can always come back home. In fact, she often says how she'd like to appear on the show again."

"You bitch!" Rhi howled, then looked around, hoping no one was watching.

She saw Marjorie Stockburn walking her dog in the distance. The last thing she needed now was a conversation with Marjorie, who didn't know the meaning of brevity. Instead, Marjorie noticed her on the steps and greeted her with a look that would freeze fire, then turned on her heel and hurried off in the opposite direction, dragging poor Rufus behind on his leash. Marjorie was always friendly. She'd obviously seen the paper.

A sob caught in Rhi's throat and she made for the safety of her house. How could her mother betray her like this? It was like the spider that eats its young. She pulled the curtains tightly closed and wondered how much tinned food she had stored away. Plan A was to bunker down and never set foot outside again. She would shrivel up and die alone, only to be found in eight years when the gas company dropped by to check on overdue bills.

There was a knock on the door. It was probably the townsfolk with pitchforks and burning crosses. Rhi swung the door open, ready to take them on. It was worse than burning crosses. It was Tad, looking thunderous.

"What's the meaning of this?" He waved the newspaper at her.

Rhi's heart dropped but she managed to fake a smile anyway. "Good morning to you too."

"You didn't think of mentioning this to me?"

Her fake smile faded. "I didn't think you'd be interested."

"Are you freaking serious?"

Rhi was appalled at the tone he was using with her. Who did he think he was? "Stop yelling at me."

"I'll stop yelling when you explain this." His face was crimson with rage.

"I don't need to explain something like this to you. It's my business."

"Your business? It's my goddamn theater."

Rhi's chin wobbled, which seemed to disarm him slightly, but she refused to completely lose it in front of him. "I don't know what any of this has to do with you."

"Could you be any more insensitive? Of *all* plays?"

Tad thrust the paper at her and Rhi realized it was folded open at the audition notice for *Hamlet*. Rhi was completely taken aback. He was talking about the audition notice, not about her being a witch.

"Did you read the article about me?"

Tad dismissed that with a wave of his hand. "I don't give a shit about that, except to say that I know some witches and they'd never pull a stunt like this."

She needed to shift gears. "Tad, I'm doing *Hamlet* because of you. I thought you wanted closure."

"You don't know me. How dare you assume I need closure?"

Rhi shook her head. Was this a dream? It was surreal. "What about the audition? *Hamlet* was your idea."

"Why would I revisit the play that killed my father? I didn't even fucking do it in high school. I was suspended for skipping a semester." Tad tossed the paper at her feet. "I'm going to call my lawyer and dissolve your lease."

Tad took off in a cloud of dust and anger, while Rhi bolted herself inside her house and shook. She took three deep breaths but still felt strange. Off kilter. Why on earth was he acting that way? And if he dissolved the lease, what the hell was she going to do?

The doorbell rang again. What now? She had half a mind to ignore it but felt it might be Tad again, and she'd do anything to sort this out. Rhi opened the door an inch and peeked through.

It wasn't Tad. It was Tye and Crystal.

"The rest of your coven has arrived," Tye joked as she pushed open the door and pulled Rhi into her embrace.

"I'm going to be chased out of town," Rhi said when she finally let go.

Crystal was next, holding Rhi while she cried. "No, you won't. People around here are very open-minded."

"I feel so betrayed. I can't believe my mother would do this."

Crystal's face was set in stone. "It's a horrible thing to do, Rhi, but that's why you need to stand tall and not let this beat you. She thinks you'll go back to New York now."

"Then she's right. I have no choice."

"You've always got a choice."

The phone rang. "Don't get it," said Rhi. "It might be her."

The machine picked up and the three women listened to Rhi's greeting and the beep, followed by: "Rhi, it's Margaret Forester speaking."

Rhi went pale. Margaret was the head of the theater appreciation society in town and instrumental in organizing students for Rhi's drama class.

"I just read this morning's paper, Rhi, and want to put my name down to help in any way I can with your production of *Hamlet*. I think it's a wonderful first choice, and the Hamlet Theater Appreciation Society will support you in whatever way possible."

Rhi glanced at Crystal.

"That's it...Oh, one other thing..." Margaret continued, "I was wondering if you know of a potion that will get rid of the bugs on my roses. Thanks, dear."

Margaret hung up but before anyone could speak, there was a knock on the door. Crystal marched over and opened it while Rhi tentatively peered down the hall.

"Morning, Crystal. Is Rhi—oh, there you are." Molly Morgan, who lived two doors down and sang in the church choir, waved at Rhi. "I just want to let you know that it doesn't matter what path we're on, Rhi, as long as we're all heading in the same direction."

"Thank you, Molly."

Molly turned to leave, but then paused and gave Rhi a look that spoke volumes. "Your mother clearly wasn't loved as a child, for she doesn't know how to parent properly. I will pray for her."

"I'd appreciate that."

"Don't close the door!" called a voice. "More people coming through."

Annie appeared in the front garden with Jake and Sam. She marched up to the steps and into the house. She looked furious and Rhi's heart plummeted a thousand feet. In the overall scheme of things, Margaret's and Molly's opinions didn't matter. It was her friends she didn't want to lose. And Annie's mouth was set in a hard line that indicated anger.

"How dare your mother do that to you! No wonder you had to leave New York."

Rhi's shoulders visibly sagged with relief.

Annie looked her square in the eye. "You could've told me." She gestured toward Tye and Crystal. "I know about those two so I don't know what the big deal is."

Sam gave a laugh. "I'm just pissed off we had to do all that work at the theater. Wasn't there a spell…?"

"I want to know if you wiggle your nose like Samantha in *Bewitched*." Jake tried it.

"No, I use a wand like in Harry Potter." Rhi was elated. Her friends didn't care.

"And I knew I vaguely recognized you. It was that TV show," Annie said. "I think I even had a few of your T-shirts when I was younger."

Rhi nodded. "I was trying to distance myself from all that."

Annie smiled at her friend. "It's who you are, honey. That doesn't mean you don't have the right to move here and live differently. But don't hide who you are."

Rhi started to cry again. Her secret was out, but it was okay. The article didn't bother them at all. If anything, they were supportive and sympathetic.

Tye headed into the kitchen. "Anyone for coffee?"

"Yes, please," Annie said. "I'll help you."

"We've got to get to work." Sam called out to Annie: "Hey, curly, are you right to get back into town if we take off?"

"I'll get a lift with Tye," she replied from the kitchen.

Sam gave Rhi a hug. "We just wanted to check you were okay."

"My turn." Jake squeezed her tight. "And perhaps you can cast a spell to make me and Sam really rich?"

"I'll sacrifice a chicken tonight," Rhi said with a straight face.

"You're a good pal," Jake said, equally serious.

Rhi waved them off and then sat down with Crystal on the sofa.

"Are you feeling better?" Crystal asked.

"A little. I had a visit from Tad this morning too."

"He wouldn't have a problem with that article. He grew up around me."

"He was apoplectic about the audition notice in the paper. He can't believe I'm auditioning for *Hamlet*."

This surprised Crystal. "But you said it was his idea."

"It was, Crystal..." Rhi bit her lip. "Do you think he has just used me to renovate the place and now intends to take over the theatre himself?"

"Definitely not."

She knew how close Crystal was to Tad, but this needed to be addressed. "Then I think there's something wrong with him. Mentally. He can't remember auditioning for me. He thinks I'm nuts."

Crystal's eyes bore into Rhi. "He definitely auditioned for you?"

"Definitely. I swear Crystal." Rhi's chin wobbled again. "He's going to get a lawyer to dissolve my lease."

Crystal patted Rhi's knee. "This is all going to work itself out, love. Just leave it to me."

"Do you think there's something wrong with him?"

Crystal shook her head. "No, I don't. I think there's another explanation for this."

Chapter 26

Crystal woke with a start. Goddamned dreams. Enough already. She reached for her clock and pressed the light on it. Two twenty. Damn it.

She clambered from her bed and slipped into her gown and slippers. There was no going back to sleep now. She made her way to the kitchen and parked herself in front of the fridge, searching through the shelves until she found the pie. Perched on a stool at the bench in the pitch dark, she held a fork over it. But before she could take a mouthful, before she could even place one piece of blueberry pie to her lips, she burst into tears.

It couldn't be.

It was. She knew it. She'd hoped beyond hope that Tad had visited the theater while Rhi was there. She'd called him and asked him as much.

"Rhi told me about your visit today. Tad, I'll only ask once...have you been inside the theater?"

"Crystal, have you?"

"Not since..."

"That makes two of us." Tad's voice shook. "I don't know what she's playing at, but I'm calling my lawyer tomorrow."

"Tad, darling...if that's what needs to be done, then you know I'll support you. But I'm asking, don't make that call for a week. Let me try to sort this out."

"My lawyer will sort this out."

Crystal decided to play to his compassionate side. "Just say Rhi is struggling with some issues. What do you think will happen if she hears from your lawyers without having some support in place?"

"He sighed. "She does need help. I might've exacerbated things recently. I really did try to stay away from her but down on the beach one day...you don't need the details, but Crystal, her reaction to me asking her out made my blood run cold. She has some serious issues."

"Let me deal with this first, before you evict her."

"Okay, Crystal."

Crystal knew she needed to sort this out now. For Rhi's sake. Her head hung as she cried tears of heartbreak, as fresh as the ones all those years ago. Time hadn't erased the pain. Nothing would. She knew that now. Back then, at least she had hope. Hope that she'd move on, meet someone who filled her heart and soul more than—or at least as much as—he did.

It never happened.

Damn it.

She placed the fork back in the cutlery drawer and the pie back in the fridge, and returned to her room, where she dressed.

It was time to have it out with him.

She grabbed a wrap on the way out and pulled it tight around herself. The crisp night air hit her and woke her up. She decided to walk. It wasn't far and would give her time to gather some strength.

The houses were dark, the streets quiet. Normally, she loved this time of night, but right now it felt ominous. Crystal glanced up at the moon and gave a little nod. She arrived at the theater and walked around the back. An owl hooted as she approached the door. She simply knew she wouldn't need a key. Sixth sense. The door was slightly ajar, although she was sure Rhi would have locked it. She pushed it open and stepped inside, waiting for her eyes to adjust. Crystal had eyes like a cat, but still regretted not bringing a torch. Finally she was able to make out the shapes and shadows of the backstage area and she went inside. She knew instinctively where to go. The silver star twinkled in the dark and she pushed the dressing room door open. Thirty years disappeared in a flash.

He was waiting there, stretched out on the sofa, his arms folded behind his head.

"I was wondering when you'd catch on."

Chapter 27

Half-a-dozen fresh oysters, followed by venison steaks with stroganoff sauce and fries, and red velvet cake for dessert. Crystal kept going through the meal in her mind. She was going to cook the most amazing St Valentine's Day meal ever. She mentally ticked every item on her list, over and over. Chocolates and wine. Tick. Bubble bath and lingerie. Tick. She wanted the night to be perfect. Crystal didn't have any money to go out and celebrate St Valentine's Day, but they could still celebrate it here. In fact, at home in bed was their favorite place in the world. So he told her, over and over.

It was one of those bone-breakingly cold New York nights, when icicles hung from your face. But Crystal felt warm; she had all winter. She was madly in love. Kip Daniels was wild and charming and loved her too. They'd been inseparable for months. At first she'd been wary. Kip could have anyone, so when he'd started chatting her up at her local cafe she was naturally suspicious. Not that Crystal had self-esteem issues—she knew she was sexy. She had one of those pinup girl–type bodies, which men loved. All curves and boobs, topped with blonde waves and baby blue eyes. But she wasn't beautiful, like Brigid. She didn't have that type of bone structure or style. Crystal always felt that she looked like she'd tumbled out of bed (she did, which was part of her appeal). She always had mismatched socks, or a button that had popped open. Her hair was always tousled, no matter how much she'd styled it. And her lipstick was always slightly worn and smudged, as if she'd been kissed long and hard.

Lately, she had been. Kip acted like he could never get enough of her, which was convenient because she certainly couldn't get enough of him. But it was more than passion and attraction that kept drawing them together. It was the meeting of two very similar minds.

Crystal was smart and sassy and Kip loved matching that. Kip was used to women fawning over him. Crystal didn't fawn. Instead, she told exactly what she thought, and she adored their verbal sparring.

He wasn't even fazed when she admitted to being a witch.

"Knowing a witch may one day come in handy," he said.

Crystal lugged the groceries through the entrance and into the kitchen. She'd arranged with Brigid for them to have the apartment to themselves. Brigid had promised to go on a date.

"I'll get some poor sucker to spring for dinner for me," she said. "I'll give you two some space."

Crystal smiled at the thought of it. She knew she was at risk of looking ridiculous most of the time now, walking through life with a goofy grin on her face. But what the hell, she was in love.

She placed the shopping on the table. She was going to cook up a storm wearing her nicest lingerie and nothing else. Kip was conveniently running late, which gave her time to dress (or undress) and freshen up a bit. She walked toward her bedroom. Strange. She couldn't remember leaving the door closed this morning.

But as she placed her hand on the doorknob, she knew. It was one of those moments when time stood still, for what felt like a century. In that space she had time to think, reflect, ponder all the outcomes...but still she chose to turn that knob. She knew, but she opened the door anyway.

And there was Kip, in all his naked splendor...having sex with someone else in her bed.

Crystal's heart cracked. She heard it. She felt it. Her world would never be the same. A sob caught in her throat, and Kip jumped, realizing she was there. Crystal saw the woman. She calmly sat up and looked at Crystal, as if she'd intruded on them. Her own room!

"We didn't expect you home for ages," Brigid said.

Brigid moved out later that night. She took Kip with her. It was two years before Crystal saw either of them again.

*

"Have you been haunting this place all this time?" Crystal was in shock. He looked exactly as he had the day he died, right down to his costume of black pants and billowy white shirt.

"I've thought of it as passing time."

"You're a ghost. You're stuck here. It's a haunting."

"Well, I'm not up-to-date on the lingo, but being a witch, you'd know."

They stared at each other, both swinging between the delight and the sheer horror of seeing each other again. And in such confronting forms.

"You're my mother's age." Kip was obviously shocked. "You look good though."

"Don't fucking lie. I look fat. You look dead. Jesus, Kip, what the hell happened to us?"

"Well, a roof fell on me and I'm guess you ate too many cream buns."

Kip and Crystal looked at each other and cracked up. She covered her face, but when she looked up again, they laughed some more. They laughed and laughed until both were doubled over in hysterics. The laughter bounced off the walls and rang out through the theater.

"The neighbors will hear us," Kip said.

"No, you idiot, they'll just hear me and think I'm laughing by myself."

That made them laugh even harder.

Crystal held her sides. "Stop making me laugh, you bastard. I need to catch my breath."

"Me too. Been trying for twenty-eight years."

And off they went again.

Finally, Kip placed a hand on his forehead. "Oh, how I needed that. How I've needed you. Where have you been?"

"Outside. I had no idea you were in here."

He was drinking her in. "It's so good to see you, Cryssie."

"Christ, I've missed you, Kip. I have. I really have." Her voice caught. She was overwhelmed with emotion.

He understood, so changed tack. "Tell me about Tad."

Crystal's face lit up at the mention of his name. "He's a wonderful man. Good and kind and talented."

"Talented? Is he an actor?"

"A musician. He's in a band with...my daughter, Tye."

Kip drew back. "You have a daughter?"

"She's twenty-eight."

The hurt was clear in his eyes. "Of course you have a child. You continued to live."

"Kip—"

He shook his head, trying to absorb the shock. "Stupid really that I never even considered that." He gave her a forced smile. "Married?"

"No...never married."

"Cryssie...why?"

"Why do you think?"

He tilted his head slightly to the side, as though absorbing her from every angle. "I don't know what hurts more. You moving on without me...or being unable to."

"Things didn't go to plan, did they?"

"I did once say I wanted to live in the theatre."

Crystal chuckled. "That's right, you did."

Kip grew serious. "I saw you. When I died, I saw you come to me. I was floating above it all. I saw the light. All those clichés were in fact happening. And you...Crystal, you took my pulse and then let out a cry."

"I'll never forget."

"It was a moment of such magnitude. Your loss. Witnessing that—it was bigger than my actual death. It was the moment that I realized how much you loved me."

"How could you not know, you fool?"

"Because I was exactly that. A fool."

"But we were in a good place when you died, weren't we?"

"We were. It was happiness I didn't deserve." Kip placed his hands on his chest. "Oh Christ, my heart hurts. Not a beat in nearly three decades and the goddamn thing aches."

It broke the tension and they both chuckled.

"What's it like, Kip?"

"Well, I can't speak for every ghost, but my experience has been rather dull."

"But what's it like?"

Kip appeared to pick each word from the ether, carefully. "You know how an amputee still feels the leg that's missing? Death is like my whole body has been amputated. I feel things in my heart, and my groin, but before I feel alive, even for a moment, the feeling has gone. The feeling is stronger than a memory, because it's actually physical, but it's fleeting. I tend to drift around, content enough, but then something will happen to cause that strong response...and I try hard to hold onto it, to feel it, to experience it as I would in life...but away it drifts..." He looked dreadfully sad. "My feelings are as ghostly as my form."

"Is that why you're drawn to Rhi? She makes you feel something?"

"She sees me. That's all."

"Oh c'mon Kip, it's more than that."

"If you're suggesting that something's going on between us, it's not. Even in death I have remained loyal to you."

"I bet you were beating back the offers."

"Rhi asked me out."

Crystal put her head in her hands. "That poor girl. You have to tell her—or I will."

"Spoil sport."

"What are you playing at?"

"Nothing."

"Yeah right, and I'm a size six."

"Yes, you've put on some poundage old girl...still as sexy as hell though." He sat up and grinned at her.

"You know, I'd forgotten what a vicious tongue you had."

"C'mon, Crystal...you never forgot my tongue."

Crystal waved a hand as though she was about to slap him. Dead for years but he still managed to get her all flustered.

"And I'm only teasing you know. About your weight. If I were alive—"

"Stop changing the subject. We're talking about Rhi."

"Okay, okay, you caught me. But it's not like I'm doing anything wrong. Perhaps some harmless flirting. She's a pretty girl and I haven't had much to do with pretty girls for way too long."

"And what a coincidence that the pretty girl is Brigid's daughter."

"Brigid who?" Kip opened his eyes wide. "Oh, psycho bitch from hell Brigid?"

"That's the one."

"Yes, that is a coincidence."

"Did you set that up?"

"I wish I could take credit for it, but I'm stuck here. It was the Fates who drew her to me."

"Did you know who she was straight away?"

"I did. But don't ask me how. Some things I just know, but only when they're in front of me. I have no idea what's going on anywhere else."

"You were like that when you were alive too."

"Ouch."

"You have no idea why she's here?"

"I'm guessing it's to undo what was done!"

"No, you egotistical idiot. Jesus, even in death it's all about you."

"Then what?"

"She's here for Tad."

Kip's face dropped at the mention of his son. "That can't be. They're not compatible."

"They're a great match."

"She's a witch."

"So am I."

"But you're a good one."

"So is she."

Kip suddenly rose up toward the ceiling, his face thunderous. "Her mother is an evil fucking bitch."

Crystal matched his temper. "You look pretty goddam scary yourself right now."

"I won't allow it."

"Settle down or I'll call a priest." She waved her finger back at the chair.

Kip drifted down but continued standing.

"You realize you'll mess it up for Tad if you keep playing with her like this. Be a good father. Lay off. What's she to you anyway?"

"She's renovating my theater for me. She keeps me company. She appreciates my acting. Damn it Crystal, before you walked in here tonight she was the only person who talked to me in three decades."

"I know you've missed having people around."

"Not people. You. And Tad. The rest is meaningless. I missed you both. I still do and you're right in front on me. Rhi is a beautiful, interesting and very alive diversion from the aching emptiness. She has the same dreams I did—to do this place up."

Crystal shook her head. "Well, that dream is about to fail—Tad wants to throw her out of here. She put an audition notice for *Hamlet* in the paper. He was furious, which of course confused the hell out of her because she thought performing *Hamlet* was his idea."

Kip pulled a face. "Oops."

"I see you still do that cute face thing when you've royally fucked up." It reminded her of the day she found him in bed with Brigid, although she didn't say that.

"I didn't mean any harm. I enjoyed pretending to be alive. I was going to play Hamlet."

"That would be an interesting performance."

"What will we do?"

"I'll work something out."

Kip fell silent. He hung his head and stared at the floor. "It's so unfair," he said. "I worked like a dog to open this theater. I wanted to see the curtain fall, not the goddamned *roof*. It was meant to be my moment. *The* moment."

"We have many moments, Kip."

"Only those living say that. You'll arrive on my side and realize there were only one or two. That was mine."

"Yes it was, just not how you expected."

They sat in silence for a while.

"So does Tad have feelings for this girl?"

"Yes, he does. Confused ones, admittedly. Given half a chance, they could be good for each other."

"Damn it, Crystal. How will I entertain myself now?"

"All about you again." Crystal smiled at him. "I'll think of something, okay?"

"And will you come back? It's been wonderful seeing you again." He gave her a cheeky grin. "All of you."

Crystal rolled her eyes. "I'd slap you if you existed."

Chapter 28

Rhi woke from a kaleidoscope of strange dreams and images. Tad had two faces and both of them were speaking to her at once. She kept trying to listen to the real Tad, but didn't know which one he was. And the more she tried, the louder his voice got, until she couldn't bear the noise and she covered her ears.

Light was pouring through her window. From sunshine, not burning crosses. It was a beautiful day and she really needed to face the rest of the world, not just her friends. She needed to face Tad and beg him to reconsider evicting her. She couldn't imagine losing the Majestic or leaving Hamlet. Not now. She needed to find out why he'd auditioned for her. What he's been playing at.

She grabbed her iPad and propped some pillows behind her back. She checked her emails. There was one from Candace, the head of the women's ministry at the Hamlet Evangelical Church, with their Bible study times attached in a PDF. Ren, the senior drama student, had emailed expressing interest in stagemanaging for Hamlet. She also added a PS: "Know any good love spells?" There were two other expressions of interest from people she didn't know, wanting to audition. She quickly replied to them both, explaining that the play had been postphoned.

Then she banged out an email to *The Examiner*, apologizing for the inconvenience but asking for a retraction on the audition notice, and the promise that a new play would be announced shortly.

She couldn't do more than that. It might be enough to appease Tad. And Crystal had promised to speak to him. For now, it would be business as usual at the Majestic. She simply would now consider the possibility of losing it.

She went downstairs and turned the coffee machine on. The box she'd brought home from the theater sat on the counter. She might save that for another day. Who knew what was in there?

She ground some coffeebeans and looked back at the box. Something twigged.

What had Pip said? *Box?*

She picked it up, carried it into the lounge room and placed it on the floor. Then she opened it, moving back slightly as a cloud of dust and a small spider made their way out the top. She pulled out the first piece of paper. An old electricity bill, overdue.

"I ain't paying that," she said.

More papers, and then the treasures began. Playbills, old tickets, invitations to the opening night of *Hamlet*. She resisted the urge to slow down and take a moment with each piece—she'd do that later. She was looking for one thing and one thing only. Unfortunately she had no idea what that one thing was, but Rhi sensed the dryad did, and she was following her advice.

Photos! She found them. Interesting shots. Some classes, some of the Majestic as it was being renovated. Three funny rehearsal shots. Good Goddess, was that a young Stan Knight? Rhi let out a laugh—until she saw the next photo.

Another of Stan, thirty years younger and beside him—Tad. Just as he looked today.

How the hell could that be?

Her hand shaking, Rhi turned the photo. On the back was scrawled, *Hamlet rehearsals. Stan Knight and Kip Daniels.*

The blood rushed to Rhi's head. She could almost hear it roar. Her eyes lost focus for a moment.

Kip Daniels? Tad's father?

Rhi's hand flew to heart, afraid for a moment that it was going to explode out of her chest.

"Holy shit. A goddamn ghost auditioned for me."

*

Rhi arrived at the theater wearing dark sunglasses and a hat. She shouldn't have bothered. A number of locals greeted her as she passed, and all were warm and friendly apart from Pastor Rawson's wife. It had been a full twenty-four hours since she'd been outed as a witch, and very few people seemed to care. She was as relieved as she was grateful. In many ways, her mother had done her a favor. Hiding who she was wasn't ideal; perhaps she could be a witch who lived in town, rather than the town witch, for there was a difference.

Of course, if people knew I was going to speak to the theater ghost they might be more worried, she thought.

She marched straight into the auditorium and made her way to center stage. And from there, she projected.

"Kip Daniels, show yourself."

Nothing happened for about thirty seconds and then she sensed someone watching her from the wings. She turned, and there he was, devastatingly handsome, even with a rather sheepish look on his face. He opened his mouth to say something, but Rhi thrust a hand up.

"You don't get to speak." She waved the photo of Kip and Stan at him. "Did you think I'd never work it out?"

"It has taken you an inordinately long time. You're not a very good witch."

"I'm trying to ignore that part of my life."

"You're doing a good job."

"I'm not taking all the cred for this. Why didn't I pick up on the fact that you're dressed like a reject from the Shakespearean wardrobe department every time I see you?"

"You almost did once. I dropped my guard that day you went to remove the star from the dressing room door."

Rhi thought about that incident. She'd put it down to a lack of sleep. "And the rest of the time?"

"I dazzled you."

"Dazzled me?"

"It's a little spirit trick."

"I'm not susceptible to shit like that."

"As you said, you're ignoring all your witchy gifts. It's made you quite vulnerable to dazzling."

"You've been taking advantage of me."

Kip threw his arms up. "I never laid a finger on you."

"I've been exploited by a ghost," Rhi spat.

"You went along with it, because you think I'm handsome."

"I think your son is handsome. You're dead."

"You still think I'm handsome."

"Okay, admittedly, you're not bad looking for a corpse." Rhi threw herself into a seat.

"You're not going to cry again are you?"

"I have made such a fool of myself because of you."

"Don't be melodramatic," he said.

"Your son asked me out. But because you'd already turned me down, I yelled at him."

"Okay, that is a little embarrassing." Kip grew serious. "Do you like him?"

"He's a very nice person."

Kip screwed his face up. "Oh god, sounds boring. Please tell me my son isn't just a *very nice person.* When women say, 'Oh, he's a very nice person,' they mean he has the appeal of porridge."

"He's smart, he's sexy, he's talented...and he thinks I'm nuts."

"You are a little quirky." Kip gave her a lazy grin. "So 'fess up...is it Tad you like, or me?"

"Holy shit, you're arrogant. I'm talking about your son and you're flirting with me."

"I was alone for nearly thirty years. Can I help it if I get carried away?" Kip grinned.

"Whatever happened to 'I'm with someone but we're in limbo right now'?"

His grin vanished and he suddenly looked very sad. "Alas, still true, still in limbo, despite some interesting recent events."

Rhi had no idea what he meant by that but could see he was deeply mourning the loss of a woman and felt a surge of sympathy for him. All her anger towards him evaporated. "Were you with this woman when you died?"

"Yes."

"What was she like?"

Kip closed his eyes briefly, as if trying to capture her. "Alive."

The weight of the moment and his lost love were almost too much for Rhi to bear. How could she stay angry with him?

Kip's eyes snapped open and he moved on. "So, do you think Tad likes you?"

"He kissed me."

"Was that before or after you acted a little weird?"

"Weird has been a regular occurrence."

"Sounds like he's interested."

Rhi shook her head. "Not any more."

"You can somehow make amends. Explain the situation to him."

"Yeah, that'll work. Sorry, Tad, I had you confused with your father who haunts the theater."

"Yes, best to not say that."

"So what now?"

She paused, tempted to tell him that she might lose the theatre because of him. But she couldn't. As frustrating as Kip's actions were, she felt sorry for him. The poor dead guy had been punished enough. "I can only hope he forgives me. Or gets amnesia."

"I mean with us."

"Oh, I don't know, Kip...perhaps you stay out of my way and I roll you out for Halloween?"

Kip sighed. "All good things come to an end."

Rhi softened a bit. "I can't have you scaring people. The theater will fail. No one will come to my shows if they think it's haunted."

Kip rolled his eyes but didn't speak.

"I need time to think this through. I've only just worked out you're dead."

He seemed to understand that she wanted to change the subject. "So what's it like out there now?"

"The weather?"

"No, the world." He searched the wall above, as if looking for memories there. "Is *Dynasty* still popular?"

"I don't even know what that is."

"Did Nintendo take off?"

"Ah...yes."

"Who's the president?"

"Barack Obama."

"What sort of name is that?'

"He's African-American."

Kip smiled. "Things certainly have changed."

Rhi's phone buzzed as a text came through. She removed it from her back pocket and read, *Want to have lunch? Annie xo*

She quickly typed back, *Sure. Same bat time, same bat channel. xo*

Kip watched her warily. "What are you doing?"

"Texting."

"Excuse me if I don't automatically know what the hell that means."

Rhi looked up at him. She thrust the phone out. "It's a smart phone."

"What's so smart about it?"

"It does lots of things." She flicked through the phone settings. "I can call people. Or I can message them…type little letters that I send through to their phone. I check emails…I'll have to explain that whole thing another day. I have my calendar, notes I make throughout the day, reminders; I take photos, shoot film, stay in touch with friends via this…er, they're called apps…so this app, and this one…and this one here."

"Everyone has one of these?"

"Most people."

"So anyone can contact you at any time? Wherever you are?"

"That's right."

"What's so smart about that?"

Rhi considered his words. "You're right. We've become so attached to our phones, it's stupid, not smart." Rhi shoved her phone back in her pocket. "So here's the deal. You stay out of my way, and I won't bring in the holy water."

"I didn't take you for a Catholic."

"Fine, I won't bring in the local space clearer with her sage and bells."

"I'd prefer a priest." Kip pulled at one of his cuffs. "Don't suppose you could spare some time for a chat now and then?"

Rhi suddenly felt sorry for him. He'd been stuck for decades and was lonely. "Sure, I can manage that." She turned and started walking out of the auditorium.

"Any idea when?" Kip called after her. "I'll need to book it in to my smart phone calendar."

Chapter 29

Annie watched as the black Aston Martin pulled up to the curb. She grabbed her small watering can and hustled over to the window to pretend to water the bamboo.

"Lord, be still my beating heart," she whispered as a tall, dark-haired god slithered out of the car, slammed the door and made his way to Captain's Realty.

The man sauntered into the store and scanned the room, finally noticing Annie behind the potted plant. He stared at her for a moment, his eyes burning into her, and then he broke out in a lazy grin.

"Do they need watering every day?"

"What?"

"Your shoes."

Annie glanced down at her feet and realized that, in her spellbound lust, she'd been busy pouring water all over her shoes and the floor.

"Oh shit. Damn...brand new as well."

She raced over to her desk and grabbed some tissues and began dabbing her feet. "Can I help you with something?" *Like taking off your clothes, or chewing on your bottom lip?* Annie stared intently at her shoes and prayed the god wouldn't notice the bright shade of red that was creeping up her neck.

"Maybe. My sister moved here recently and I don't know her address. Her name is Rhiannon…Wall."

Annie's head jerked up. "You're Rhi's brother?"

"One of them."

Annie stood and pulled herself together. She could see a vague similarity: the shape of the chin; high cheekbones. But his long, haughty nose, full lips and smooth tan skin were pure male. He was wearing a light gray sweater that clung to every ripple and dark blue jeans that sat around his hips and ass in a way that should be illegal. He was tall, perhaps six foot two, with spotless black sneakers on his feet and shining black wavy hair on his head, like ebony bookending the most magnificent man she had ever seen.

"I'm Annie Anderson, her estate agent…and friend," she said as she thrust out her hand.

"Taran. Nice to meet you." He clasped Annie's hand and shook it. She tried not to faint, or throw herself into his arms.

Taran gave Annie the once over. "So can I have her address?"

"You can, but she won't be there. She's meeting me for lunch in ten minutes, so you might as well come along with me."

Annie grabbed her bag, locked the door and led Taran up the street to Crystal's. He walked like a man used to being watched. He was aloof and smooth, his handsome head held high. He scanned the street without giving his thoughts of it away, although one glance at him was enough to presume that he'd rather shoot himself in the foot than leave New York for somewhere like Hamlet.

"Are you here for long?" Annie asked. Perhaps she could have some fun. After all, everyone agreed it was time the whole Annie, Sam and Jake love triangle was dismantled.

What better way to do it than with someone who was freak-of-nature gorgeous?

"Depends on what comes up," Taran said.

Annie was just about to make a flirtatious remark when she stopped short. She realized she didn't want to flirt with him. She wanted to stare at him, as one would a movie star or a piece of art, but she actually wasn't attracted to him. She couldn't imagine kissing him, or snuggling up and watching reruns of *True Blood* with him. Taran Dee might be the best-looking man she'd ever seen, but she wasn't interested. And with that comprehension came the overwhelming awareness that the reason for this was that she already had someone she wanted all that with. She did not want to lose the Knight men—one of them in particular.

"Are you okay?" asked Taran.

"Sorry...I just realized my feet are wet." Annie slipped her shoes off, much to Taran's amusement, and they kept walking.

The door to Crystal's jangled as they entered. There were people at a couple of tables but the main lunch rush was over, so Annie led Taran to a table and sat down. She wasn't thrilled with her new epiphany, but at least she'd stopped acting like her mother's terrier during the spring.

"They have excellent food here."

Taran picked up the menu with a look that said he seriously doubted it.

"I love the portobello and mozzarella baguette, although the vegie lasagna is sublime," Annie chattered. "Do you see anything that you want?"

Annie glanced up from the menu and saw that Taran had indeed seen something desirable. She followed his gaze across the room to Tye, who was placing an order of cheesecake and coffee in front of another couple.

Tye turned and grinned at Annie, before noticing Taran. The smile froze and she turned and hurried out to the kitchen

Taran chuckled. "She seems friendly." He leaned back in his chair and stretched his legs out under the table. "You were right, Annie Anderson. The menu here looks interesting."

*

Tye leaned against the kitchen wall and forced herself to take three long, deep breaths. Thankfully her mother was doing a reading. She didn't need any witnesses to this. She needed to think. It was him! Or was it? She wasn't sure. He looked exactly like him. The gaze was there. The familiarity. The mesmerizing beauty. But he was different. This man had dark hair and the man she had dreamed of all her life was blond.

Tye grabbed a glass of water and pulled herself together. She calmed herself and then sauntered back out into the cafe and over to the table.

"You okay, honey?" asked Annie.

"Something was burning." *Yeah, his eyes, straight through my lie.*

Annie watched Taran and Tye with mounting amusement. "Tye, this is Taran, Rhi's brother."

Tye seemed taken aback. Rhi's brother? She'd dreamed about Rhi's brother? She pasted a smile on her face. "Tye Hemmingway. Rhi has told me so much about you."

He seemed pleased. "Really?"

"No, I lied. She barely mentions her family."

"Good, then you have no preconceived images of me."

Little do you know. "Are you ready to order?"

"I hear your lasagna is great."

"The regular orders can't be wrong."

"Then I'll have that."

Tye nodded and turned to Annie. "The usual?"

"Yes. Has Rhi been by today?"

"She's on her way." Tye ran her eyes across Taran. "She didn't mention a visit from her brother."

"It's a surprise."

There was an excited squeal as Rhi came hurtling into the cafe. Taran bounded out of his chair and scooped his sister up into his arms then twirled her around in a big hug. Annie and Tye exchanged an amused look that said it all: they both immediately decided that, despite his arrogance, they liked him.

"What are you doing here?" screeched Rhi.

"I missed you."

"Right, so you just decided on a drive."

"There's a gallery in Boston that wants to show my work so I decided to kill two birds with one stone. Look at you, you look great!"

"It's living in Hamlet," Rhi admitted. "And you've met my friends. Sit down. You all must get to know each other."

"Good idea," Taran said as he stared at Tye.

Rhi pulled up a chair and called out to Tye, who was once again backing out the door: "Come and join us!"

Tye suddenly felt quite trapped. "I'll get your lunches first."

She made her way into the small kitchen and began preparing the meals. This *was not* how it was meant to happen. She'd always expected their first moment to be more of an *Aha!* rather than this confused *Er, is it?*

But was it?

She placed the lasagna in the microwave and stood staring at it as it heated.

It was him, no doubt about it. So what if his coloring was all wrong? Perhaps the blond hair in her dreams was symbolic of something. The goodness of his heart? Yeah right, Taran was like a stalking panther. He exuded wild sex and heartbreak, not love and light.

She removed the lasagna and placed it on a plate, garnishing it with salad. It wasn't fair. She wasn't meant to be struggling with her fate. Was she? Perhaps one's fate always included an element of struggle and then surrender.

Tye took the meals out and placed them on the table, and then pulled up a chair. Let the struggle begin.

Chapter 30

"Well, what do you think?"

Taran looked down at Rhi's eager face. "I love it."

"Really? You really like it?" All of a sudden Rhi desperately needed Taran's approval—his confirmation that the theater was indeed as amazing as she believed it was.

Taran sat on the edge of the stage. "Would I lie to you?"

Rhi knew she was the one woman on earth he *wouldn't* lie to. "It inspired me. One look and I just knew, Taran. It's like it speaks to me."

"I know Mom expects you to scamper back to New York, tail between your legs, soon. And while I never envisioned a tail...I must admit I thought she might be right."

"What! You traitor."

Taran laughed. "I know, I'm sorry. Believe me, I'd much prefer to never agree with her on anything, but this adventure of yours is quite extreme. I didn't understand it really. Until now. I get it, Rhi. I see it. I get it. And I really think you're going to succeed."

Rhi bit back tears. His support meant everything to her.

"As for this place." Taran did a full turn and scanned the auditorium. "It's missing something."

Rhi watched him closely. He had that look—the look that anyone who'd ever watched him work knew well. He stood and walked to the wall and ran his long fingers along the fresh paint.

"The Greeks, theaters, playwrights, an explosion of imagination and politics and sharing of ideas. Masks. Movement. Theater around the world. The Globe, Elizabethan England, *A Midsummer Night's Dream*, the forest, Puck's forest, filled with magic, creatures of the night, of other realms, darkness and light, watching, protecting this space without ever overtaking it."

Rhi had crept up beside him, listening, riding the wave of his imagination. She slipped her hand into his and together they stared at the wall that was already filled with his images.

"You'd paint here, Taran? You'd really do that?"

"I have to now. Once it exists in my mind it needs to exist on a wall, on a canvas...I have to, Rhi." He swung his head around and scanned the rest of the space. "I thought you'd gone mad moving here, Rhi. Now I understand. There's life in this place. It's inspiring."

"It's haunted, you know."

Taran grinned and slung an arm around Rhi's shoulders as he led her to the door. "Of course it is, sis. No self-respecting theater is complete without a ghost."

"I'm serious. It's really haunted."

"Like Casper the Ghost haunted, some cute little poltergeist moving shit around? Or seriously haunted, with spinning heads and blood coming down the walls and creepy twins?"

"Haunted as in me!" boomed a voice from behind them.

Taran jumped back. "Christ!"

"No...although I did play him once in a Christmas play."

Taran blinked a few times, which made Rhi laugh. He'd never been a huge fan of ghosts.

"And this is?"

Taran stepped forward to meet Kip. "Taran Dee. Rhi's brother."

Kip's eyes narrowed slightly. "Same mother?"

"Yes. Why?"

"Curious, that's all."

"And your name is?"

"Kip Daniels. I own this place."

"Actually, Tad owns it." Rhi turned to Taran. "Tad's his son. I rented this from him."

Kip smiled at Rhi, teasing her. "She also has a little bit of a crush on him."

"Oh, will you shut up."

"Well, you do."

"Whatever." Rhi laughed.

"And he looks just like me—"

"Yes, apart from the dead thing, you can't tell them apart."

"*You* couldn't."

"Thanks to your dazzling."

Taran watched the conversation between Rhi and Kip as if he were watching a tennis match.

"This is weird," he said.

"I find it refreshing," Kip said. "So did I hear something about you being an artist?

"Taran's an amazing artist, Kip, and he's going to paint a mural on the wall."

"Oh, here we go. Spray cans? Cheap acrylics?"

Taran raised an eyebrow. "The National Theater in Berlin has one of my murals on the wall, as does the Chicago Opera."

Kip looked impressed. "That's a relief. You're a real artist. I was just checking that Rhi wasn't giving a sympathy job to an out-of-work sibling."

Taran looked at Rhi and she shrugged. "I know, I know—the scary *Exorcist*-type ghost would be easier."

"Yes, instead you got the ghost who actually gives a damn about art and theater. Now that's never been done before."

Taran scraped his hair back off his face. "That was *The Ghost and Mrs Muir*."

"He was a sea captain, Taran. Hardly an esthete." Kip gave Taran the once over again. "I'll see you around, Taran." And he was gone.

Taran looked at Rhi. "Did someone spike my coffee?"

Rhi shrugged. "It's an unusual situation."

"Is it true about his son?"

Rhi picked up her purse and led Taran toward the door. "I was very confused for a while...made a complete ass of myself in front of Tad, thinking we'd met here in the theater. They're identical, Taran."

Taran stood on the theater steps while Rhi locked the doors. "Like those scary twins in *The Shining*?"

"Yes, that identical. Not quite as terrifying though. Kip's harmless. He was killed here at the theater and has been stuck ever since."

"And his son?"

Rhi felt the heat rise on her cheeks. "He thinks I'm crazy."

Taran gave her a playful punch on the arm. "You are crazy. But delightfully so."

"No, really crazy. He's threatened to dissolve my lease."

"That's harsh. Any point me painting a mural then?"

Rhi gave her brother a look of steel. "He'll be taking this place over my dead body. You paint, I'll deal with this."

"Yes mam." Taran gave her a peck on the cheek. "I dig it when you get all tough. It suits you."

"Thanks. So what do you think of Hamlet?"

"I think it's a bizarre little place. Ghosts, probable legal battles, and you've got some hot friends. I'm more than happy to stick around."

Chapter 31

Rhi had her first potential rental for the theater. She'd received a phone call from Nathan Parker, the head of drama at Harris Valley High, about twenty miles north. A fire had gutted the school's auditorium and they were looking for an alternative venue for their school production of *Hairspray*.

"It runs over four nights, but we'd also book it for a week of rehearsals beforehand, including dress rehearsal," Nathan explained. "It's a fabulous show. Wait till you see it."

"I'll show you the rehearsal studios first." Rhi led Nathan into the theater, but just as they hit the base of the steps she saw Kip standing at the top, glaring down at them. *Boo*, he mouthed at her.

She quickly steered Nathan in the opposite direction. "Second thoughts, let's check out the theater first." She guided him over to the theater doors but before she could reach out to open them, they opened themselves.

Nathan jumped twenty feet. "Jesus, Mary, Lucifer."

"Oh for—I should have warned you, Nathan. There's an unusual amount of hot air in this theater and sometimes it blows the doors open. Gave me an awful fright the first time too."

"I've heard stories about this place being haunted."

Rhi threw her head back and laughed, three years of drama training worth every cent. "Haunted! Aren't people funny—the stories they make up! Believe me, if this place was haunted, I'd know."

A massive thump from above.

"Squirrels in the roof," Rhi explained. "Whole family of them."

"I met that actor you know, only once...the one who died here. Lovely man."

"Word has it he starred in porn films." Rhi spoke in a stage whisper.

Nathan's eyes nearly fell out of his head. "Oh my, really? I thought he was a serious actor."

"Yeah, seriously perverted. Google the Altar Boy series...they might not sell it any more, but it was definitely him."

Rhi could see Nathan mentally jotting that one down. Then he took one sweeping look at the theater and said, "This looks fine. It's a school play and we need the space, so let's book it."

Rhi noticed Kip standing at the side of the wings. She grabbed Nathan's arm and led him swiftly from the theater, something she had a feeling poor Nathan was grateful for.

Outside, he confirmed the dates and she promised to invoice the school, and then she waved him off with a huge smile on her face. A smile that disappeared the minute he'd gone.

"Get your dead ass out here," she bellowed as she stormed back into the theater.

"I'm here." Kip was sitting in the foyer, reading a magazine.

"I need this theater to be a success. You can't scare everyone."

"He's easily scared." Kip flicked over a page. "Porn, hey? Nice one."

"Why did you do that?"

"I thought it was funny." He thrust a magazine at Rhi and pointed to a photo of Demi Moore. "She used to be my favorite actress. What does she look like today?"

"That is her today."

"Don't be ridiculous. She looks exactly the same. This magazine must be twenty years old." He turned it over to check the date. "It's this year. How does she do that?"

"You have so much to learn."

"She's scarier than me."

"What am I going to do with you, Kip?"

"The last time a woman asked that I ended up covered in whipped cream."

"You're bored."

"Only for the past twenty-five years. The first couple of years I was dead I was just confused."

"Perhaps...I could give you a job."

Kip rolled his eyes. "I'd make a fabulous ghost writer."

"I'm serious. You're bored. You need a job."

Kip looked offended. "What as? Front of house? Perhaps I could show people to their seats?"

"It was just a suggestion."

"I'm an actor."

"I get that. But you were more than that too. You did exactly what I'm doing thirty years ago. You left New York and renovated this place with your own blood, sweat and tears. I'm following your path here."

"You'd better make sure that stage roof is secure then."

Rhi looked horrified. "That's not nice. All I'm saying is, perhaps I could learn something from you. You could be my advisor."

Kip watched her for a moment. "I have no answer for that. Your suggestion makes me want to sob, and yet...it's oddly appealing." Kip raised an eyebrow. "What's the salary?"

"I'll pay you exactly what I'm paying myself."

"Fabulous. I'll be dead and broke. It's a deal." He thrust out his hand.

"I'd shake, but I've a feeling it would be creepy."

Kip drew his hand back and they smiled at each other

Rhi put her hands on her hips. "I have work to do."

Kip copied her. "Me too. Now tell me what it is."

Rhi thought for a minute and then grabbed her bag and drew out her iPad. She sat down on one of the seats while Kip chose one nearby. "I need to pick your brains."

"I don't have any."

Rhi ignored him and opened her notes. "I heard that you held drama classes here. That's my plan too. What did you teach the kids?"

"I didn't teach kids. I don't like them."

"You don't like kids?"

"Not really. Adored my son, quite liked my niece, but other children...meh. I taught adult classes."

Rhi looked thoughtful. "I should probably offer an adult class too."

"I had the classes up and running three months before the show. Women came from far and wide for them."

"What about men?"

"There was one."

"You only had one male in your class?"

"Teddy Breneger. Does he still own the bakery?"

"Yes. With his boyfriend." Rhi pulled her hair back and wrapped a band around it. "Were you a real ladies' man?"

"I had my moments. And then I met my love. Rough start—because of me, not her. But once we got on track, it was grand."

"Did you have any male friends?"

"A couple. But I was never a sports-and-beer type of guy. I'm fascinated by women." He moved forward. "I'm quite fascinated by you."

Rhi held a hand up in front of her face. "You're not really fishing from a big pond."

"You're not the only woman I talk to."

This surprised Rhi. "Someone else talks to you?"

He retreated to a seat further away from her. "Maybe."

"Who?"

Kip ran his hand across his lips, as though zipping them.

Rhi pretended she wasn't interested anyway, and turned her attention back to the iPad. "I notice you're now acting like a ghost. Drifting around, hovering and all that."

Suddenly he was hovering above her. "What's that thing? Is it another phone?"

"It's an iPad. It does a lot of the same things as my smart phone, but it doesn't actually phone anyone."

"So it's less intelligent."

Rhi thrust it at him. "It has a lot going for it."

"And you're constantly hooked up to these things?"

"They are a big part of our lives now," Rhi said.

"Scary."

"You might look my age, but you definitely sound like my father's generation."

Kip looked miffed. "So what do you want to know about the classes?"

"Should I ask students to pay annually?"

"They won't do it. Break it into school semesters. Even for adults."

"Yeah, good idea."

"One afternoon a week and Saturday for kids. One evening for the adult classes, but make it the same as the day you teach the monsters. Don't waste too much time on classes right now, but it can be a solid little money spinner."

Rhi jotted everything down. "I'm going to put an ad in the *Examiner* this week. Online editions as well?"

"On what?"

"Do you know nothing of the outside world?"

"The day you walked in was the most exciting thing that has happened to me in nearly thirty years." He drifted closer to her, not threatening, but simply to be near.

"I know, Kip. I feel for you, I do."

"I didn't mean to make a mess of things for you."

"I know."

"I'm stuck, Rhiannon."

"How can I help you?" she asked softly.

"You can't. No one can. Not even her...not even now she's back."

Rhi's brain started to piece it together. "Your girlfriend visits you?"

He nodded, misery etched across his beautiful features.

She joined the dots quickly. It was impossible to miss. The woman he loved could see him. The woman he loved had looked after his son.

"Crystal."

Chapter 32

Word had spread that Rhi's devastatingly handsome brother, a well-known artist in his own right, was painting a mural on the theater wall. Like bees to honey, anyone who was S/F/ 18–50 took to walking by the theater each day, with freshly baked cookies, or a jug of iced tea. One overeager high school senior started forgetting to put on underwear in the morning, until her father caught wind of her plan—or should that be, the wind caught hold of her skirt? Taran became the talk of Hamlet and a Mecca for all females.

All apart from one.

Tye had no idea why she was so wary of him. Really, she should be thrilled that the guy from her dreams had finally shown up. But as much as his physical appearance was slightly off, so were her feelings for him. Yes, he was hot. But he wasn't right. And he was definitely dangerous.

To be fair to Taran, he wasn't exactly using his sex symbol status to his advantage. He was clearly aware of his affect on the female of the species, and reveled in this magnetism whenever it suited his purposes. But he was more focussed on his work, and the women—even pretty blonds carrying warm, buttery cookies, sexy divorcees or pantless high school prom queens—didn't seem to interest him. Dressed in baggy shorts and a T-shirt, Taran worked with an intensity more suited to brain surgery. Tye recognized his passion as he painted, the images in his head making an urgent and howling exit onto the wall via his brush. She was the same when she wrote music.

Tye couldn't escape him completely. She stopped meeting Rhi at the theatre, but she couldn't stop Taran coming into the shop.

"You should drop by and see my mural." Taran rubbed a splatter of paint off his hand, leaned back in his chair and stretched his muscular arms.

"I hear you have enough interruptions over there." Tye placed his coffee on the table.

"You wouldn't be an interruption."

"Maybe I'll drop by some time."

"I'm going to take you out to dinner." On anyone else, such arrogance would have sounded ridiculous. On Taran it sat well. He didn't need to ask a question, just make a statement.

"No. I can't."

If he was surprised he didn't show it. "Why not?"

"I have plans tonight."

"I didn't mean tonight."

"Then I have plans every night."

"So change them."

Tye was tempted for a moment, but that moment quickly passed. "What do you want?"

"The coffee's fine."

"I mean from me."

This seemed to throw him for a moment. "Do I need to know?"

"With me, yes. I'm not blind, Taran. You're an attractive guy. But I'm waiting for someone who knows immediately what I will be to them."

"That's asking an awful lot from mere mortal men."

"I'm aware that it narrows the field down."

Taran finished his coffee and placed the cup on the table. "I get what you're talking about. It actually happened to me once. But even that didn't work out. I saw you and thought, She's attractive, smart... dinner would be nice. That's a good starting point for all sorts of things." Taran walked over to the counter and paid for his coffee. "I'll see you soon."

Tye watched him leave and then breathed a sigh of relief. He was unnerving. But then, perhaps she was being unreasonable. Being a witch didn't necessarily mean there would be a magical overtone to every aspect of her life. She still experienced the ups and downs everyone else did. She couldn't just wave a magic wand and solve everything. (Actually that wasn't entirely true, but as a witch she had to choose her moments, as every spell she put out there also returned to impact on her.) Despite her upbringing, she was quite a practical person. And yet, on this one issue, she had been unwaveringly wistful. She didn't date. She didn't ever give guys a chance. She was loyal to a dream. And she waited.

Thinking about it now, she felt rather foolish.

She should probably give Taran a chance and at least have dinner with him, but she needed to get a handle on how she was feeling first. She'd always thought that meeting the man she dreamed about would be easy. Instead, she was awash with conflicting emotions. He wasn't at all what she'd expected. She felt betrayed by her own psychic gifts. She didn't feel the way she thought she should. She wasn't even sure it was him.

She looked around the shop, which was now empty. She was grateful for a quiet afternoon. Her mom was having lunch with an old friend. Strange that the old friend didn't come to the shop. Perhaps she was meeting Larry for an afternoon romp.

She noticed a text: *Make me a latte. I'll be there in 10.* X Tad.

She went to put her phone down but then remembered that she'd been meaning to update it and download all the recent pics. She hooked it up to her computer and then left it while she made Tad a coffee. She was just filling the glass with milk when he arrived.

"Quiet today?" Tad said as he gave her a kiss.

"That suits me."

"Anything wrong?"

"Not really." She wasn't quite ready to share her feelings about Taran yet. Instead, she turned her attention back to the computer while Tad sat on a stool near the counter.

"You're close to Rhi now, aren't you?" Tad asked.

Tye nodded. "We've become good friends."

"And you wouldn't be good friends with a total weirdo would you?"

Tye's attention was elsewhere. "I'm friends with you."

Tad laughed. "Apart from me."

She flicked through some photos, giving Tad only a sideways glance. "What makes you think Rhi is weird?"

"We've had a few extremely weird exchanges."

"Perhaps she's just shy around you. She can be reserved, but—" Tye froze.

"Tye? You okay?"

Tye looked at Tad and then back at the computer. "I didn't realize you were in this photo."

"What photo?"

"At the theater."

Tad paled. "The Majestic? Tye, I haven't been near the theater for years. I was just telling your mom the same thing the other day."

"But you're in this photo, Tad. Here, look."

Tad jumped up and moved to her side. He stared at the screen, which clearly showed a photo of Tye, Rhi, Annie, Sam and Jake on the steps of the finished theater. And then his eyes moved to the door behind them, to a sixth person.

Tye looked at him. "Rhi told me you'd been there, but I didn't see you that day."

Tad's voice was barely above a whisper. "That's because I wasn't there."

Chapter 33

"And so there we were, stuck in that beach house for a week with wild weather raging around us. No television. Nothing. And I thought Tad and Tye would tear each other apart...but the owner of the house had a music room. So the kids went in one afternoon and Tad sat down at the piano and Tye picked up the violin, and I didn't see them until dinner. I didn't see them much for the rest of the holiday. They were obsessed. And that's where it all began."

Kip stared at her, a smile filled with both admiration and gratitude on his face. "I've missed so much."

"That's the way it goes, love."

"You kept your promise though."

"I would've anyway. Even without you asking me, I'd have kept an eye on him."

Crystal's phone buzzed. She knew it was a text from Larry, so ignored it.

"Not you too!" Kip exclaimed. "One of those dumb phones. You of all people, Crystal."

"Mine's not that fancy, Kip. Just calls and texts. I'm a luddite."

"So who would be contacting you at this time of the night?"

"None of your business, that's who."

"A boyfriend?"

"Kip!"

"You're not answering my question. Why not? Do you have a lover?"

"Do you have a lover?"

"The last lover I had was you!"

They stared at each other for a moment, blazing heat filling the space between them, erasing both his death and her age.

"Kip, I won't apologize for surviving."

"Nor should you. You have every right to have a lover, even now that we're back together."

"What do you mean by that?"

"I'm grateful that you spend so much time with me, Cryssie, and I know I can't satisfy all your needs."

"Jesus, Kip. The thought of going there with you makes me feel like a cougar."

"A cat?"

"It's a modern term for an older woman who has sex with a younger man."

Kip still looked confused. "I don't see you as an older woman. I just see you. And I'm jealous of you being with someone else. But that's my problem."

"No—it's my problem too. You were my great love. I always knew you were."

"I wish I'd been so clear about things, Cryssie."

"You were toward the end, Kip."

"But those early days—"

"We were young. You were young. It's not important now."

Kip nodded. "You're right. We're here now, and that's what's important."

Crystal refrained from saying anything. As much as she loved him, spending time with him was a no-win situation for both of them. "I have to go. I've been here all evening. I need some sleep."

Kip looked disappointed. "Just another hour?"

"I'm not a vampire, Kip. I need sleep at night. I'll see you soon, okay?"

"Okay, okay."

Crystal left via the back door of the theater, walking down the steps and along the side fence to the pavement. The street was isolated, the night still. She was glad for some time alone now, to walk and think and clear her mind. She heard her phone buzz again. She'd ignored the texts from Larry, even though she sensed his growing confusion with each one. She slipped her phone from her coat pocket and read them now.

How about dinner tonight beautiful?

Hellllooo Crystal!!!!

Have I done something wrong?

Just checking you got my message, darling.

It wasn't Larry's fault. He was a perfectly nice man: funny, smart and attractive. No mental baggage or obvious medical conditions—a huge bonus once you reached a certain age.

No, there was nothing wrong with Larry. He just wasn't Kip. No one ever had been.

Unfortunately, even Kip wasn't Kip any more, just an ephemeral version of himself. He was also exactly as he had been when he died, whereas she'd done a lot in nearly thirty years. She'd travelled. Raised Tye, and virtually raised Tad. She'd built a successful small business in New York, sold it, and built another one here in Hamlet. And she'd done it all alone. No man supporting her. Not that she'd ever been adverse to the idea...but no man had ever rocked her world the way Kip had.

The way he still did. Damn it! Despite his arrogance, and insularity and him being dead, the connection between them was more powerful than ever. He was her soul mate and while

Crystal was the first to admit he was an unfortunate choice for one, he was hers and there was nothing she could do about that.

She knew she couldn't be with him. But she couldn't bear to let him go either. What the hell was she going to do?

She'd start by having some manners. She texted Larry back.

Sorry Larry, I have some personal matters I need to attend to this week. Will explain when I see you next. Xo

She let herself into the house and noticed a light on. Tye was obviously staying the night.

"Mom, where have you been?"

Both Tad and Tye were sitting on the lounge, ashen faced. Beside them was Tye's computer, a photograph filling the screen.

"Can you explain this?" asked Tad.

Crystal sat on the edge of the lounge and looked at the photo. Her stomach dropped. What was he thinking? The bastard was standing there for the entire world to see. Goddamn him.

"Mom, please explain this." Tye sounded panicked.

"It's your father."

"That's impossible," Tad said.

"No, honey, it's not," Crystal said. "He's haunting the theater."

"How do you know that?" asked Tye.

"I've been with him all night."

Tad's eyes nearly fell from his head. "That's my father?"

Tye took a deep breath and turned to him. "He's my father too."

Chapter 34

"Crystal!"

"I'm right here, Kip."

"I can't find my tights!" Kip was frantic, pulling clothes out of a pile of washing.

"Now there's something I never thought I'd hear you say."

Crystal grabbed Kip's tights from a drawer and threw them at him.

"What would I do without you?"

"Perform Hamlet bare-legged probably."

Kip gave her a kiss and started dressing.

"Kip...there's something I need to speak to you about."

"Is it important?"

"Yes."

"Then let's save it until after the show. I'm a bundle of nerves, Cryssie...I just need to get through opening night."

Crystal turned to the mirror and applied some lipstick. "Okay, we've got plenty of time to talk about it."

He moved behind her and wrapped her arms around her. "You look beautiful."

Her eyes shone, as they always did when he paid her a compliment.

"And after the show, we'll have our own private celebration."

Crystal nodded. "Perfect."

Kip kissed her neck and moved off in search of the rest of his costume.

She could wait. She wanted the time to be right. She knew this was huge, but also felt that Kip would be happy. She'd tell him she was pregnant later. After opening night, when he was hers alone again.

She looked at him now, so handsome and so obviously nervous. "You'll be fantastic, Kip. I just know it."

Which wasn't actually true. She had the most awful feeling he was going to fail.

But that's okay, she thought to herself. I'll be there to catch him.

*

"But I wasn't," Crystal sobbed. "I wasn't."

Tye reached out and held her mother, even though she knew she was upset with her.

Crystal was inconsolable. "You weren't to say anything, Tye. You promised me."

"Things have changed. If my father is in that theatre, then I want to meet him. And for me to do that, Tad needed to know."

"But—"

"No buts! It's an outdated promise. It's not like she can stop him from seeing us now."

The night seemed to close in around the three of them. The living room lamps cast shadows on the wall that flickered strange images on the ceiling. Tad's face was indecipherable. He didn't move.

"I promised, Tye."

"You didn't break that promise. I did." Tye turned to Tad. "I wanted to tell you a million times, but I couldn't."

"Why not?" Tad asked quietly.

Tye looked at Crystal. "Tell him."

"Please don't ask me that."

"I'll tell him if you don't."

Crystal reached out a hand to calm her daughter. And then she turned to Tad.

*

The wind howled, rattling the windows, knocking at the roof, threatening to blow the house apart. Crystal lay on the floor, in fetal position, unsure if the turmoil was actually a storm outside Kip's house, or inside of her. She was shattered. Completely destroyed. Her man, the only man she had ever loved, or would ever love, was dead. She'd been dragged away from his broken body by paramedics who, concerned for her, had injected her with sedatives and brought her home.

The first night passed. Then the first day of her new life, the one where Kip was dead. There were times she stopped crying and instead would sit, staring at the clock, catatonic. Each minute that ticked away took her further and further from him. His kiss, his touch, his smell, his laugh, his frustrating and all-consuming goddamn behavior…Each tick of the clock was yet another death knell, further and further into a world she already despised.

The doorbell rang but she ignored it, just like all the others she'd ignored all day. But then she heard Collette call out her name. She wanted to take no notice, but a little voice told her she must open the door. Collette had Tad and Crystal needed to know that he was okay.

Collette stood on the doorstep. She was immaculate as usual, with her high-maintenance hair and red lipstick. But her eyes were bloodshot and puffy. She'd loved Kip in her own way.

"Hello, Crystal."

"Hello, Collette." Crystal's eyes drifted to the world outside. It was still. A beautiful fall evening, not a breeze in the sky.

"Can we talk?"

Crystal led Collette into the house and they sat on a sofa in the living room. Crystal didn't offer her anything. Collette clearly wanted to make the visit as brief as possible. Crystal's pain was excruciating to witness.

"You do realize that this is now Tad's house," Collette said.

"I haven't thought about it."

"You can't live here."

"Okay." Like she wanted to anyway. It was the last place on earth she'd live now that Kip was gone.

"I'm taking Tad back to New York after the funeral. My lawyers will tie everything up here."

"Okay."

"I know you're pregnant."

Crystal looked her in the eye for the first time since she'd arrived, the full force of her grief evident. Even Collette seemed shocked by it.

"Are you sure it's Kip's?"

"Of course I am."

"Well, you can't tell anyone. He'd dead, so there's no point announcing it anyway, right?"

"Tad needs to know."

"I'm Tad's only parent now and I get to make those decisions, so I'm saying he doesn't. It will be confusing for him. Everyone treats him as Kip's only child. It makes him special. I won't take that away from him." Her eyes narrowed. "And of course, there's the inheritance. I funded Kip's life. The theater. This house. Our son gets it all."

Crystal came to her senses. Collette had the wrong idea about her. "I would never—"

Collette held a heavily bejeweled hand up. "I haven't finished yet. I know you have a special bond with Tad, and I don't want to stand in the way of it. I'm happy for you to be in his life as a family friend. But mention that baby and you'll never see him again."

"I promised Kip I'd always keep an eye on him."

"That's sweet, but Kip's dead. I make the decisions now. Clear?"

Crystal was dissolving. She was disappearing into an abyss of invisible sludge, weighing heavily around her and suffocating her. For a moment, a brief moment, she considered taking a razor to her wrist. She could join Kip. They could be together, as they'd planned. But then she felt the tiniest flutter...a baby's movement inside. It was the first time she'd felt anything. New life, amid this overwhelming death. Kip lived on in this child, just as he lived on in Tad. She thought of Tad, who she loved as her own. They would be okay. They would be a family. She would do what she had to.

"Fine, Collette. I won't say a word. But I'm begging you, don't take him away from me." Crystal's eyes pleaded with her, one woman to another. "I can't lose him too. My heart—I won't survive it."

Collette actually seemed moved. She turned her head away and wiped a tear from her eye. "I'm glad we've worked that out. To be honest, I need some help raising him anyway. As long as we both know where we stand."

Relief flooded her body and Crystal knew she'd survive.

Collette stood and made her way to the door. She paused at the entrance and turned back to Crystal.

"I'm sorry. I know you loved him."

*

Crystal blew her nose. "And so we came to an agreement. And though you might feel hurt right now…it worked out for us all."

"Sounds like my mother," Tad said, his face set in stone. "How dare she?"

"We've grown to respect each other over the years, Tad, but at the time, she was a star and I didn't have the resources to fight her. And I couldn't lose you. I'd made a pact with your father that if anything ever happened to him, I'd be there. And I had to be. I decided to do everything in my power to raise you two as siblings. You might not have known Tye was your sister, but you felt it. I know you did."

Tye looked at Tad. "She's right."

"How long have you known?"

Tye shrugged. "I've always known."

A sob caught in Crystal's throat. "I am so sorry that I took this from you."

Tad's voice was gentle and filled with emotion. "Crystal, you have given me more than you have ever taken." He turned to Tye. "I'm more worried about you, Tye. You missed out on being acknowledged by my—our grandparents because of my mother."

Tye took Tad's hand while she kept her other arm around her mom. "We were both so young when they died, it wouldn't have made much difference. As long as you were in my life, I didn't care. You were my connection to him. I used to look for him in you, Tad. I looked for myself in you. I always knew Mom did the right thing."

Tad's eyes widened. "Thank god I never hit on you. I occasionally wondered why I never even wanted to."

Tye let out a laugh. "I think that's partly why Mom told me."

Crystal pulled an apologetic face. "I really pushed the idea of us being family when you were young, so thankfully that was never an issue."

"Why haven't you told us about him being at the theater, Mom?" Tye asked.

"I've only just found out. When Rhi said that Tad had performed the Hamlet soliloquy for her—"

Tad visibly paled. "She what?"

"Kip has been communicating with Rhi since she took possession of the theater. She thought it was you."

Tad's eyes widened. "Jesus, he's really there?"

"Yes."

"Oh god, I feel sick. I was planning to take legal action. I've treated her like she's crazy." Tad took his head into his hands. "I feel like *I'm* going crazy. It's easy to accept that you're my sister, Tye. But that my father is haunting the theater is not."

"How do you explain the photo?"

"I can't."

"Do you believe it's possible?" Crystal asked him.

"Yes. I don't know. Anything is possible, Crystal. You taught me that. You opened up a world to me that I clearly remember my father rejecting. He was fearful of it, wasn't he?"

Crystal knew they were moving into complicated territory again. "He feared certain things but only because he was very much a believer."

"What did he fear?" Tye asked.

"Witches," Crystal said simply.

Tye laughed, but stopped when she realized her mother was serious. "But you're a witch."

Crystal shrugged. She didn't want to go into this now. She couldn't. She'd had enough of sordid tales from the past tonight, and this next one made the one she'd just told the kids look like an episode of *Howdy Doody*.

The doorbell rang and broke the tension.

"Goodness, who could that be at this time of night?" Crystal made her way down the hall to the entrance, and opened the door.

"Why didn't you tell me your boyfriend is haunting my theater?" Rhi was clearly in no mood for small talk. She looked at Crystal for a response, but then her eyes drifted toward the end of the hallway, where Tye and Tad stood, listening to her. "Oh shit."

Crystal drew Rhi inside. "It's okay, love. They know."

Rhi's eyes were locked on Tad's. Crystal could almost see the energy thick in the space between them. Her heart went out to them both, struggling as they were with this attraction that had been manipulated by Kip. Of course he hadn't meant to. Kip never really meant to hurt anyone. But he was so bloody narcissistic, even in death. Especially in death.

"I bet you thought I was certified," Rhi said to Tad.

"Yes. But I also think you're lovely." He walked over to her and ever so gently gave her a kiss on the forehead. And then, turning to all three women, he said, "Do what you have to do. I trust you all. But I need some time."

And with that he walked out the door.

Chapter 35

Crystal's home above the shop was a spacious two-bedroom apartment that had been renovated to her taste. It was as unusual as its owner; it wasn't quirky but it had an offbeat flair. There were hardwood floors and beams throughout, with whitewashed walls and colorful curtains. Crystal headed for the kitchen.

"I need some comfort food," she explained, as she motioned for Tye and Rhi to follow her.

"I might go home and check on Tad," said Tye.

"No, you'll stay here tonight. Give him space."

"I should check that he's okay."

"I'll know if he's not."

Rhi and Tye pulled stools up while Crystal got busy cooking. Her kitchen had the wood floors and beams overhead like the rest of the apartment, but the features were its deep red cabinets and granite bench tops. It was spacious, with a large pine island in the center, where the girls now sat. Above the island were two brass light fittings. There were baskets scattered around the kitchen, lined with gingham to hold fruit and vegies. One contained only lemons. There was a wooden pot rack in the corner, and off it hung a range of cast iron and copper pans. It was a kitchen belonging to a woman who was strong, creative and who loved to cook.

Rhi thought there was something extremely comforting about this space. She watched as Crystal set about blending cashews, vanilla, coconut oil and agave syrup. She toasted shredded coconut, sliced some figs, poured cream over them, and garnished with the coconut and grated dark chocolate.

"So why didn't you tell me, Crystal?"

"I only realised he was there recently, because of things you'd told me." She passed a plate to the girls. "Munch on these while I bake for the shop."

Tye and Rhi did as they were told, and Tye filled Rhi in on the evening's events.

Rhi was still shaking her head in disbelief when Crystal put the first of her pies in the oven.

"I see it," she said. "It never occurred to me that you could be related, but now that you've told me...you actually do look alike. You're both tall, with perfect features."

Tye chuckled. "Perfect, hey? Thanks."

"Tye has my coloring. But I would watch them growing up, mesmerised by their beauty, and think, how can no one see this? I saw the resemblance right from day one." Crystal poured the mix for a white chocolate coconut cake into a baking tin and put the bowl and a spoon in front of Rhi.

"Want to lick the bowl?"

Rhi's eyes lit up. "I don't think I've ever licked a cake mix bowl."

Tye and Crystal both stared at her in amazement.

"How can that be?" asked Crystal.

"My mom isn't much of a cook. And I took after her."

Crystal shook her head. "Then the bowl is yours."

Tye put her hands up in defeat. "All yours."

"So what are we going to do about Kip?" Rhi asked, scraping out cake mix with her finger.

Crystal put her wooden spoon down and pulled up a stool opposite. "He needs to cross over. As soon as possible."

Tye looked shocked. "What do you mean by that? You've been spending time with him. Why can't I?"

Crystal looked lovingly at her daughter. "Because that's not your father in that theater."

"It's as close to it as I'll ever get," Tye said, her voice rising slightly.

"True. It's also as close to my soul mate as I'll get. I spent years loving this man when he was alive, and thirty years mourning his death. When I discovered him in that theater, I wanted to grab hold of that, embrace it, and hide it—keep it mine in case it vanished again. And that's what I've done for the past week, spending every spare minute with him. But it's not him."

"I don't understand."

"He can't touch me. He can't hold me. He can't understand what my life is like outside the theater. He's trapped there. I think he has unfinished business. As much as I'd like to continue my visits with him, they make me yearn for something I stopped grieving for years ago. The very nature of grief is that we grow into it...we learn to wear it. This has changed everything. It's fresh again for me." Crystal's eyes teared up. "He has to go."

Tye turned to Rhi. "What do you think? You know him."

Rhi shuffled on her seat, embarrassed. "He became stuck at the moment of his death. Something happened."

Crystal shuffled on her stool. "I know what it was. I just haven't worked out how to fix it."

"What was it, Mom?" Tye asked.

"Not something I can talk about yet."

"What was he like?" asked Rhi. "As a boyfriend?"

Crystal wiped her tears, and cracked a smile. "He's been flirting with you, hasn't he?"

"No!" Rhi lied, badly.

"He was always an incorrigible flirt. It caused untold heartache for me back then."

This was all new to Tye. "Really? I've always heard you speak highly of him."

"There are many truths," said Crystal "He was the smartest, funniest man. His heart huge and, Goddess, he was blessed physically."

"But," Tye said.

"Yes, but."

"He is a flirt, but he was always clear that he had someone in his life...or death. His loyalty is to you, Crystal. He knows where to draw the line."

"Pity he didn't always know how to do that while he was alive." She smiled at Rhi. "It's easy to forgive him though. You've done it even though he's been playing tricks with you for months."

Rhi looked from Crystal to Tye. "Sometimes I separate the two men easily, but other times the lines are blurred and Kip took advantage of that. I would like to know Tad better, but it's Kip I spend time with."

"What he like?" Tye asked.

"All the things Crystal said. Interesting. And entertaining. But he's lonely. He's so very lost." Rhi looked at Tye. She knew this couldn't be easy for her. "I'm really fond of him. That's why I agree with Crystal. He needs to cross over."

Crystal sighed. "The anniversary of his death is coming up next month. The fourth."

Rhi pushed the rest of the bowl away. Tye picked at a vase of flowers.

"Shall we throw him a party?" she said wryly.

To their surprise, Crystal nodded. "Yes, but not a normal party. Rhi, we need to stage *Hamlet*. Only then will he cross over."

"*Hamlet*? In less than a month?"

"He needs to get to the end of the play." Crystal was already making plans in her head.

"Less than a month?" Rhi reiterated.

"The moment of both our birth and death is very powerful," Crystal explained. "The veils are thinner. You know that. It has to be that day."

Rhi knew she was right. "It won't be easy to pull off."

"It will with the right people. You'll have to perform with him, while I watch. His ego won't be thrilled with an audience of one."

"We can have a bigger audience, Crystal. We both see him. All we need is an audience of people like us."

"Yes, between us we could pull in an audience of witches and psychics. Right?" Tye said.

Crystal nodded, excited. "This is exactly what we need to do. Rhi, you start looking into staging this thing, and I'll deal with Kip."

"And Annie?" Rhi said.

"What about her?"

"You realize Tye is Annie's cousin too," Rhi said.

"It's why I made sure they knew each other growing up. And I guess you can tell her now too."

"You did good, Mom." Tye reached for her mother's hand. "Overnight I've got this family that I actually would've chosen anyway." She gave Rhi a sideways hug. "Now all I need is a link to you."

"Marry my brother," Rhi said.

Tye laughed. "Taran is gorgeous...and there's something there, but—"

"Then marry my other one."

"What other brother?"

"Taran's twin."

"Taran has a twin! Are they identical?" Tye's eyes looked like they would drop out of her head they were so wide.

Rhi was a little lost by her reaction. "Yeah, Finn. They're almost identical, only Finn is blond."

Tye's face lit up. "Are you serious?"

"Ah... yeah."

"Blond?"

"Yes. Otherwise they're identical."

"Did you hear that, Mom?"

"Sure did, honey."

"How about that? A brother, a father, a cousin—and hey, you have a brother I'm yet to meet. My stars really are aligned."

Crystal gave her daughter a wink and turned to check the oven, leaving Rhi wondering what the hell they were so happy about.

Chapter 36

"Tad? Are you home?"

Rhi followed Tye into the home she shared with Tad. Tye actually lived in the guesthouse at the back, but spent most of her time in the main house with Tad. Or in the recording studio he'd built in the basement. She had been to Tye's before, but she'd always entered around the back—this was the first time she'd been inside Tad's domain, and she was impressed. Tye led her into one large open space—kitchen, dining and lounge room—filled with simple furniture in browns and creams. The main focus of the room was a grand piano. The house was facing east, and sun streamed through the large windows. The guy had taste. His house wasn't large, but it was beautiful.

"I'll check the rest of the house," Tye said and disappeared down the hall.

Rhi walked out onto his balcony. The air was salty and she breathed the ocean in. How she loved it in this part of the world. She noticed a large telescope and wondered if Tad was into astronomy. There were so many things she wanted to know about him. But right now, she just wanted to know he was okay. His phone had been switched off. He wasn't responding to texts.

"He's not here." Tye appeared behind her holding a note. "I knew he wouldn't just disappear. He doesn't like to worry people."

Rhi took the note from Tye and read it out loud. "'Taking some time out. See you soon. Don't forget to water the plants.'"

"Even when he's upset he's still responsible."

"Any ideas where he'd be?"

Tye shrugged. "Who knows? New York, maybe. His favorite guitar is missing. That tells me that he's hit the road for a while."

Rhi stared out at the ocean.

Tye joined her and put her arms around her. "Don't worry...he'll be back."

"It's so weird, yearning for someone I barely know."

"I know exactly what you mean." Tye turned and walked back into the house. "Come on, we've got to go see my cousin."

Rhi didn't move, her confusion evident.

"Annie!" Tye clarified.

Rhi took off after Tye. "Oh god, yes, I want to see this."

*

It turns out Annie wasn't overly surprised. Thrilled, but not surprised.

"There were rumors when I was growing up that Crystal had been pregnant when Uncle Kip died. I heard my mother talking about it once. My grandparents refused to believe it, so I guess she let it go. God rest their souls."

"What did your mother say?" Tye asked.

"You mean your aunt?"

"Oh my—of course."

"You were up here one summer—we were about thirteen, I think—and I overheard Mom say that you looked a lot like Kip...like a young colt. She said she'd bet her house on it, and then some, but my grandmother told her to shush." Annie drifted away for a moment, thoughtful. "I admire Crystal. Imagine fighting to have your child make those family connections, under those circumstances. Collette always was a bitch. And poor Crystal; to deal with losing the love of your life, being pregnant and told your baby could never know her family." Annie's eyes glistened. "I obviously don't know much about spirits and things, but if there is any way I can help you get this play on, let me know. I know I can't see him...but I believe what you're saying."

"There is one thing," Rhi said. "I need a house for two weeks. Somewhere for the actors to stay while they're here."

"How many actors in *Hamlet*?"

"I don't know yet, but given the time frame I'm thinking of cutting the play right back and giving each actor multiple roles."

Rhi could see Annie mentally going through her list. "I've got the apartment near the wharf. That has three bedrooms. And then the Lilac Cottage down the street from you, Rhi, is empty. I'm going to renovate the kitchen so I'm not taking bookings for that."

"I think that should house everyone. I'll let you know the final numbers once I've discussed it with Kip."

Annie's eyes grew wide. "You actually talk to him?"

"Yes."

"Isn't that scary?"

"The only thing frightening about it was that I thought he was Tad, so I've spent a couple of months making a total dick of myself."

"My mother always said that she loved him, but that he was up his own ass."

Rhi laughed. "Yes, death hasn't changed that."

"Hey, this is my dad you're talking about."

The three women looked at each other and then burst into howling laughter.

Chapter 37

Crystal hurled open the door of Kip's dressing room. "The game has changed, darling."

"In what way?" Kip was hanging upside down from the ceiling.

"What are you doing?"

Kip pointed at an open magazine on the sofa. "It says inversions are good for you. They help you live longer." He let out a barking laugh. "Doesn't work for me."

Crystal placed her hands on her hips. "I'm not interested in that. What I want to know is why you'd stand in the way of a group of people having their photo taken."

"You've lost me."

"When Rhi and her friends had their photo taken on the theater steps?"

"Oh that. I was looking at the dumb phone. I didn't realize it took photos too. I didn't think I'd end up *in* the photo...being dead and all."

"So who's the dumb one? You are now in a photo on Tye's camera."

"And she saw?"

"She did. And so did Tad."

"Oh, that's not good." Kip drifted to the sofa, looking upset with himself.

"You think?"

"How did he take it?" he asked quietly.

"No idea, he's disappeared."

Kip rose above her, panicked. "You must find him. What if something happens to him?"

"He's a grown man. He needs some space to deal with this—and the fact that he has a sister."

Kip's eyes bulged. "Jesus. Collette had another baby? The woman must be pushing sixty."

"I'm talking about me, you idiot."

"You're pregnant? That would explain the weight gain."

"You know, death has turned you into a moron. Obviously I'm not pregnant at my age."

"Oh...well how do I know what advances they've made in those areas? Those smart phones are quite unnerving, as is Demi Moore...Hold on—sister?"

Crystal shook her head. "The penny drops."

"Oh god, Crystal...your daughter is twenty-eight, right?"

"Our daughter is twenty-eight."

And with that Kip began to moan. He began to wail. He hunched over himself, curled tight in a ball, and let out the most hideous, haunting cry.

Crystal rushed to his side. "Oh darling, please don't."

"I didn't even know that I could cry, Cryssie." He kept going. "I have a daughter?"

"You do. And she's wonderful and talented and you'd be very proud of her."

"Oh, Cryssie."

"She wants to meet you."

His eyes bulged. "No, impossible. I'd scare her. I'm not me. I have nothing to give. Oh god that fucking roof really screwed things up for me."

"No, love, it was your time."

"It wasn't, it wasn't…"

Crystal tried to calm him down. "Kip, Rhi, Tye and I have been talking."

"Like a little coven."

"You need to cross over. We want to help you cross over."

He lifted him head, hurt. "Don't you want me around?"

"I wish I could have you around forever. But it's not fair to Tye and Tad. And, my love…it's not fair to you. You're stuck."

"It is a bit endless," he admitted.

"We're going to stage *Hamlet*."

Kip cracked a smile. "That's funny."

"I'm serious. We're going to cast actors who can see you, and invite an audience of psychics. You will have your moment."

Kip went quiet. He moved to the corner and hovered there, his form hazier than usual.

"You don't want that?"

"I've always wanted that, Crystal."

"Then what's the problem?"

His form disappeared and then became visible again. It was as though there was a short circuit. Each time he reappeared he had his hands to his head, as though trying to shake off a terrible memory.

"Darling, speak to me." Crystal stood and moved toward him. Each step closer became more difficult. His energy was shaky and heavy. "Don't you want to finish *Hamlet*, Kip?"

He turned to her, grief etched across his spectacular features. "I always wanted that. And you think I want to be here? I didn't choose this. I never would've have chosen this." He began to shake, and as he did, his form rose and grew clear, filled with rage.

Crystal stepped back. "Kip…calm down."

He began to spin. Around him a vortex of energy and shadows collected a pile of papers and they rotated faster and faster in a whirlwind of fury.

"Kip, please."

Faster and faster until a specter of darkness filled the room.

"*I'm here because of her!*"

The full force of Kip's rage threw Crystal across the room. She felt her body slam against the wall, and then everything went black.

*

Crystal felt faint from shock. Kip was standing in the doorway of her shop, an apologetic grin on his face and a baby in his arms. It had been just over two years since she'd seen him. Each day had been a battle between her heart and her mind. She had moved on from the old apartment. She'd opened her first shop, a tiny hovel of a place on the Lower East Side, where she provided readings and mixed charms. It didn't take long for people to talk about how good she was, so her client list had grown exponentially and she was now looking for a new place to rent. She'd even been on a few dates, but no one could erase her feelings for Kip.

And looking at him now, he knew it.

"This is my son, Tad."

The baby beamed up at Crystal and her heart shifted gears. She knew immediately she was a goner, for him as much as his father.

"It's good to see you Crystal."

"I'm not sure if it's good to see you, Kip."

He at least had the decency to look embarrassed.

Kip peered around at the small table where Crystal's tarot cards were placed, a chair either side. By the curtained window was a two-seater mahogany settee with a hand-reeded seat. The walls were lined with shelves containing all sorts of magical tools and potion jars. In the corner was a cash register.

"I like your shop." He seemed nervous.

"Why are you here?"

Kip burst into tears. "I have nowhere else to go."

Crystal closed the shop for the day and took Kip back to her studio apartment three blocks away. After putting Tad down for a nap, Kip told her the mess he was in.

"I'm not sure how I ended up in a relationship with Brigid."

"Would you like me to remind you?"

"God, Cryssie...I know, I know. I fucked up so badly. But what I mean is...I've never really liked her. She's beautiful and cool...and a stupid part of me saw conquering her as a challenge, but I never felt comfortable with her, like I did with you."

"You make me sound like a pair of old slippers."

"Is that so bad?"

"Obviously it was. You ran a mile."

"I'm so sorry, Cryssie. So very sorry. I'll admit I wasn't ready to settle down, but that's exactly what I saw happening with you. It scared the hell out of me. I loved you. I don't know what possessed me to throw that away." Kip stared down at his hands, which were still shaking. "Brigid and I found a place in Astoria. Things were difficult right from the start. Then about a year ago I got a small role on *The World Turns and Turns*. Only a week's work, but I met Collette."

"Collette Kelly?" Even Crystal knew of her and she'd never watched the show. "Are you telling me that little boy in there is Collette's, not Brigid's?"

Kip's eyes widened when he realized what Crystal had been thinking. "Tad's not Brigid's. Hell, Crystal, that woman will devour her young when she has them. I would never..." He paused for a moment and sighed. "Mind you, I didn't expect *this either. It was a one-night thing. But Collette and I...She's cool. She doesn't want a relationship with me but we're on the same page with Tad."*

"And Brigid?"

"It's over."

Crystal took a deep breath. She needed to muster as much strength as she could right now. He was single. He had a child. Of course he'd come back to her. But this time she would not be a pushover.

"I didn't have the guts to tell Brigid about Collette until just before Tad was born. She scares me, Crystal. I was trying to extract myself first, but the night I told her...she went nuts. Crazy. She screamed and made threats and threw things at me...and then—"

Kip paled, as if all the blood from his body had drained out the soles of his feet.

"What happened, Kip?"

"She cursed me."

Ice coursed through Brigid's veins. "Are you sure?"

"One hundred percent. She cursed me, Crystal, and I feel it. Every day since, I've felt doomed." He turned to her, grabbed her hands as if clutching hold for dear life. "It's why I'm here. If something happens to me, I'm begging you to keep an eye on Tad."

Crystal was shocked to the core. "Of course."

"You're the only person I trust."

*

"Crystal? Cryssie, please wake up."

Crystal slowly opened her eyes and the room spun into view. She looked at Kip, who was kneeling beside her.

"I'm so sorry." He looked like he was about to cry.

Crystal carefully sat up. "No, Kip, I'm sorry. I failed you."

Kip wouldn't hear of such a thing. "You're the one person who never failed me. The one person I could always trust."

"That's not actually true."

He leaned closer to her, until she looked him in the eyes. "I love you. I always have, ever since I first saw you in that cafe eating that apple pie. All those other women who wouldn't eat because they were watching their weight, and you there, with a slab of pie covered in cream—you were as gorgeous and delicious as what you were digging into."

"And now look at me. I should've steered clear of that pie."

"You're still that girl to me."

Crystal began to sob. "I wish we'd grown old together. I wish you could touch me, Kip."

And in that moment, the Fates took pity on the lovers. The universe opened its veils and Kip reached forward and touched her. The tips of his fingers stroked her face. It was brief, but real and precious. Then the veils closed again. And they stared into each other's eyes, more grief-stricken then ever.

"I'll make everything right for you, Kip, but you must promise me something."

"Anything."

"Start rehearsing *Hamlet*."

"What's the point if I can't cross over?"

"You concentrate on *Hamlet*, and leave that one to me."

Kip nodded. "Anyone else...but you, I trust."

"I wish you hadn't."

Chapter 38

Rhi racked her brain about how to approach *Hamlet*. She could hardly stage a fully rehearsed version in two weeks. She pored over the play and decided that with some careful editing, it could be performed with seven actors.

Kip wasn't sold. "Seven? Impossible."

"It's not impossible. In fact, I saw the play performed in New York a couple of years ago with a cast of four, and it was excellent. It got amazing reviews."

"From who? *Staten Island Express*?"

"The *New York Times* and *New York Magazine*."

Kip was suddenly interested, although he still pretended not to be. "Is that so? I guess we could be a little experimental."

"In our production, the actor playing Hamlet is dead. That's about as experimental as it gets."

"Shall I direct?"

"Kip, I'm directing. My theater now, my rules."

"I'm glad Tad likes feisty women. He takes after me."

It was agreed, they would perform with a small cast. But even more complicated, Rhi needed actors who could see Kip. At a point in her life when she wanted to reject her roots, she needed to draw on them. Her extended Wiccan family was filled with actors and performers. Spellcrafting often involved great performance and theatrics, so it was natural that the arts and magical crafts often went together.

Rhi thought long and hard about who could help her. Toby was an obvious choice for lighting design, while his girlfriend Darna was both a gifted actress and seer. Ren agreed to stage manage. Apparently her grandmother read tea leaves, so she didn't think the reason for the performance strange at all. Finn would do sound. Rhi's friend Anton was both a witch and a Julliard graduate, while an old friend from Columbia, Juan, was one of the most powerful psychics she knew. Both were working regularly in TV and film and Anton had just been signed for a pilot.

"I'd prefer if no one knew about this," he said. "They're predicting big things for this series I'm in and I don't want me being a witch to overshadow my work on that."

"I hear you, Anton. And I promise, this is a closed performance, with only family and friends who are practitioners of the craft in the audience."

"You aren't inviting Dee Dee Duprey are you?"

"Goddess, no. She always puts her celebrity gossip column before the craft."

"Okay, count me in."

Word spread around the small but diverse community of witch actors that a very unusual production of *Hamlet* was casting. Rhi received about two dozen calls, which were whittled down to a list of seven who were willing to drive to Hamlet to audition.

"Won't you be holding auditions in New York?" asked one actress.

"Impossible. The actors need to meet our Hamlet and he can't travel."

"He sounds difficult."

Never truer words spoken, thought Rhi as she sat through the casting process, listening to Kip bitch and moan. She'd grown to care deeply about him. She enjoyed his company. He often had her in hysterics. He was handsome—Rhi had to stop herself from staring, he was so exquisitely carved—but right now he also reminded her that she hadn't heard from Tad. No one had. And she was worried. She didn't mention anything to Kip—he was unbearable enough when he was stressed. So she kept her mouth shut, and tried not to look at him too often. Difficult to do when he was sprawled out across three seats near her. Instead, she focused on the actors who were making their way out onto the stage one by one.

"Clare, first let's talk about your physic abilities. Can you see anyone but me in this room?"

Clare pointed to Kip. "Him."

Kip slapped a hand across his face and covered his eyes, as if it was too much to witness. "I have a name."

"And how would you explain your gifts, Clare?" Rhi continued.

"I'm clairaudient, clairvoyant and clairsentient."

Kip burst into howls of laughter. "No pun intended, right?"

Rhi cracked up too, covering her face with her clipboard. She couldn't help it. Kip made her laugh.

Clare looked baffled. "Did I say something funny?"

"The whole 'My name is Clare and I'm clairvoyant, clair-sentient' thing is a scream," said Kip.

"Oh, I'd never even thought about that."

Kip turned his attention away from her and shouted, "Next!"

A confused Clare was hustled out the door and in her place came Yolo, in his early twenties. Kip took an immediate dislike to him and vice versa.

"What sort of name is Yolo? You don't look Asian," Kip snapped.

"It's my life motto, dude, and it kind of caught on so now everyone calls me Yolo: you only live once."

Kip rolled his eyes. "I could argue that, but what joy would I gain from waging wits with you?"

"Let's just concentrate on the scene I gave you, between Hamlet and Horatio," Rhi suggested.

"So you want me to read this Hamlet dude?" Yolo asked.

"Oh for heaven's sake, the man is a twit." Kip turned to Yolo. "I know you act like you had a roof fall on your head, but since that actually happened to me, Hamlet is mine."

"Okay, chill. I'll read Horace."

"Horatio," Rhi corrected.

Kip tilted his head back and relayed the lines. Even in his frustration, he was superb.

"So much for this, sir: now shall you see the other; You do remember all the circumstance?"

Yolo followed from the script. "Yeah, like remember it, my lord?"

Kip threw his hands into the air. "Enough. I refuse to share the stage with this barbarian. He's crucifying the Bard's language."

"Fine by me, dude. You take it all too seriously, anyway," Yolo said dismissively, leaving the stage.

"Of course I take it seriously, you imbecile. I was killed during this play. It tends to color things."

Kip was furious with Rhi. "Where did you find him?"

"Through a friend. He channels."

"I want to change channels every time he opens his mouth."

"Settle down, you'll have a coronary," Rhi teased and then pretended she realized something. "Oh no, already dead, so rage away."

"Ha ha. And I won't settle down. I'm absolutely amazed that anyone on the spiritual plane would use that dipstick as a vessel to pass on wisdom. Please tell me the next actor is of a higher caliber."

"Kip, beggars can't be choosers. Actors who can also see ghosts are a little thin on the ground."

"Rubbish. I spent years around actors and they'll all tell you how they've seen a ghost at some stage. They're metaphysically open by nature."

"They also all like to drink and talk crap."

Fortunately, Kip liked the next applicant. Perhaps a little too much.

"Jessica. That's a pretty name."

"Thanks."

"Do you get a lot of work, Jessica? You should. You're stunning."

"I'm focused on taking character roles at the moment."

"Are you nuts? You're a knockout. Milk it, you foolish girl."

"I'm looking for longevity in the industry."

Kip snorted. "So was I, and look where it got me. I should've taken that pretty-boy role on *Days of Our Lives*...but no, I wanted to be a serious actor. Can't get much more serious than being stuck in a regional theater for thirty fucking years."

Jessica didn't bat a long eyelash. "Yeah, well, if I find myself in a similar situation, I know who to call."

Kip didn't miss a beat. "Ghostbusters?"

Jessica cracked up, and both Rhi and Kip joined in.

"I like her," Kip shouted to the stars. "Give her the role."

The cast was announced. Rhi would play Ophelia and Osric. The other main characters were divvied up between Darna, Jessica, Anton and Juan. There were just a few minor characters left, but they'd run out of options of who should play them.

"Chandler Wheeler," Kip said.

"The local Chandler Wheeler, who occasionally reads tarots at Crystal's shop?"

"That one. He will do it for me. He was a friend."

Rhi tried to be diplomatic. "He's not the greatest tarot reader. He's a little hit and miss."

"Same goes for his acting. But he'll understand what's happening and he will support me."

It turned out that Chandler was more than happy to be involved. He was very emotional when Rhi explained what was going on. When he heard that Kip had been stuck in the theater all these years, he burst into tears.

"If only I knew he was there. Oh darling Kip, what a fine man he was. A good and dear friend. I will do whatever I can to help him."

Rhi realized why Kip liked Chandler so much. The guy worshipped him.

Rhi plotted out the play, and worked out ways for the cast to make simple, quick changes from character to character.

"We'll talk to Toby about lighting. We won't use elaborate costumes."

"I'll have to wear this." Kip waved his hands down his body. "I'm a little bored with it but have no choice."

"Oh, I've never noticed," Rhi teased.

"Ha ha."

"I think we'll all wear something similar."

"My advice would be to wear something fabulous, just in case you die halfway through."

"Do you always have to be flippant?"

"Flippant? I'm being thoughtful. You do not want to be wearing cheap nylon for all eternity."

The actors were emailed the edited script and would arrive in Hamlet the following Monday for two weeks of rehearsals. Annie had arranged their housing. It wasn't going to be easy.

Not only would they be learning lines in an inordinately short space of time, but they'd also be performing opposite a dead man. They were gifted actors, and each of them was excited about the challenge. They saw this as a spiritual exercise as much as a theatrical one. But mostly, like the good theater folk they were, every single one of them knew that this experience would be grade-A dinner party fodder for years to come. And being part of a good story was priceless.

Chapter 39

Annie had "Song to the Siren" on a loop. The Cocteau Twins blared out from her iPod and filled the car with heartbreak. Spurred on by her soundtrack, Annie sobbed, tossing one soggy tissue after another into a pile at her feet. She'd just seen Sal going into Knight and Day Music, which had triggered the wave of misery that was now engulfing her. She'd managed to drive to the far end of the beach and park away from prying eyes, and then this—half an hour of uncontrollable howling. What the hell was wrong with her?

Love, that's what. Damn fool.

She knew it couldn't last forever. She knew one of them would eventually meet someone, move on, and change the dynamic. But why'd it have to be him?

She'd always adored both Jake and Sam. They'd been great friends growing up. Annie had been a bit of a tomboy, and the brothers were a fantastic fit for her as playmates: smart, sporty, a little bit naughty, and lots of fun.

It wasn't until she was a senior in high school that their relationship first shifted. She went to the prom with Jake, who was in her year. At the end of the night he kissed her. It was her first ever kiss and it was utterly perfect.

Unfortunately someone had spiked the prom punch and not long after the kiss, Jake passed out. Big brother Sam came to the rescue and gave them a lift home. Jake was sprawled across the back seat. Annie was in the front with Sam, hands on her lap, her mind a million miles away—or rather, back at the school hall, reliving the kiss. Sam, ever the gentleman, walked her to her front door and then, to her utter surprise, pulled her into his arms and kissed her too.

"Couldn't help myself, curly. You look gorgeous in that dress."

Annie's legs held until she reached her room, where they buckled and she spent the night tossing and turning in confusion. The following morning she went to the beach with a group of friends, including Sam and Jake. There was no mention of either kiss.

And that was that. The three continued their friendship, but now it was filled with flirting. The brothers were competing for the affections of the same girl, and yet it never affected their own relationship, probably because she never chose one brother over the other.

Years passed, until a final shift, not long ago, when a slow dawning occurred. Annie was at a stage in life where she was starting to think about marriage and babies. Her career was secure and she loved it. Financially, she was doing well. She was generally happy. She wanted a family. And whenever she imagined that family, one man's face kept appearing. Only one.

She'd tried to ignore it. She'd even attempted to block it out with booze, but she wasn't a very committed alcoholic—it didn't suit her. He suited her. Perfectly. And the more she tried to block him from her mind, the more he interrupted her thoughts.

She considered telling him how she felt, but how, after a lifetime of being three, could she change it to two? Someone she cared about deeply would get hurt. The dynamic between them all would irrevocably change. She'd never once considered for a moment that he was actually interested in someone else.

Annie liked Sal. She was a great gal. But dammit it—she wanted him!

Annie tossed another wet tissue on the floor, just as someone tapped on the window. She jumped, and realised Taran was staring through the passenger side window.

"You okay?" he mouthed.

Annie smiled. It was as fake as her fingernails. She was too embarrassed to wind the window down. It didn't deter him. He opened the door and slid into the passenger seat.

"Cockteau Twins? Would you like to borrow my razor?"

Annie turned the music down. "Why not? It's clear you're not using it."

Taran ran his hand over his stubbled chin. "I haven't been sleeping. Or shaving."

"Anything wrong?"

Taran stretched his legs out as far as her small car would allow. "I've got a lot of stuff on my mind. How about you?"

"I just needed a howl and what better place for that than a public car park?"

"Couldn't make it home?"

Annie shook her head, tears threatening to explode again.

"Want to tell me what's going on?"

"No."

"Okay."

And with that she burst into tears. "I'm in love with someone I don't want to be in love with," she wailed.

Taran reached out and took her into his arms. "Yeah, I know how you feel. So am I."

Annie pulled back. "You are? Who?"

"Her name's Calypso. She's English, but we met in New York and I fell for her, big time. Anyway, I told her and

245

she disappeared. Gave me a kiss, sent me into the shower, and when I got out she was gone."

"Ouch."

"Yep."

Annie pulled her hair off her face. The curls were sticking to her wet cheeks. "You didn't go after her?"

"No... I retreated to lick my wounds." Taran grinned at Annie. "I figured I'd get over her, but it's been a year and I haven't. And then I've just had this offer from a gallery in London that wants to exhibit my work. Huge opportunity for me but it would mean living there for a few months.

"And that's where she lives?"

"Correct."

"You can at least see her and ask why she just took off."

"Not sure my ego could take another battering."

Annie gave his arm a pat and teased. "Oh, I don't know, Taran, it's pretty huge. A few dents won't do it any harm."

"Thanks. You've made me feel so much better. How about you? Are you going to confront the guy you're crying over? Tell him how you feel?"

Annie pulled a face. "I want to...but..."

"But?"

"He's met someone else."

Taran passed Annie another tissue. "Then Annie, you'd better get in there quick."

Chapter 40

The theater was suddenly filled with life, a little jarring after being tainted by death and on the brink demolition for so long. But the changes suited it. Rhi had her office set up and the phone connected, and other companies were now calling to enquire about the space. The Hamlet Majestic was officially open for business.

Rhi had hired Annabelle Hampton to teach dance and Vaniqua was teaching a Saturday morning singing class. Children were being herded in and out of classes. The foyer was filled with laughter, running, and parents' raised voices. Any stress Rhi initially felt about the classes quickly vanished once they began. She enjoyed being with the kids and they certainly had fun. By the second week, her numbers had doubled thanks to word of mouth.

The theater was rarely dark. The *Hamlet* actors were there late into the night, drinking black coffee and rehearsing their scenes over and over. Everyone was off script from the very first rehearsal, which was incredible—unheard of—and helped ease the pressure of the terribly short rehearsal period. She'd spoken to each member of the cast individually: this wasn't a career move; this was almost like a charity gig. They all joked about what could be printed on the tickets.

Hamlet to Help the Ghost Pass Over.

The Ghostly Gala.

The Phantom Fundraiser.

Half-price spirits after the show.

Many of the normal opening night stresses didn't exist. It was a one-off performance in front of a hand-picked audience chosen for their psychic abilities, not their industry contacts. They wouldn't be there to evaluate the play, but to exorcize Hamlet. And although the cast gelled right from the start, it was not intended to be an ensemble piece. There was one star, and that was Kip.

And he knew it.

"Kip, I think you should move downstage for that exchange."

"When I directed this play I blocked this scene upstage."

"I'm blocking it differently," Rhi said.

Kip wouldn't budge. "I don't feel it. The motivation's not there to move downstage."

"Then how about you do this crazy little trick I picked up at drama school called *acting*."

"Are you asking me to fake my emotion?"

"Kip, can you stop bitching? You're driving me mad."

"Good. Use it for Ophelia. That last run through you did, she didn't seem mad at all."

The rest of the cast was exceedingly patient with him. Jessica laughed at him at lot, while Darna flirted, two approaches that defused him every time. Kip liked Anton and was a little wary of Juan's powerful psychic abilities, so he never picked on him. And Chandler, the weak link in the play, received nothing but encouragement.

"Chandler, if you can enter stage right...yes, that's right, and now deliver that line directly to Hamlet." Rhi waited for him to do it. "Ah...the line, Chandler."

Chandler stood on stage, face to face with Kip. They were both silent for a moment. Finally Kip turned to Rhi.

"He can't see me."

She noticed that Chandler had no reaction to that, which meant he couldn't hear him either. She moved to the corner of the room and motioned for Kip to join her for a private chat.

"This is going to be a problem," Rhi whispered.

"Give the guy a break," snapped Kip. "He'll be alright on the night."

"Perhaps we can recast his roles?"

Kip's eyes flashed angrily. "Chandler was there for me last time. He'll be there on the night."

Rhi took a deep, calming breath. It didn't help, but she returned to the others anyway. "Okay, we'll block these scenes very carefully. Chandler, if you can see Kip during the performance, great. But if not, you'll know exactly where he is, as long as he hits his mark."

Chandler spoke to thin air in front of him, unaware that Kip was now floating just above his head. "I'm good with that. How about you, Kip?"

The cast rehearsed hour after hour, day after day. Around them, friends rallied to build sets. Vaniqua was running front of house. Hilary was sewing costumes. Toby, who'd come up with Darna, was getting the tech box ready to go.

Each night, Rhi went home to the cottage, where she'd have dinner with Taran and then fall into an exhausted sleep. Exhausted but content. She was filling her days with things she loved. She was busy, and often stressed, but not for one second did she regret taking any of this on.

There were only two things marring her happiness: Tad and Kip. Tad, because no one had heard from him, and she missed him. And Kip, because she knew he too was about to disappear from her life. They'd become friends. And it was going to be hard to let that go.

Chapter 41

Crystal watched as Manhattan came into view out the window as the train made its way into Penn Station. How had it been two years since she'd made this trip? She still loved this city. She couldn't live here again, but it would always hold a piece of her heart.

She'd been born and raised in Brooklyn by her mother and her mother's sister, both witches who kept to themselves. Her aunt had never married, and had moved to be with Crystal's mother after she was widowed when Crystal was only a baby. Crystal's father had been a policeman who'd died on the job, so her mother lived off a small pension and the readings they did. It had been a fairly normal childhood, considering. People respected the sisters and didn't bother them. They were low key and didn't like to draw attention to themselves. They were involved in the community when needed, but never stuck their noses into other people's business. They were both loving women who hugged a lot and laughed loudly. And at home, behind closed doors, they worshipped the Goddess. Crystal grew up knowing two things: women were strong, and the craft was personal.

Her mother and aunt died, in that order, not long after she'd graduated college. Crystal was grief stricken, but keeping in mind how strong her parents expected her to be, she moved into Manhattan to start a new life. She found a ratty old two-bedroom apartment that with some elbow grease and creativity turned into a quirky home. She advertised for a roommate, knowing it wasn't good for a woman her age to live alone. She needed a bit of a push to be social. Three people answered the ad. One was Brigid, who had just arrived in New York from London.

It had been one of those meetings that both young women just knew was fated. Their first meeting was like looking into the eyes of a long-lost friend. That's what they believed they were. And they became inseparable. Crystal forgave Brigid's shortcomings. She could be moody. She was vain and self-absorbed. She never did any housework. Crystal forgave it all, because Brigid made her laugh. She forgave it all because Brigid could be great company. But mostly, she forgave it all because without Brigid, she was alone.

Until that night when Brigid did the unforgivable, and stole Kip from her. Of course Crystal knew that no man could be stolen; Kip had made himself available and was just as guilty. But men would fail women over and over again. Women should never betray their friends.

The train came to a standstill and Crystal made her way through the carriage and onto the concourse. She was swallowed by the crowd and thrust into the bowels of hell that was Penn Station. Her mother used to tell her about how it was once a grand old station, the most beautiful building in Manhattan. But all that had been destroyed. "In the name of progress," her mother would hiss each time they were there. "They call this progress?"

Memories of her mother gave her strength, something Crystal needed right now. She eventually found her way out of the station and flagged a cab. She'd forgotten how busy the city was. Her whole life spent traversing its streets and then they were so easily forgotten when she left.

"East Eighty-first thanks."

The driver pulled into traffic, which was heavy. It had taken Crystal two weeks to garner the courage to make this trip. Rehearsals for *Hamlet* were winding up and the performance was tomorrow. Kip was keeping up his side of the bargain: he was performing. Now it was her turn. She needed to make sure he'd cross over.

She dug through her purse and pulled out her cosmetics bag. She flipped open a mirror and sighed. Never a kind sight under the harsh light of day. She'd been so gorgeous once. Did the mirror know that? Surely if it did it wouldn't be so cruel now. She combed her hair and put on some fresh lipstick. What else could she do? She wished there was an effective anti-aging spell. Concealer was as close as she'd get. She shoved the makeup back into her bag. No point getting worked up over a few wrinkles. This was who she was now.

She thought back to the day Kip had arrived at her small shop with Tad in his arms. There wasn't a single second she didn't know for sure that she'd take him back. But she did it slowly. She'd made him work for it. She'd made him prove he was worthy. And, to be fair, he had been.

They'd started as friends. She came to rely on him as much as he did on her. He helped her move into her new shop. He fixed her toilet, and put an extra lock on her door, and mixed a mean cocktail. For over four years she loved him as a friend, while together they spent time with Tad. She was Aunt Crystal. Weekends were spent at Central Park. She babysat Tad when Kip had a casting or a rare job.

She figured Kip had other women, but he never flaunted them, never discussed them; most weekends were spent with her. And then he found the theater in Hamlet. He was so excited about the prospect of a life there with Tad. It was in that excitement, and her enthusiastic support, mixed with a bottle of wine, that they became lovers again. The minute he touched her she felt like she was home after a long and arduous journey. His scent, his breath, his body—all as familiar as anything in this world. It was her world.

Once their bodies reconnected, they both knew there was no going back. But still she encouraged him to move north, promising to visit. And she did visit. And then again. This time their love was more respectful. He was still a flirt, but Crystal began to trust that it wouldn't go any further because he valued her. She'd become indispensible. He was still unpredictable and crazy and self-centered. But he was passionate in his feelings for her, and often talked of their future together.

Brigid's name occasionally came up. He never was able to shake the feeling that she'd cursed him. In his mind, Crystal was his savior. The good witch. Who always defeated the bad. Only Crystal knew the truth.

A sob caught in her throat, but she shook it off. Not now. This was no pity party. She paid the driver then made her way up the brownstone's steps, and rang the doorbell. She braced herself—it was time to admit how she'd failed Kip. It wouldn't be easy. There was only one person who could help to free him. The door opened and the two old friends came face to face for the first time in nearly thirty years.

"Hello, Brigid."

Chapter 42

Brigid was not prepared for this. She should've been. She didn't need to be psychic to know it was inevitable, especially now that Rhi's path had crossed with Crystal's. They were bound to meet again.

At first, Crystal's appearance shocked her. She'd aged, of course, but she'd done nothing obvious to delay the march of time. No cosmetic work. No dermas and fillers. And she'd certainly piled on the pounds. But then, in a second, more careful look at the woman she'd once been so close to, Brigid saw the vivacity on her face. Years of laughter and lust for life, something she occasionally searched her own face for in the mirror. She'd accidentally erased all that. Or her dermatologist had. If it had ever been there to begin with.

Crystal was wearing black pants, a gray blouse and a beautifully cut black-and-white patterned jacket over the top, but still her ample cleavage threatened to spill. Lucky thing. Brigid had had to buy her breasts. Crystal's hair looked messed up, in a delightful way. Mostly, Crystal still looked like she'd just tumbled out of bed after a marathon shag. So despite, or perhaps because of, the ample curves and laughter lines, Crystal looked sexier now than she had at twenty-five, and she'd been a showstopper then.

Brigid was immediately envious.

"You look fabulous, Brigid."

"I look like every other woman over fifty who visits Dr Godfrey." Brigid waited for Crystal to say something. She didn't. Brigid was grateful that Lugh was out for the day. Whatever this was about, she didn't want him to know. "You had best come in," she finally said.

Brigid led Crystal through the entrance and along the hall. She glanced around at her home, wondering what Crystal thought of the understated antiques, or the living room she'd just had decorated in whites and neutral shades. The fireplace, the curtains, the walls, everything was a brilliant white. The sofas were a delicious taupe, apart from one oversized chair covered in animal print fabric.

Brigid watched Crystal for a reaction, but there wasn't one. Even now she couldn't impress Crystal. She didn't even seem to notice the brass pentacles on the light fittings or the foot-high statue of the Goddess Brigid carved from marble in the corner.

Brigid led Crystal over to the bay windows and two French Rococo chairs, with a small table in between. She could watch for Lugh coming home from here.

"Would you like some tea? Or water?"

Crystal shook her head. "I won't take up too much of your time."

Thanks Goddess for that, thought Brigid.

Crystal appeared to be nervous. She stared out the window at the street below. "Rhi is lovely."

"I'm aware of that. She's my daughter."

Crystal perked up a bit. "Are you going to be a bitch?"

"It seems to be my natural state of late."

"Of late?" Crystal sniffed.

"Listen, Crystal, you're in my house, taking up my time, so get to it."

"Firstly, Rhi is happy up there. She's made good friends and she's worked her butt off to renovate that theater."

Despite herself, Brigid felt a surge of pride. "That's nice but it's not her home."

"It is now. And she gets to make that decision, not you. You cut her money off and outed her as a witch, and still she's soldiered on and made something of her life up there."

"Thanks for the update on my daughter."

"She's in love, you know," Crystal said. "With Kip's son."

"You can't be serious. Please tell me he's not an alley cat like his father?"

"Imagine all Kip's decent qualities and none of the ego or vanity."

"You didn't come here to tell me about my daughter's love life."

"No...I came to talk about Kip," Crystal said.

Brigid was annoyed now. "Crystal, get over it. It all happened so long ago. I've moved on."

"So have I—but Kip hasn't. He's haunting the theater."

Brigid felt the room tilt off balance. "He's haunting Rhiannon's theater?"

"Yes."

"You've seen him."

"Yes."

"Has Rhi?"

"Yes."

Brigid spoke in controlled but very icy tones. "Does she know?"

"She knows nothing."

"Oh, come on. Surely you've told her about us."

"No."

This shocked Brigid. "You haven't?'

"I knew you wouldn't want me to."

"You knew, did you? Like you know me now."

"I believe I still do. Your desperate attempts to get her to leave Hamlet indicated how you felt about Rhi being near me. But mostly, people don't change."

"Kip has."

"Not as much as you'd think."

"So she knows nothing of us, or Kip?"

"She knows nothing of you and Kip. That's your story to tell, Brigid, not mine. However, she does know about Kip and me. She's friends with our daughter."

Brigid didn't say anything for the longest time. Memories surfaced, the late night banging on the door. Crystal on her doorstep, looking swollen, her eyes, her breasts.

*

"He's dead, Brigid." Crystal's face was a mask of pure pain.

"Shhh, you'll wake my boys." Brigid didn't let her in. Instead, she stepped onto the doorstep. "What's going on?"

"Kip is dead."

Brigid felt it like a kick to the guts. The breath was knocked from her body.

"The stage ceiling collapsed on him. He's gone."

Brigid actually took Crystal into her arms then, for what else could she do? But she didn't shed a tear herself. She was afraid that if she did, she'd never stop.

Finally, Crystal drew breath. "I thought you should know."

"Thank you. Yes." Brigid looked at Crystal's bust, more swollen than ever. "Crystal, are you...?"

"Am I?"

Brigid realized she couldn't bear the answer she knew she'd get. So instead she said, "Are you going to be okay?"

"I'm going to try." Crystal turned and disappeared down the street.

*

"Yes, I suspected you were pregnant that night you came to tell me he'd died. What's her name?"

"Tye."

Brigid's face remained composed, but she'd be lying if she said this information didn't hurt. She'd loved Kip. She'd known from the very start that he wasn't hers, but the heart wants what it wants. She turned and stared out the window.

"Why are you here?"

"Kip was killed before he got to the end of *Hamlet*."

"I know."

"Rhi is in rehearsals with him right now, to finish the play. She's cast some Wiccan actors and they're performing *Hamlet* to an audience of psychics, so Kip can finish the play and cross over."

"I'd be very careful about who else you relay that information to. People get locked up for less."

"You obviously haven't received an invitation."

Brigid wasn't going to let Crystal know that Lugh had mentioned an invitation to Rhi's opening night, but that she'd taken no notice because she had no intention of going. "I'm busy at the moment. I don't have time to be traipsing all the way up there."

"Surely you want Rhi to succeed?"

"Of course I do."

"Well, her first play will bomb. He won't cross over. None of this will work. He's not trapped there because he didn't get to finish the play. He's trapped there because of us."

"Us? There is no *us*."

"You cursed him."

Brigid glanced at the door and then the street below the window, afraid someone would overhear. "We've talked about this. Years ago. Why are you bringing it up again?"

Crystal's eyes welled up with tears. "Because I didn't tell him."

The color rose in Brigid's face. "You continued to let him believe I cursed him?"

"Yes. I didn't want him going back to you. When he was afraid of you, he needed me."

"Kip died thinking I cursed him?" Her voice grew louder.

"I'm sorry, Brigid."

Brigid stood, towering over Crystal. "Get out of my house."

Crystal didn't move. "All I ask is that you come and talk to him. He needs to hear it from you. Tell him the truth."

"I told you the truth that night, even though I knew it could be the end of everything I'd worked for."

"I've never told a living soul. Ever."

"You were meant to tell one. Him." Brigid was furious. "You cursed him more than I did. You have his blood on your hands, not me."

Crystal grabbed her purse and walked quickly from the house without uttering another word.

It was only after she'd slammed the door on her that Brigid fell to her knees and finally cried for Kip.

*

Outside on the pavement, Crystal was doubled over. She couldn't breathe. Oh Goddess, don't let her die here, on Brigid's doorstep. Even though she knew she deserved to. Brigid was right. She had Kip's blood on her hands.

"Are you okay?"

Crystal looked up into the face of Taran's brother. She knew it was him, not only because they were identical in all but coloring, but also because she recognized him from the dozens of drawings Tye had made of him over the years.

"I live in Hamlet," she managed to say.

"You know Rhi?"

"I do. And Taran." She drew strength from his kind eyes. "You need to go to Hamlet immediately. My daughter has been dreaming of you her whole life."

Finn didn't question her. He didn't falter. He simply said, "Would you like a lift home? I could do with the company on the drive up there."

Chapter 43

Crystal watched the full moon rise over Connecticut from the passenger seat window in Finn's car. They were already firm friends.

"You don't have to stop for anything? Clothes, a tooth-brush?" Crystal had asked.

"I have a bag in the trunk."

"Are you always that prepared?"

"I was on the way to Hamlet tonight anyway. Rhi asked me to help with the show tomorrow. I was just dropping by to see if Dad wanted a lift. I entered through the poor door, as Mom always calls it."

Crystal had no idea what he meant.

"The house was built with a maid's entrance," Finn explained. "It's rarely used now, but we kids used it when we were teens. Anyway, it was the only key I had on me, so I let myself in and overheard you and Mom."

Crystal put her hands to her face. "Brigid will be so furious with me."

"Not to mention how Kip will feel."

Crystal's chest felt tight again. "I've made such a mess of things."

Finn laughed, glanced at her and then returned his gaze to the road. "We've always known about Mom. Do you think my father wouldn't quickly realize that she was a powerless witch? But he loves her so much that he's always let her think he has no idea. He covers for her when they work. Taran also picked it up years ago, and so my father sat us both down, told us the truth, and said if we ever let on to Mom, he'd skin us alive."

"She has no idea."

"Not that I'm aware of."

"Does Rhi know about her?"

"I don't think so."

"If this got out…if the press caught wind of it…"

"I know. She'd be ruined. But the only people who know care about her enough to never say a word."

Crystal knew that was true. She'd watched Brigid's rise to fame and although she knew she held knowledge that could bring her down, she'd never considered it, not even for a moment. She was pleased Brigid had got what she'd so desperately wanted. All their history, all the heartache…and Crystal had never wanted anything but good things for her. "So you heard everything?"

"Enough. And Rhi had told me a few things about this Kip guy. I've pieced together enough to know what's going on in Hamlet," Finn said. "Can I ask why you didn't tell him about the curse?"

Crystal stared out the window. "I guess I loved him too much."

*

"Kip says you cursed him when you found out about Collette."

Brigid slammed the door shut so her new boyfriend Lugh couldn't hear them.

"So what if I did?"

"Then you need to lift it. He's obsessed with the idea that he's going to die, and he has a baby now."

Brigid was distressed. She paced the room. *"He actually thinks I cursed him? That I would do that?"*

"He does."

"You say it's affecting him? How?"

"He's depressed. He's fearful. He's thinking he should give Tad back to Collette, in case something happens to him."

"Oh for fuck's sake!" Brigid placed her hand on her flat stomach. "I'm pregnant. Twins apparently."

"To Lugh?"

"Of course to Lugh."

"Congratulations. I didn't think he was your type." Crystal couldn't help herself. She'd always had foot in mouth.

"I was wrong. We've got our radio show and a new magazine column and Lugh is in talks for a book deal for us both."

Crystal smiled. "Then he is your type."

Brigid glanced at the door. "I'm telling you all this so you know that I've got a new life. It's the one I've always wanted."

"I'm pleased for you, Brigid." She actually was. Although she had no idea what this all had to do with Kip.

"I didn't curse him."

"Then why does he say you did?"

"I pretended to. I went through the theatrics. I shrieked and pointed and summoned different demons."

"Brigid, that sounds like a curse to me. And it shows. He's scared."

Brigid moved toward Crystal. "I'm going to tell you something now that could ruin everything I'm working for. I need to trust you."

"I think I've shown I'm trustworthy."

"Share this information with Kip, the best way you know how, but then I ask that you never utter it to another living soul."

"You have my word."

"Ever! I'm serious."

"I hear you."

"And after tonight, stay away from me. I don't want to be reminded that you know this."

"Know what?"

Brigid stepped forward and whispered. "I can't curse."

"Why not?"

"I have no magic."

Crystal's eyes bulged. "You're a powerless witch?"

"Don't you fucking tell anyone."

"I said I wouldn't."

"It's why I left London. My parents kept it a secret but I could always see the disappointment in their eyes. My lineage is virtually royal in the witch world."

"I know." It was Crystal's turn to glance at the door. "Does Lugh know?"

"Absolutely not. No one but my parents and now you. Lugh is powerful enough for both of us, and I'm good enough at faking it. But...there is no way I can curse someone." Brigid's eyes narrowed. "And if you ever tell another living soul apart from Kip, I'll learn to curse."

"Why tell me? Is it because you're pregnant? You feel for him?" Crystal was surprised by Brigid's compassion.

"No, you naïve idiot. It's because I'm in love with him. Probably always will be."

Crystal decided Kip didn't need to know anything of her visit to Brigid.

*

"I was so insecure. So worried he'd go back to Brigid. I wanted him to need me..." Crystal felt weary. "It sounds pathetic to me now, but I was so young."

Finn reached out and gave her hand a squeeze. "You weren't to know he was going to die. And he didn't die because of that. Two separate things. A bit of bad luck really."

"But he's been stuck for thirty years because of it. Just thinking he's been cursed was enough to trap him." Her voice wavered. "I'm so ashamed."

"Everyone makes mistakes, Crystal. Just think...you have the opportunity to fix this one."

"True. I hadn't thought about it like that." She smiled at him. "I'm very pleased I ran into you today. So are you going to be in the audience?"

"Rhi has asked me to do sound. Should be an interesting gig."

"She said it'll be a full house."

"It'll be like the New York Psychic Fair." Finn gave Crystal a cheeky smile. "So is your daughter attractive?"

"I feel like a marriage broker. I'll give her to you for four camels."

"She must be attractive. I've never paid *four* camels for a woman before."

Crystal let out a husky laugh. She liked Finn. He had a good heart and a good sense of humor. What more could one ask for? Oh and those looks. While Taran was sex-on-a-stick, Finn was gloriously golden. He had all of Taran's features, but on Finn they looked like the boy next door. He was approachable. Not that she disliked Taran—she liked him a lot based on the few times she'd met him, but he was a predator while his twin was a loyal pup.

Finn pointed to a sign for Hamlet. "Not long to go."

Crystal curled up on her seat and decided to enjoy these last miles with Finn. She wasn't looking forward to facing Kip. "Drive slowly," she said to Finn. "I'm in no rush."

Chapter 44

Tye used Rhi's key to open the backstage door. She was so nervous her hands were shaking. She shone the torch into back of house to get her bearings, and then walked over to the backstage lights and switched them on. It was so quiet she could hear a pin drop. The place smelled of fresh paint, and looked shiny and clean, but still there was an eerie air to the place, being there alone.

"Hello? Kip?"

She opened the door to the dressing room where Rhi said he often hung out, but it was empty. She checked the second dressing room, behind the proscenium, on stage and then in the auditorium. She switched on light after light.

"Kip? It's Tye…Crystal's daughter. Your daughter." She ran upstairs, a trail of light in her wake. "I want to meet you."

The foyer was empty, the bathroom was empty, Rhi's office was empty. Eventually the whole theater was alight, but Kip was nowhere to be found.

Tye retreated, going back over her path, flicking off one light after another, checking each room one last time. Finally, she stood at the backstage door again, unable to speak now. All that anticipation and excitement and hope for nothing.

She flicked off the final light and closed the door behind her, unaware that she had been watched every step of the way.

*

Kip drifted to the door, listening as she locked it from the other side.

His daughter. That was his daughter.

She was beautiful.

He floated to the base of the door, his hand pressed against it...he couldn't feel the door, but he could feel her. How badly he wanted to swing that door open and yell, "Wait for me, Tye!" He'd give anything to run outside to her, to walk along the beach, to wave to people as they passed him by, seeing him...How he missed the world.

"Tye...I see you." His words were nothing but wisps of wind. He was nothing but a shadow. He wanted to show himself to her, but how could he? He couldn't allow her only memory of him to be this. This outline was no father. No image for her to hold on to and draw strength from. No. Crystal would tell her stories of him. Tad could show her photos. Those things were real.

This wasn't. He wasn't.

As much as he wanted to have a conversation with her, the only gift he could ever give her now, as her father, was to be invisible.

Kip drifted around the door for hours, wishing there was something more than death that could swallow him, and take him away from his pain.

*

Annie flicked the TV off and checked her phone. Nothing. She hadn't heard from either Sam or Jake for a few days. It was her own fault; ever since the clambake, she'd been distant. They all needed to date other people, and she'd finally said exactly that to them. There'd been an immediate shift. She'd run into Jake near work and he'd been a quite distant. And then tonight, as she was driving home, she'd seen Sam's car outside Sal's restaurant. Damn them. They were all just friends, right? Always had been. You didn't cut friends off. Why were they rejecting her now?

She picked up her phone and pressed Jake's number. It went straight to voicemail. "Hi Jake...it's me...just calling to say hi."

She hung up and cringed. "Hi! *Hi!* Idiot." No, she wouldn't let her friendships be changed by this. She dialed Sam's number. This time, he answered.

"Hey, curly, what's up?"

She smiled at his use of her childhood nickname. "Just wondering how you are? Haven't seen you for a few days. I miss your ugly head."

"Just busy that's all."

Annie could hear laughter in the background, more than one person and definitely a woman. "Sorry, have I interrupted something?"

"I'm over at Jake's. Sal is here. Come over."

I'd rather wash my eyes with acid, thought Annie. "I would, but I'm exhausted. I'm already in my pajamas. It's been a big week at work. Say hello to everyone though."

"I will."

"Okay. See ya."

"See ya, curly."

She turned her phone off and sat motionless for a second, before hurling it against the wall and watching it smash to pieces.

*

Rhi sat in her garden reading her emails on her iPad. It was a beautiful warm evening. Even the sun was taking its time to go inside.

There were more responses to her Hamlet invite, most of them affirmative. It looked like she'd pull in a full house for the show.

And then she saw the email from Victoria. Her first reaction was to trash it, but years of friendship and months of hurt made her read it.

Dear Rhiannon,

I'm hoping you'll read this. I know your first reaction will be to trash it. I'm currently in the Hope Springs Rehabilitation Facility. I've been here for a month, and am going very well in an alcohol recovery program. At this stage of my recovery, I am to contact anyone I've hurt as a result of my drinking. It's a long list, I'm embarrassed to say. But you are at the top.

What I did to you was unforgivable. I know I betrayed your trust, and never expect that to heal. I've been carrying a lot of pain for a long time, which Dad's death magnified. I felt like that pain gave me the right to do whatever I wanted. I've discovered it didn't. Chandra, along with numerous other men during that time, made me feel adored, for a brief second, and that feeling was addictive and seductive, and therefore I easily crossed lines for the sake of it, with no thought of the pain it would later cause. And by pain, I not only mean yours, but also mine. Losing you from my life has been unfathomable. But at least it was the thing that got me seeking help.

I am so dreadfully sorry for hurting you. I can only hope that your new life out of New York has brought you happiness.

Victoria

Rhi stared at the email for a moment and analyzed how it made her feel. She realized the betrayal and hurt had passed. There was a shred of sadness there for the death of the friendship, but perhaps that would always remain. She didn't mourn Victoria now. She thought of Kip. It was almost too much for her to bear at the moment, this looming goodbye. But life is filled with goodbyes and relationships you mourn. And despite ourselves, our pain, and the belief that we'll never survive some of these things, we do.

Rhi pressed reply. For her own sake and for Vic's, she had to respond.

> *Dear Vic,*
> *I forgive you.*
> *I am happy here. I hope you find happiness too.*
> *Love Rhiannon*

She pressed send.

"Look at you, sitting in the garden but still working."

Rhi looked up at Taran. "I love it out here."

"It's pretty special." He sat on the end of her sunlounger. "I'm thinking I might take off."

"You can't. Not before the play."

"I need to make a decision about this show in London. All my work is there and I need to go through it before I make the call."

Rhi knew Taran was struggling with his feelings for the woman in London. It was good for him. "You need to go."

He ran his fingers through his hair. "Can I have a key to the theater? I want to check the mural one last time before I leave. Perhaps say goodbye to Kip."

"I gave the key to Tye. If you go down now, she might still be there."

Taran gave her a kiss on the forehead. "By the way, did you know there's a dryad in that oak?"

Rhi looked across the lawn and saw Pip fluttering her eyes at Taran.

"We tend to ignore each other now. It's like living with a teenager."

*

Tye walked along the beachfront, away from the theater. Disappointment filled her limbs and threatened to swamp her. And yet, what did she expect? That he'd step out of the shadows and they'd head down to O'Reilly's and catch up over a few beers? That meeting him would fill the empty space that had always been inside her? Even her mother was now missing him more than ever, having spent the time with him at the theater. Grief and loss was meant to be a process. If she'd seen him tonight, would it have propelled her backward?

She'd never know.

She noticed a figure up ahead, running. It took a moment for her to recognize Taran.

"Tye!"

"Hey, what are you doing?"

"I was heading down to the theater to grab the key off you."

Tye handed it to him. "I thought you'd finished your work there."

"I have. But I'm hitting the road, so thought I'd go down for one last look and say goodbye to...the place."

"You mean my father."

"Yes, Rhi told me about that."

"So you've talked to him too?"

"We've chatted."

Tye burst into tears.

"Hey, are you okay? What's happened?"

"It's stupid. I just went to the theater to talk to Kip, but apparently I'm the only person in town he won't appear to."

"Of course he won't."

That surprised Tye. "But everyone else talks to him."

Taran lifted her chin so she was looking at him. "That's an exaggeration, but even if it were true, everyone else is not his daughter."

"You'd think that he'd want to speak to me most of all," Tye said.

"I'm sure he does. But you know what love is?"

Tye rolled her eyes. "Oh no, guru Taran is going to teach me the true meaning of love, is he? Go on, hit me with it."

"Knowing what someone else needs and giving it to them, no matter how difficult that is for you. You don't think Kip wants to talk to you? Of course he does. But you went in there looking for a father. That's what you need. He can't give that to you because he's dead."

Tye nodded. "By all accounts, he was an excellent father to Tad."

"And would've been to you, had he lived. Hold on to that."

"You think that's it?"

"I really do. The guy is a total perfectionist. Even now you get that feeling from him. He watched me paint each day, making sure it met his approval. And the stories Rhi tells me about rehearsals—it's all or nothing with him." Taran took Tye's face in his hands. "He's proud. He knows he can't be your father, so he won't be anything."

Tye sighed. "I get a bum deal."

"To be fair, his hasn't been great either."

Her eyes searched his face. "True."

"Why do I always get the feeling that you know me?" Taran asked.

"Taran, I've dreamed about your brother my whole life." She said it simply and with love.

"It's Finn you recognize?"

"Yes, it is." She smiled up at him.

"I'm leaving town tomorrow. And even though I'll probably regret this..." Taran pulled her into his arms. "I'm not leaving without a kiss." And his lips crushed down on hers.

"Christ, Taran, you heard what the lady said."

Taran and Tye broke apart to see Finn and Crystal standing nearby.

Finn looked at his twin. He was calm and icy cold. "I've forgiven so much, but this one might be too tough."

Tye turned to Taran, her eyes filled with fury. "You ruined the moment for me." She turned and bolted. She ran until she reached the beach. It was finally him. And she'd seen the look on his face when he realized who the woman in Taran's arms was. That was not meant to be their first moment. That wasn't how she'd dreamed it. Taran had ruined everything.

She collapsed in the sand and sobbed. What a shit of a night. First her father, and now this. She never, ever pictured meeting her soul mate like this! And surely he wouldn't want her now that his brother had been there first. She had known Taran was trouble from the moment he walked into the cafe.

"You left before we were properly introduced. I'm Finn." He sat beside her in the sand.

She smiled through her tears. "I'm Tye."

"We're meant to meet."

She nodded. "Yes, but not like that."

Finn shrugged. "It doesn't matter how it happened, just that it did."

Tye looked into his eyes and had her *aha* moment. She saw it in him too. And then they sat side by side, comfortable together, as they had been for all eternity.

*

Annie knew she was acting like a stalker, but she couldn't help herself. The minute she smashed the phone she regretted it. She wanted to call Sam back and say yes, I'll be over in ten minutes. Don't have any fun without me. Tell everyone to sit still and wait for me to arrive. But her phone was broken.

So instead she acted like a crazy person and drove over to Jake's house, wearing her pajamas, and parked outside the house.

"What now?" she muttered to herself.

Annie got out of the car and crossed the road. Her nightgown was totally inappropriate for wearing in public, as were her pig slippers, but she didn't care. She was like a woman possessed. She ran along a hedge, hunched over so no one could see her. She paused at a lemon tree at the side of Jake's house and peered around. All clear. She bolted to his side window and peeked over the sill. The kitchen was empty, but the table was piled high with food and empty wine bottles.

Annie's eyes narrowed. What were they celebrating?

She crept around the side of the house. A car drove past and she dived behind a trashcan. One of her pig slippers got caught between two potted plants. She yanked it off, and then shoved it back on her foot, aware that she had gone beyond idiotic, all in the name of jealousy.

But she couldn't stop herself. She stuck her head around the side of the house. She heard voices first. A woman's laugh. And then she noticed them on the front porch, in each other's arms. It was Sal…and—well, it was difficult to tell from where she was crouched but she was certain it was him.

This had to stop immediately.

She moved in on them, out of the shadows of the garden and up the front steps onto the porch.

"Sam Knight, don't kiss her, kiss me."

The couple jumped in fright. Sal screamed, pulling at her blouse, while Jake, not Sam, stared at Annie in amusement.

"Jake?"

"What are you doing, Annie?" he said.

Annie pulled her nightgown around her. She looked down at her pig slippers. The ear on one had torn off. "I thought you were Sam."

"Why would I be kissing Sal?" asked Sam from behind her, "When I'm in love with you?"

Annie turned, face-to-face with the man she'd dreamed about since prom night. "I love you too. Clearly, or I wouldn't have made such a fool of myself." Annie shot Sal a look. "Sorry."

Sal smiled back at her. "I'd do the same for Jake."

Sam strode across the porch and pulled Annie into his arms. "Do you know what a mess you've caused? I wouldn't kiss you because I thought you were in love with Jake. And he wouldn't ask Sal out because he didn't want to hurt you, even though they've liked each other for ages."

"I'm really sorry about that," Annie whispered.

"Jesus, Sam, kiss the woman," Jake said.

And Sam did.

*

Rhi gazed at the moon outside her bedroom window. She was full. All the hard work, the heartache, the dreams were coming to fruition. Tomorrow, as the moon waned, it was time to let go. The first production would be what it would be. Kip would pass over. The theater would be hers alone. Only one thing marred her happiness.

"Bring him home," she whispered to the moon.

She noticed something moving down in the garden. She stuck her head further out the window and peered down. There was a shaft of pure white moonlight illuminating the garden. And in the center of it, an old woman danced.

"Ishbel."

She was so free, so in the moment. She was everything Rhi aspired to be. Rhi raced downstairs and out to the yard. She saw Ishbel spinning and turning, arms raised to the sky, a look of bliss on her face. She stepped into the moonlight...but Ishbel disappeared.

"Ishbel?"

Pip drifted past her, shaking her head, as though Rhi still didn't understand.

"Just dance, Rhi."

Rhi lifted her face to the stars and spun around and around, her arms stretched out to the moon.

Chapter 45

"Okay everyone, it's opening night—"

"And closing night," Anton said.

"And the night Kip finally crosses over and meets his maker," Jessica said dryly.

"I wonder if you'll be going up...or *down*," Juan said.

Darna winked at Kip. "You excited, honey?"

"It's right up with the episode of *Dallas* where we found out who shot JR."

"What did he say?" Chandler still couldn't see or hear Kip.

"He's jumping up and down, he's so excited," said Rhi. "Right beside you."

Chandler beamed at thin air. "I'm so happy for you, buddy."

Kip rolled his eyes and floated to the side of the stage.

Rhi called for everyone's attention. "So let's focus. We hit a few bumps in the dress rehearsal, but you know the old saying?"

"Bad dress, good opening night," everyone said.

"Come to think of it," Kip said, "the last dress rehearsal I had was fabulous. No wonder the roof collapsed during the show." He looked like he'd had an epiphany and everyone nodded. Actors were notoriously superstitious.

Rhi turned and looked up at the tech box. "Are you guys ready up there?"

Toby and Finn gave her a wave.

"Okay, let's head backstage. Audience will be arriving soon."

Everyone did as they were told apart from Kip. Instead he stood face to face with Rhi. They both knew it would be the last moment they had alone.

"Are you nervous?" Rhi asked.

"Not in the living sense of the word, but I'm definitely edgy."

"About the play...or about...?"

"Both," he admitted.

"You know your lines?"

"I've known them for twenty-nine years."

"And as for the other thing...you'll see a light. Just step into it."

"Right."

There was nothing to be said that their eyes weren't already saying.

Kip took a tentative step toward her. "Thank you, Rhiannon."

"Please don't." Rhi placed her fingers across her lips. Her hand was shaking. She desperately needed to keep it together to get through the play. "I cannot say goodbye to you," she whispered.

Kip gave her a sad nod and turned to leave.

"I will never forget."

He nodded and disappeared out the back. Rhi held a chair, shaking her head to draw strength. She had to get through this. Yes, he was going, but that wouldn't happen if she lost it now.

"I hope you've saved seats for us."

Rhi spun around and found her parents standing in the doorway. She ran to her father and hugged him. "I wasn't sure you would come."

"Wild horses wouldn't keep us away, love." Lugh looked at his wife. "Right Brigid?"

Brigid stepped tentatively up to her daughter. "Perhaps wild horses, but certainly not family arguments. Those can be healed."

Rhi hugged her mother. It was awkward, but a start. "It means a lot to me. And to Kip. I'll introduce you to him."

Brigid shot Lugh a look. "No need, Rhi. We've met."

"You knew Kip too?"

Lugh took his daughter by the arm and led her away. "Long story, and we'll explain later, but how about we catch up alone while your mother attends to some long overdue business?"

*

Crystal sat on the sofa in Kip's dressing room, her hands clutched in her lap.

"But what if it happens again?" Kip had a look of dread on his face.

"Even if the ceiling falls on you, darling, it's not like it can kill you again."

"But what if I don't cross over?" He looked at Crystal like she was the font of all knowledge.

"If you want to, you will." Crystal felt the weight of his fear, her heart heavy. "You do want to cross over, don't you?"

He came to kneel in front of her. "I do. I'm tired of this. The only thing keeping me here is you, but we'll be together again, won't we?"

"I believe so, Kip. It's that thought that has kept me going for three decades."

He smiled at her, his eyes filled with love. "You have been the one true and real thing in my life. And my death," He chuckled. "If I don't cross over tonight, it won't be because of you."

Crystal stood. "Actually there's something you need to know."

"What, Cryssie?"

"She wants you to know that if you don't cross over it will be because of me," said Brigid's voice as she flung open the door. The woman had a grander entrance than Harrods.

Kip flew up to the roof. "Who the fuck invited you?"

"It's my daughter's theater and you didn't memo her to keep me off the guest list."

"You really are the devil's daughter. Look at your face. How can you not age? You're like a fucking vampire."

"Says my dead ex-lover, as if talking to him is completely normal." Brigid shot Crystal a look, one perfectly plucked eyebrow raised.

Crystal was surprised to see compassion in her eyes. She'd forgotten that it ever resided in Brigid.

"Crystal came to me recently to ask me to lift the curse. I initially refused, because I prefer to err on the side of bitch. But then I thought, poor bastard, you've suffered enough, right?"

"I think I have." Kip sounded nervous.

Brigid reached into her purse and pulled out two peacock feathers. Then, holding one in each hand, she marched to the center of the room and began to moan.

"What the hell are you doing?" Kip stuttered.

"Lifting the curse. Now shut up while I work." Brigid gave Crystal a sly wink. "Demon forces, hear me now...Begone this curse, release my vow...Free this ghoul, let him pass...even though he was an ass..."

Crystal bowed her head and bit her lip so she wouldn't laugh. What the hell was Brigid doing?

"Curse be broken, from now, tonight...Let thy spirit find the light. Break this curse, and set Kip free...This limbo has been the cause of me. But now, tonight, on that there stage...Kip Daniels will pass to the next age."

Brigid shook her head a little more, and waved the feathers around, stamped her feet and bit and pulled a face that looked strangely sexual. And then, with one wild, yodeling yelp, she flung the feathers to the sky and stood still as they fluttered down around her. She scooped them up, put them back in the bag, and straightened her skirt.

"You're free now, Kip. Enjoy the show." She turned to leave.

"Brigid," Crystal said. "Thank you."

"You'd do the same for me." She looked at Crystal for a moment and then up at Kip. "The life I have with Lugh...I can't imagine having that torn away from me, the way you two did. I'll leave you alone now."

Brigid closed the door quietly behind her and Kip floated down to Crystal. His face was beaming.

"I feel it, Cryssie. It's gone. The curse has been lifted."

"Yes it has." She felt it too.

Chapter 46

The Majestic was even more beautiful than it had been in its heyday. The façade was now a brilliant white, the windows shining with light from within. The building looked alive, defiant in its elegance, as if to say, "You ran me into the ground with your fears and pain. But look what I've become again." Rhi had done an amazing job.

Tad felt small, standing outside the theater, looking up at this grand dame. There was a feeling of déjà vu to the evening, and yet he was no longer five years old. He wasn't vulnerable any more. Sure, it had taken courage to come tonight, but he was ready and it was time.

The performance had already begun inside–he could hear faint voices, theatrical shouts and muted screams, mood music and sound effects. He walked around the back, marveling at all the work that had taken place. He felt like he was being watched by the theater itself, as if it was allowing him the privilege of circling and admiring. He could almost sense the structure watching him for signs of remorse. He'd certainly let her fall to pieces. And Rhi had brought her back to life.

He slipped through the stage door. The place looked very different to how it had nearly thirty years ago. Then he spotted the silver star on his father's dressing room door; some things never changed. There were a couple of people milling around—actors, watching the performances on stage. He noticed Tye on the other side of the wings, but she didn't see him. She was sitting quietly by herself, head bowed, hands in her lap. He stepped behind a curtain, where he had a clear view. He was just in time to see the end. He'd planned it that way. It was one thing to sit through the whole play, struggling with his emotions, another to turn up and share this moment with Rhi. And his dad. He trusted Crystal enough to believe it was possible.

The stage was strewn with swords, chalices and the bodies of the King and Queen. He could see the first few rows of the audience from where he stood, and everyone seemed mesmerized.

He watched the actors talk to thin air. Was that his father they were talking to? Was he actually there? It was strange to watch, and made him highly uncomfortable. Horatio fell to his knees. He seemed to be cradling someone. Perhaps they were all just pulling his leg.

He glanced down at his hands...they were shaking. It was too soon for him to be back here. Perhaps another few decades. Yes, he was weak. Or at least that's how he felt. He'd chosen to ignore this place, ignore it all, rather than relive what had happened that night exactly twenty-nine years ago. Exactly.

Damn Collette. He'd arrived in New York to confront her about Crystal and Tye. To his surprise, she'd apologized immediately.

"I'm so sorry. I'd do it differently now," she'd said. "I'm glad you know."

This had disarmed him. "You owe Crystal and Tye an apology."

"I agree. And now this is out in the open, they'll get one. I admire Crystal immensely for how she's handled everything."

Then there was nothing to do but mope around his mother's place for a couple of weeks, occasionally visiting friends for the night. Finally, she'd snapped.

"Why are you still here?"

He had no idea himself, and it showed.

"Are you going to this play they're putting on up there?" She'd let it be known that she thought it was weird, but as Shakespeare himself had said, "There are more things in heaven and earth…?Than are dreamt of in your philosophy."

"I'm going to give it a miss this time 'round."

"What about this woman you like?"

"How do you know there's a woman?"

"It's written all over you." She challenged him, hands on her hips. "What *are* you so afraid of?"

He couldn't answer her. He didn't know.

"Christ, Tad, you know what I really loved about you father? He was a go-getter. He wouldn't sit there bitching about his feelings for someone…He was a Neanderthal. When he liked a woman, he'd pretty much club her over the head. When he wanted a theater, he asked me for the cash and he bought one. When he became a dad—did he run for the hills? No. He not only embraced it, but he was the one who got up night after night, feeding you and singing you back to sleep. He was so goddamn present. Alive."

"And now he's been stuck in that theater for thirty years."

"Yes, but he's dead. What's your excuse?"

His mother was right. He'd been frozen to this very spot in the theater for nearly three decades. He needed to move on too. And he couldn't even fathom doing that without Rhi, despite everything that had happened between them. He felt someone watching him. He looked across the stage to the wings opposite and saw Tye. They locked eyes, their own silent language shared in one look, and he smiled.

And at that very moment, he heard his father's voice.

"O, I die, Horatio."

Tad's head jerked back toward the stage. He saw a man lying in Horatio's arms.

The final moments of the play took place. Horatio and Fortinbras finished their lines. The lights faded to black...there was a moment of awed silence...

And then the applause began.

Tye knew when Tad arrived. She sensed him. And right away, she knew she'd get through the night. She'd hung around feeling quite useless. She watched the play from the wings for a while, but her father remained invisible to her. So she found a seat, away from everyone, and waited for it all to end. It was like being by someone's bedside, waiting for death to put everyone out of their misery. Each minute was endless, but not long enough.

Then Tad arrived. She made her way to the wings and watched him across the stage. She was so happy to see him, safe and sound. She saw him as she always had, as her brother, but more than that—her everything. He was her friend. Her creative partner. Her inspiration. Her sounding board. Her pain in the ass at times. She was blessed to have him. She knew him like she knew herself. And right now, he was struggling.

"I'm here Tad," she whispered.

It was as though he could hear her. His looked up, away from the stage, directly at her. Their eyes locked and he smiled. It washed away the hurt, it made everything okay. It was never meant to be about 'a father'—her journey was with her brother.

And at that very moment, she heard a voice.

"O, I die, Horatio."

Tye's head jerked toward the stage. She saw a man lying in Horatio's arms.

The final moments of the play took place. Horatio and Fortinbras finished their lines. The lights faded to black...there was a moment of awed silence...

And then the applause began.

Chapter 47

Kip was filled with joy. He was performing again and it felt so good. Rhiannon had cast well. These actors were even better than the last lot he'd performed with. He was nervous, admittedly, but they were all with him, every step of the way. Including Chandler, who could suddenly see him.

It was tough as he closed in on his soliloquy. Line by line he drew nearer to the moment that had failed him before, but there was no way he'd let it beat him. Not this time.

He could feel the audience. If only actors knew how freaking fabulous it was performing to an audience of witches. They were sending him so much love and light and goodwill. He felt so alive!

And then, it was upon him.

"To be or not to be..."

He was there, back in this moment. There was no time to be confused, or fearful...He felt every word he spoke with passion and pain. He finished the soliloquy to cheers.

It was a piece of cake from there. And a thrill!

The play came to an end and there was a standing ovation for him. He stood center stage of his very own theater, just like he always knew he would. This was the moment he wanted. And it was his.

"Thank you. Thank you. Thank you so much."

He noticed someone watching him in the wings and realized Tad was standing there. He had returned for him. He knew he would. Tad was a man now, not the boy he was last time. This time he was confident and calm. And he was staring straight at him, as though he could see him. Kip smiled at his son and he smiled back…A nod—it's okay to go.

Kip knew Tad would be fine. But there was one more person. Where was she? He scanned the wings. He looked down at the audience. And then he spotted her, at the front of the audience with Brigid at her side. Crystal did not clap. She did not cry. She locked eyes with him, held her hand to her heart and nodded goodbye.

And then he saw it, that intense, welcoming light. It was time. He had finished what he'd wanted to do.

The audience roared its approval. The clapping filled him. He took one more bow and, looking at no one but Crystal, he stepped into the light.

The final curtain descended on Kip Daniels.

Chapter 48

Rhi was alone on the stage. She could hear the audience still milling around in the foyer drinking wine. They had worked hard to raise the energy for Kip. What a gift they'd all given him. What a wonderful group of people. It made her oddly proud of her ancient faith. Many of them would soon head down to O'Reilly's for the cast party, where even more spirits would be raised. Rhi would join them to celebrate. It was a success. And yet, she felt so deeply and profoundly sad. How long would it take for her to stop expecting him just to pop out from behind the curtains?

"Rhi?"

Rhi stepped back, startled. "Kip?"

He laughed. "No, it's me, Tad...Do you want me to show you my ID?"

Rhi resisted the urge to throw herself into his arms. "It's so good to see you."

"You too Rhi." He nodded at the theatre. "I like what you've done with the place."

"Thank you." She peered into his face, concerned. "You've missed the play, Tad. He's gone."

"I caught the end from the wings." He smiled, a mix of sadness and also relief. "This production ended better than last time."

Rhi gave a wry chuckle. "Yes. I'm sure he'd approve."

He looked deep into Rhi's eyes. "I saw him, Rhi. I saw him go."

The tears began to flow. "Oh shit, Tad… I'm sorry. It's just…I'm going to miss him around here."

"Then we'll miss him together." Tad moved toward her. "Don't be sad."

"I'm sad and happy."

"You're sappy."

"I am sappy."

They smiled at each other.

"He's at peace," Rhi said. "And I'm so glad you came for back him."

"I came back for you."

"Oh." That threw her.

Tad pulled her up into his arms. "Tonight I'm letting go of the past. And I'm really hoping you'll be part of my future."

"Are you still evicting me?"

"Depends on how you answer my last question."

"I'd very much like to be a part of your future."

"Good answer. I'll extend your lease." Tad ran his fingers through her hair.

She couldn't bear it a second longer. She needed him. "Can I have a rerun of that kiss on the beach?"

"Without the crazy afterward?"

"Definitely without that."

And so he kissed her. But it was even better than the kiss on the beach. She was clear now. She knew who he was, no confusion, no misunderstanding. She wrapped her arms around him. Every sense exploded. She could smell him, taste him, touch him. He was real. She dissolved into him. There was no return. Everything that had happened had brought her to this moment.

And she felt so alive.

"If you two have finished your love scene up there, can we get this party started?" called Sam from the back of the room.

Rhi looked at Sam, his arm draped around Annie. Beside them were Tye and Finn. They all looked excited, ready to move on.

Rhi realized that's how she felt now too.

"You know what I'm really looking forward to?" Tad whispered in her ear.

She raised an eyebrow. "What?"

"Having a conversation with you where you don't sound crazy."

"I'm looking forward to having a conversation with you where you don't act like two different people."

Tad laughed. "Yeah, I'm looking forward to that."

Rhi grabbed his hand and pulled him off the stage and toward the theater door. She paused as she got there, turning to look at her theater.

"I'm looking forward to it all."

Acknowledgments

Thank you to the crew at Momentum for giving my book a home. It means a lot to me.

A heartfelt hug to Ulrike Sturm for getting me on a plane and putting me up in her wonderful artist's studio, where I started *Hamlet's Ghost*.

Thanks to my dear friends Lord David and Lord Mark for taking me out of Sydney to finish the book, and for protecting me from zombies while we were there. And to Steve Griffiths for letting me use his fabulous house as a writer's retreat. Inspiration hit. Thank you.

As always, I'm grateful to my mother Yvonne Pfeiffer, whose support and love knows no bounds.

To RIOT... for understanding that dinner is ready when the fire alarm goes off and that I'd much rather be writing than cooking... thanks guys!

My guy, Dominique Sweeney: you have read, critiqued, and supported yet another novel. You've given me chocolate and wine when needed. You have enthusiastically embraced this genre despite the shit people heap on it. For months you shared our bed with a ghost—a fictional one at that. You understood completely why I fell in love with Kip and why I mourned him after he'd left me. You held my hand through it all. It's no wonder I'm with you.

And finally, there is a unique ending to my journey with this book. No matter what I write in the future, this story will hold a precious place in my heart.

I did the final proof read of *Hamlet's Ghost* at the bedside of my former acting teacher and dear friend, Zika Nester. It was definitely a unique place to finish any book, but to be surrounded by theatre folk helping a friend pass over while finishing a novel about exactly the same thing was extraordinary.

To the seven women I shared closing night with: Sharon, Jo, Jodie, Cath, Kate, Margaret and Rebecca—you are all magnificent. I have so much love for you all.

And beautiful Zika: I'm so glad you got to share *Hamlet's Ghost* with me. As you always said, *"Use it!"* So I did. I dedicate this book to you.

www.ingramcontent.com/pod-product-compliance
Lightning Source LLC
Chambersburg PA
CBHW030956260626
47169CB00002B/562